John Burroughs

Riverby

John Burroughs

Riverby

ISBN/EAN: 9783337301286

Printed in Europe, USA, Canada, Australia, Japan

Cover: Foto ©Andreas Hilbeck / pixelio.de

More available books at **www.hansebooks.com**

RIVERBY

BY

JOHN BURROUGHS

BOSTON AND NEW YORK
HOUGHTON, MIFFLIN AND COMPANY
The Riverside Press, Cambridge
1897

The Riverside Press, Cambridge, Mass. U. S. A.
Electrotyped and Printed by H. O. Houghton & Co

PREFATORY NOTE

I HAVE often said to myself, "Why should not one name his books as he names his children, arbitrarily, and let the name come to mean much or little, as the case may be?" In the case of the present volume — probably my last collection of Out-of-door Papers — I have taken this course, and have given to the book the name of my place here on the Hudson, "Riverby," by the river, where the sketches were written, and where for so many years I have been an interested spectator of the life of nature, as, with the changing seasons, it has ebbed and flowed past my door.

J. B.

CONTENTS

RIVERBY

AMONG THE WILD-FLOWERS

I

NEARLY every season I make the acquaintance of one or more new flowers. It takes years to exhaust the botanical treasures of any one considerable neighborhood, unless one makes a dead set at it, like an herbalist. One likes to have his floral acquaintances come to him easily and naturally, like his other friends. Some pleasant occasion should bring you together. You meet in a walk, or touch elbows on a picnic under a tree, or get acquainted on a fishing or camping-out expedition. What comes to you in the way of birds or flowers while wooing only the large spirit of open-air nature seems like special good fortune. At any rate, one does not want to bolt his botany, but rather to prolong the course. One likes to have something in reserve, something to be on the lookout for on his walks. I have never yet found the orchid called Calypso, a large, variegated purple and yellow flower, Gray says, which grows in cold, wet woods and bogs, very beautiful, and very rare. Calypso, you know, was the nymph who fell in love with Ulysses and detained him seven years upon her island, and died of a broken heart after he left her. I have a keen desire to see her in her floral guise, reigning over some silent bog, or rising above the moss of some dark glen in the woods, and would gladly be the Ulysses to be detained at least a few hours by her.

I will describe her by the aid of Gray, so that if any of my readers come across her they may know what a rarity they have found. She may be looked for in cold, mossy, boggy places in our Northern woods. You will see a low flower somewhat like a lady's slipper; that is, with an inflated sac-shaped lip, the petals and sepals much alike, rising and spreading, the color mingled purple and yellow, the stem, or scape, from three to five inches high, with but one leaf, — that one thin and slightly heart-shaped, with a stem which starts from a solid bulb. That is the nymph of our boggy solitudes, waiting to break her heart for any adventurous hero who may penetrate her domain.

Several of our harmless little wild-flowers have been absurdly named out of the old mythologies: thus, Indian cucumber root, one of Thoreau's favorite flowers, is named after the sorceress Medea, and is called "medeola," because it was at one time thought to possess rare medicinal properties; and medicine and sorcery have always been more or less confounded in the opinion of mankind. It is a pretty and decorative sort of plant, with, when perfect, two stages or platforms of leaves, one

above the other. You see a whorl of five or
six leaves, a foot or more from the ground,
which seems to bear a standard with another
whorl of three leaves at the top of it. The
small, colorless, recurved flowers shoot out
from above this top whorl. The whole expression of the plant is singularly slender and graceful. Sometimes, probably the first year, it
only attains to the first circle of leaves. This
is the platform from which it will rear its
flower column the next year. Its white,
tuberous root is crisp and tender, and leaves in
the mouth distinctly the taste of cucumber.
Whether or not the Indians used it as a relish
as we do the cucumber, I do not know.

Still another pretty flower that perpetuates
the name of a Grecian nymph, a flower that was
a new find to me a few summers ago, is the Arethusa. Arethusa was one of the nymphs who
attended Diana, and was by that goddess turned
into a fountain, that she might escape the god
of the river Alpheus, who became desperately
in love with her on seeing her at her bath.
Our Arethusa is one of the prettiest of the
orchids, and has been pursued through many a
marsh and quaking bog by her lovers. She is
a bright pink-purple flower an inch or more
long, with the odor of sweet violets. The
sepals and petals rise up and arch over the
column, which we may call the heart of the
flower, as if shielding it. In Plymouth County,
Massachusetts, where the Arethusa seems common, I have heard it called Indian pink.

But I was going to recount my new finds. One sprang up in the footsteps of that destroying angel, Dynamite. A new railroad cut across my tramping-ground, with its hordes of Italian laborers and its mountains of giant-powder, etc., was enough to banish all the gentler deities forever from the place. But it did not. Scarcely had the earthquake passed when, walking at the base of a rocky cliff that had been partly blown away in the search for stone for two huge abutments that stood near by, I beheld the débris at the base of the cliff draped and festooned by one of our most beautiful foliage plants, and one I had long been on the lookout for, namely, the climbing fumitory. It was growing everywhere in the greatest profusion, affording by its tenderness, delicacy, and grace the most striking contrast to the destruction the black giant had wrought. The power that had smote the rock seemed to have called it into being. Probably the seeds had lain dormant in cracks and crevices for years, and when the catastrophe came, and they found themselves in new soil amid the wreck of the old order of things, they sprang into new life, and grew as if the world had been created anew for them, as, in a sense, it had. Certainly, they grew most luxuriantly, and never was the ruin wrought by powder veiled by more delicate lace-like foliage.[1] The panicles of droop-

[1] Strange to say, the plant did not appear in that locality the next season, and has never appeared since. Perhaps it will take another dynamite earthquake to wake it up.

ing, pale flesh-colored flowers heightened the effect of the whole. This plant is a regular climber; it has no extra appendages for that purpose, and does not wind, but climbs by means of its young leaf-stalks, which lay hold like tiny hands or hooks. The end of every branch is armed with a multitude of these baby hands. The flowers are pendent and swing like ear jewels. They are slightly heart-shaped, and when examined closely look like little pockets made of crumpled silk, nearly white on the inside, or under side, and pale purple on the side toward the light, and shirred up at the bottom. And pockets they are in quite a literal sense, for, though they fade, they do not fall, but become pockets full of seeds. The fumitory is a perpetual bloomer from July till killed by the autumn frosts.

The closely allied species of this plant, the dicentra (Dutchman's breeches and squirrel corn), are much more common, and are among our prettiest spring flowers. I have an eye out for the white-hearts (related to the bleeding-hearts of the gardens, and absurdly called "Dutchman's breeches") the last week in April. It is a rock-loving plant, and springs up on the shelves of the ledges or in the débris at their base as if by magic. As soon as blood-root has begun to star the waste, stony places, and the first swallow has been heard in the sky, we are on the lookout for dicentra. The more northern species, called "squirrel corn" from the small golden tubers at its root, blooms in May, and has the fragrance of hyacinths. It does not affect the rocks, like all the other flowers of this family.

My second new acquaintance the same season was the showy lady's slipper. Most of the floral ladies leave their slippers in swampy places in the woods ; only the stemless one (*acaule*) leaves hers on dry ground before she reaches the swamp, commonly under evergreen trees, where the carpet of pine needles will not hurt her feet. But one may penetrate many wet, mucky places in the woods before he finds the prettiest of them all, the showy lady's slipper, — the prettiest slipper, but the stoutest and coarsest plant; the flower large and very showy, white, tinged with purple in front: the stem two feet high, very leafy, and coarser than bear-weed. Report had come to me through my botanizing neighbor, that in a certain quaking sphagnum bog in the woods the showy lady's slipper could be found. The locality proved to be the marrowy grave of an extinct lake or black tarn. On the borders of it the white azalea was in bloom, fast fading. In the midst of it were spruces and black ash and giant ferns, and low in the spongy, mossy bottom, the pitcher plant. The lady's slipper grew in little groups and companies all about. Never have I beheld a prettier sight, — so gay, so festive, so holiday-looking. Were they so many gay bonnets rising above the foliage, or were they flocks of white doves with purple-stained breasts just lifting up their wings. to take flight, or were they little fleets of fairy boats, with sail set, tossing on a mimic sea of wild weedy growths? Such images throng the mind on recalling the scene, and only faintly hint its beauty and animation. The long, erect, white sepals do much to give the alert, tossing look which the flower wears. The dim light, too, of its secluded haunts, and its snowy purity and freshness, contribute to the impression it makes. The purple tinge is like a stain of wine which has slightly overflowed the brim of the inflated lip or sac and run part way down its snowy sides.

This lady's slipper is one of the rarest and choicest of our wild-flowers, and its haunts and its beauty are known only to the few. Those who have the secret guard it closely, lest their favorite be exterminated. A well-known botanist in one of the large New England cities told me that it was found in but one place in that neighborhood, and that the secret, so far as he knew, was known to but three persons, and was carefully kept by them.

A friend of mine, an enthusiast on orchids, came one June day a long way by rail, to see this flower. I conducted him to the edge of the swamp, lifted up the branches as I would a curtain, and said, "There they are."

"Where?" said he, peering far into the dim recesses.

"Within six feet of you," I replied.

He narrowed his vision, and such an expression of surprise and delight as came over his face ! A group of a dozen or more of the plants, some of them twin-flowered, were there almost within reach, the first he had ever seen, and his appreciation of the scene, visible in every look and gesture, was greatly satisfying. In the fall he came and moved a few of the plants to a tamarack swamp in his own vicinity, where they throve and bloomed finely for a few years, and then for some unknown reason failed.

Nearly every June, my friend still comes to feast his eyes upon this queen of the cypripediums.

While returning from my first search for the lady's slipper, my hat fairly brushed the nest of the red-eyed vireo, which was so cunningly concealed, such an open secret, in the dim, leafless underwoods, that I could but pause and regard it. It was suspended from the end of a small, curving sapling, was flecked here and there by some whitish substance so as to blend it with the gray mottled boles of the trees, and, in the dimly lighted ground-floor of the woods, was sure to escape any but the most prolonged scrutiny. A couple of large leaves formed a canopy above it. It was not so much hidden as it was rendered invisible by texture and position with reference to light and shade.

A few summers ago I struck a new and beautiful plant, in the shape of a weed that had only recently appeared in that part of the country. I was walking through an August meadow when I saw, on a little knoll, a bit of most vivid orange, verging on a crimson. I knew of no flower of such a complexion frequenting such a place as that. On investigation, it proved to be a· stranger. It had a rough, hairy, leafless stem about a foot high, surmounted by a corymbose cluster of flowers or flower-heads of dark vivid orange-color. The leaves were deeply notched and toothed, very bristly, and were pressed flat to the ground. The whole plant was a veritable Esau for hairs, and it seemed to lay hold upon the ground as if it was not going to let go easily. And what a fiery plume it had! The next day, in another field a mile away, I chanced upon more of the flowers. On making inquiry, I found that a small patch or colony of the plants had appeared that season, or first been noticed then, in a meadow well known to me from boyhood. They had been cut down with the grass in early July, and the first week in August had shot up and bloomed again. I found the spot aflame with them. Their leaves covered every inch of the surface where they stood, and not a spear of grass grew there. They were taking slow but complete possession; they were devouring the meadow by inches. The plant seemed to be a species of hieracium, or hawkweed, or some closely allied species of the composite family, but I could not find it mentioned in our botanies.

A few days later, on the edge of an adjoining county ten miles distant, I found, probably, its headquarters. It had appeared there a few years before, and was thought to have escaped

from some farmer's door-yard. Patches of it
were appearing here and there in the fields, and
the farmers were thoroughly alive to the danger
and were fighting it like fire. Its seeds are
winged like those of the dandelion, and it sows
itself far and near. It would be a beautiful
acquisition to our midsummer fields, supplying
a tint as brilliant as that given by the scarlet
poppies to English grain-fields. But it would
be an expensive one, as it usurps the land completely.[1]

Parts of New England have already a midsummer flower nearly as brilliant and probably
far less aggressive and noxious, in meadow
beauty, or rhexia, the sole northern genus of a
family of tropical plants. I found it very
abundant in August in the country bordering
on Buzzard's Bay. It was a new flower to me,
and I was puzzled to make it out. It seemed
like some sort of scarlet evening-primrose.
The parts were in fours, the petals slightly
heart-shaped and convoluted in the bud, the
leaves bristly, the calyx-tube prolonged, etc.;
but the stem was square, the leaves opposite,
and the tube urn-shaped. The flowers were
an inch across, and bright purple or scarlet. It
grew in large patches in dry, sandy fields, making the desert gay with color; and also on the
edges of marshy places. It eclipses any flower

---

[1] This observation was made ten years ago. I have since
learned that the plant is *Hieracium aurantiacum* from
Europe, a kind of hawkweed. It is fast becoming a common weed in New York and New England.

of the open fields known to me farther inland. When we come to improve our wild garden, as recommended by Mr. Robinson in his book on wild gardening, we must not forget the rhexia.

Our seacoast flowers are probably more brilliant in color than the same flowers in the interior. I thought the wild rose on the Massachusetts coast deeper tinted and more fragrant than those I was used to. The steeple-bush, or hardhack, had more color, as had the rose-gerardia and several other plants.

But when vivid color is wanted, what can surpass or equal our cardinal-flower? There is a glow about this flower as if color emanated from it as from a live coal. The eye is baffled and does not seem to reach the surface of the petal; it does not see the texture or material part as it does in other flowers, but rests in a steady, still radiance. It is not so much something colored as it is color itself. And then the moist, cool, shady places it affects, usually where it has no floral rivals, and where the large, dark shadows need just such a dab of fire. Often, too, we see it double, its reflected image in some dark pool heightening its effect. I have never found it with its only rival in color, the monarda or bee-balm, a species of mint. Farther north, the cardinal-flower seems to fail, and the monarda takes its place, growing in similar localities. One may see it about a mountain spring, or along a meadow brook, or glowing in the shade around the head of a wild mountain lake It stands up two feet high or more, and the flowers show like a broad scarlet cap.

The only thing I have seen in this country that calls to mind the green grain-fields of Britain splashed with scarlet poppies may be witnessed in August in the marshes of the lower Hudson, when the broad sedgy and flaggy spaces are sprinkled with the great marsh-mallow. It is a most pleasing spectacle, — level stretches of dark green flag or waving marsh-grass kindled on every square yard by these bright pink blossoms like great burning coals fanned in the breeze. The mallow is not so deeply colored as the poppy, but it is much larger, and has the tint of youth and happiness. It is an immigrant from Europe, but it is making itself thoroughly at home in our great river meadows.

The same day your eye is attracted by the mallows: as your train skirts or cuts through the broad marshes, it will revel with delight in the masses of fresh bright color afforded by the purple loosestrife, which grows in similar localities, and shows here and there like purple bonfires. It is a tall plant, grows in dense masses, and affords a most striking border to the broad spaces dotted with the mallow. It, too, came to us from over seas, and first appeared along the Wallkill, many years ago. It used to be thought by the farmers in that vicinity that its seed was first brought in wool imported to this country from Australia, and washed in the Wallkill at Walden, where there was a woolen factory. This is not probable, as it is a European species, and I should sooner think it had escaped from cultivation. If one were to act upon the suggestions of Robinson's "Wild Garden," already alluded to, he would gather the seeds of these plants and sow them in the marshes and along the sluggish inland streams, till the banks of all our rivers were gay with these brilliant exotics.

Among our native plants, the one that takes broad marshes to itself and presents vast sheets of color is the marsh milkweed, far less brilliant than the loosestrife or the mallow; still a missionary in the wilderness, lighting up many waste places with its humbler tints of purple.

One sometimes seems to discover a familiar wild-flower anew by coming upon it in some peculiar and striking situation. Our columbine is at all times and in all places one of the most exquisitely beautiful of flowers; yet one spring day, when I saw it growing out of a small seam on the face of a great lichen-covered wall of rock, where no soil or mould was visible, — a jet of foliage and color shooting out of a black line on the face of a perpendicular mountain wall and rising up like a tiny fountain, its drops turning to flame-colored jewels that hung and danced in the air against the gray rocky surface, — its beauty became something magical and audacious. On little narrow shelves in the rocky wall the corydalis was blooming, and among the loose boulders at its base the bloodroot shone conspicuous, suggesting snow rather than anything more sanguine.

Certain flowers one makes special expeditions for every season. They are limited in their ranges, and must generally be sought for in particular haunts. How many excursions to the woods does the delicious trailing arbutus give rise to! How can one let the spring go by without gathering it himself when it hides in the moss! There are arbutus days in one's calendar, days when the trailing flower fairly calls him to the woods. With me, they come the latter part of April. The grass is greening here and there on the moist slopes and by the spring runs; the first furrow has been struck by the farmer; the liverleaf is in the height of its beauty, and the bright constellations of the bloodroot shine out here and there; one has had his first taste and his second taste of the spring and of the woods, and his tongue is sharpened rather than cloyed. Now he will take the most delicious and satisfying draught of all, the very essence and soul of the early season, of the tender brooding days, with all their prophecies and awakenings, in the handful of trailing arbutus which he gathers in his walk. At the mere thought of it, one sees the sunlight flooding the woods, smells the warm earthy odors which the heat liberates from beneath the dry leaves, hears the mellow bass of the first bumble-bee,

" Rover of the underwoods,"

or the finer chord of the adventurous honey-bee seeking store for his empty comb. The arriving swallows twitter above the woods; the first chewink rustles the dry leaves; the northward bound thrushes, the hermit and the gray-cheeked, flit here and there before you. The robin, the sparrow, and the bluebird are building their first nests, and the first shad are making their way slowly up the Hudson. Indeed, the season is fairly under way when the trailing arbutus comes. Now look out for troops of boys and girls going to the woods to gather it! and let them look out that in their greed they do not exterminate it. Within reach of our large towns the choicer spring wild-flowers are hunted mercilessly. Every fresh party from town raids them as if bent upon their destruction. One day, about ten miles from one of our Hudson River cities, there got into the train six young women loaded down with vast sheaves and bundles of trailing arbutus. Each one of them had enough for forty. They had apparently made a clean sweep of the woods. It was a pretty sight, — the pink and white of the girls and the pink and white of the flowers! and the car too was suddenly filled with perfume, — the breath of spring loaded the air, but I thought it a pity to ravish the woods in that way. The next party was probably equally greedy, and because a handful was desirable, thought an armful proportionately so; till, by and by, the flower will be driven from those woods.

Another flower that one makes special excursions for is the pond lily. The pond lily is a

star, and easily takes the first place among
lilies; and the expeditions to her haunts, and
the gathering her where she rocks upon the
dark secluded waters of some pool or lakelet,
are the crown and summit of the floral expeditions of summer. It .is the expedition about
which more things gather than almost any
other: you want your boat, you want your
lunch, you want your friend or friends with
you. You are going to put in the greater part
of the day; you are going to picnic in the
woods, and indulge in a "green thought in a
green shade." When my friend and I go for
pond lilies, we have to traverse a distance of
three miles with our boat in a wagon. The
road is what is called a "back road," and leads
through woods most of the way. Black Pond,
where the lilies grow, lies about one hundred
feet higher than the Hudson, from which it is
separated by a range of rather bold wooded
heights, one of which might well be called
Mount Hymettus, for I have found a great deal
of wild honey in the forest that covers it. The
stream which flows out of the pond takes a
northward course for two or three miles, till it
finds an opening through the rocky hills, when
it makes rapidly for the Hudson. Its career
all the way from the lake is a series of alter-
nating pools and cascades. Now a long, deep,
level stretch, where the perch and the bass and
the pickerel lurk, and where the willow-herb
and the royal osmunda fern line the shores;
then a sudden leap of eight, ten, or fifteen

feet down rocks to another level stretch, where the water again loiters and suns itself; and so on through its adventurous course till the hills are cleared and the river is in sight. Our road leads us along this stream, across its rude bridges, through dark hemlock and pine woods, under gray, rocky walls, now past a black pool, then within sight or hearing of a foaming rapid or fall, till we strike the outlet of the long level that leads to the lake. In this we launch our boat and paddle slowly upward over its dark surface, now pushing our way through half-submerged treetops, then ducking under the trunk of an overturned tree which bridges the stream and makes a convenient way for the squirrels and wood-mice, or else forcing the boat over it when it is sunk a few inches below the surface. We are traversing what was once a continuation of the lake; the forest floor is as level as the water and but a few inches above it, even in summer; it sweeps back a half mile or more, densely covered with black ash, red maple, and other deciduous trees, to the foot of the rocky hills which shut us in. What glimpses we get, as we steal along, into the heart of the rank, dense, silent woods! I carry in my eye yet the vision I had on one occasion, of a solitary meadow lily hanging like a fairy bell there at the end of a chance opening, where a ray of sunlight fell full upon it and brought out its brilliant orange against the dark green background. It appeared to be the only bit of bright color in all the woods.

Then the song of a single hermit-thrush immediately after did even more for the ear than the
lily did for the eye. Presently the swamp-
sparrow, one of the rarest of the sparrows, was
seen and heard; and that nest there in a small
bough a few feet over the water proves to be
hers — in appearance, a ground bird's nest in
a bough, with the same four speckled eggs.
As we come in sight of the lilies, where they
cover the water at the outlet of the lake, a
brisk gust of wind, as if it had been waiting
to surprise us, sweeps down and causes every
leaf to leap from the water and show its pink
under side. Was it a fluttering of hundreds of
wings, or the clapping of a multitude of hands?
But there rocked the lilies with their golden
hearts open to the sun, and their tender white
petals as fresh as crystals of snow. What a
queenly flower indeed, the type of unsullied
purity and sweetness! Its root, like a black,
corrugated, ugly reptile, clinging to the slime,
but its flower in purity and whiteness like a
star. There is something very pretty in the
closed bud making its way up through the
water to meet the sun, and there is something
touching in the flower closing itself up again
after its brief career, and slowly burying itself
beneath the dark wave. One almost fancies a
sad, regretful look in it as the stem draws it
downward to mature its seed on the sunless
bottom. The pond lily is a flower of the
morning; it closes a little after noon, but after
you have plucked it and carried it home, it still

feels the call of the morning sun, and will open to him if you give it a good chance. Coil their stems up in the grass on the lawn, where the sun's rays can reach them, and sprinkle them copiously. By the time you are ready for your morning walk, there they sit upon the moist grass, almost as charmingly as upon the wave.

Our more choice wild-flowers, the rarer and finer spirits among them, please us by their individual beauty and charm; others, more coarse and common, delight us by mass and profusion; we regard not the one, but the many, as did Wordsworth his golden daffodils: —

> " Ten thousand saw I at a glance
> Tossing their heads in sprightly dance."

Of such is the marsh-marigold, giving a golden lining to many a dark, marshy place in the leafless April woods, or marking a little watercourse through a greening meadow with a broad line of new gold. One glances up from his walk, and his eye falls upon something like fixed and heaped-up sunshine there beneath the alders, or yonder in the freshening field.

In a measure, the same is true of our wild sunflowers, lighting up many a neglected bushy fence corner or weedy roadside with their bright, beaming faces. The evening primrose is a coarse, rankly growing plant; but, in late summer, how many an untrimmed bank is painted over by it with the most fresh and delicate canary yellow!

We have one flower which grows in vast multitudes, yet which is exquisitely delicate and beautiful in and of itself: I mean the houstonia, or bluets. In May, in certain parts of the country, I see vast sheets of it; in old, low meadow bottoms that have never known the plough, it covers the ground like a dull bluish or purplish snow which has blown unevenly about. In the mass it is not especially pleasing; it has a faded, indefinite sort of look. Its color is not strong and positive enough to be effective in the mass, yet each single flower is a gem of itself. The color of the common violet is much more firm and pronounced; and how many a grassy bank is made gay with it in the mid-May days! We have a great variety of violets, and they are very capricious as to perfume. The only species which are uniformly fragrant are the tall Canada violet, so common in our Northern woods, — white, with a tinge of purple to the under side of its petals, — and the small white violet of the marshy places; yet one summer I came upon a host of the spurred violet in a sunny place in the woods which filled the air with a delicate perfume. A handful of them yielded a perceptible fragrance, but a single flower none that I could detect. The Canada violet very frequently blooms in the fall, and is more fragrant at such times than in its earlier blooming. I must not forget to mention that delicate and lovely flower of May, the fringed polygala. You gather it when you go for the

fragrant, showy orchis, — that is, if you are
lucky enough to find it. It is rather a shy
flower, and is not found in every woods. One
day we went up and down through the woods
looking for it, — woods of mingled oak, chestnut, pine, and hemlock, — and were about giving it up when suddenly we came upon a gay
company of them beside an old wood-road. It
was as if a flock of small rose-purple butterflies
had alighted there on the ground before us.
The whole plant has a singularly fresh and
tender aspect. Its foliage is of a slightly purple tinge, and of very delicate texture. Not
the least interesting feature about the plant is
the concealed fertile flower which it bears on a
subterranean shoot, keeping, as it were, one
flower for beauty and one for use.

II

In our walks we note the most showy and
beautiful flowers, but not always the most
interesting. Who, for instance, pauses to consider that early species of everlasting, commonly
called mouse-ear, that grows nearly everywhere by the roadside or about poor fields?
It begins to be noticeable in May, its whitish
downy appearance, its groups of slender stalks
crowned with a corymb of paper-like buds, con-
trasting it with the fresh green of surrounding
grass or weeds. It is a member of a very large
family, the Compositæ, and does not attract one

by its beauty; but it is interesting, because of
its many curious traits and habits. For instance, it is diœcious, that is, the two sexes are
represented by separate plants; and what is
more curious, these plants are usually found
separated from each other in well defined
groups, like the men and women in an old-
fashioned country church, — always in groups;
here a group of females, there a few yards
away, a group of males. The females may be
known by their more slender and graceful
appearance, and, as the season advances, by
their outstripping the males in growth. Indeed, they become real amazons in comparison
with their brothers. The staminate or male
plants grow but a few inches high; the heads
are round, and have a more dusky or freckled
appearance than do the pistillate; and as soon
as they have shed their pollen their work is
done, they are of no further use, and by the
middle of May or before, their heads droop,
their stalks wither, and their general collapse
sets in. Then the other sex, or pistillate
plants, seem to have taken a new lease of life;
they wax strong, they shoot up with the growing grass and keep their heads above it; they
are alert and active, they bend in the breeze;
their long, tapering flower-heads take on a tinge
of color, and life seems full of purpose and
enjoyment with them. I have discovered, too,
that they are real sun worshipers; that they
turn their faces to the east in the morning, and
follow the sun in his course across the sky till

they all bend to the west at his going down. On the other hand, their brothers have stood stiff and stupid and unresponsive to any influence of sky and air, so far as I could see, till they drooped and died.

Another curious thing is that the females seem vastly more numerous. I should say almost ten times as abundant. You have to hunt for the males ; the others you see far off. One season I used every day to pass several groups or circles of females in the grass by the roadside. I noted how they grew and turned their faces sunward. I observed how alert and vigorous they were, and what a purplish tinge came over their mammæ-shaped flower-heads as June approached. I looked for the males ; to the east, south, west, none could be found for hundreds of yards. On the north, about two hundred feet away, I found a small colony of meek and lowly males. I wondered by what agency fertilization would take place, by insects, or by the wind? I suspected it would not take place. No insects seemed to visit the flowers, and the wind surely could not be relied upon to hit the mark so far off, and from such an unlikely corner, too. But by some means the vitalizing dust seemed to have been conveyed. Early in June the plants began to shed their down, or seed-bearing pappus, still carrying their heads at the top of the grass, so that the breezes could have free access to them and sow the seeds far and wide.

As the seeds are sown broadcast by the wind,

I was at first puzzled to know how the two sexes were kept separate, and always in little communities, till I perceived what I might have read in the botany, that the plant is perennial and spreads by offsets and runners like the strawberry. This would of course keep the two kinds in groups by themselves.

Another plant which has interesting ways and is beautiful besides is the adder's-tongue, or yellow *erythronium*, the earliest of the lilies, and one of the most pleasing. The April sunshine is fairly reflected in its revolute flowers. The lilies have bulbs that sit on or near the top of the ground. The onion is a fair type of the lily in this respect. But here is a lily with the bulb deep in the ground. How it gets there is well worth investigating. The botany says the bulb is deep in the ground but offers no explanation. Now it is only the bulbs of the older or flowering plants that are deep in the ground. The bulbs of the young plants are near the top of the ground. The young plants have but one leaf, the older or flowering ones have two. If you happen to be in the woods at the right time in early April you may see these leaves compactly rolled together, piercing the matted coating of scar leaves that covers the ground like some sharp-pointed instrument. They do not burst their covering or lift it up, but pierce through it like an awl.

But how does the old bulb get so deep into the ground? In digging some of them up one spring in an old meadow bottom, I had to cleave the tough fibrous sod to a depth of eight inches. The smaller ones were barely two inches below the surface. Of course they all started from the seed at the surface of the soil. The young botanist, or nature lover, will find here a field for original research. If, in late May or early June, after the leaves of the plant have disappeared, he finds the ground where they stood showing curious, looping, twisting growths or roots, of a greenish white color, let him examine them. They are as smooth and as large as an angle-worm and very brittle. Both ends will be found in the ground, one attached to the old bulb, the other boring or drilling downward and enlarged till it suggests the new bulb. I do not know that this mother root in all cases comes to the surface. Why it should come at all is a mystery, unless it be in some way to get more power for the downward thrust. My own observations upon the subject are not complete, but I think in the foregoing I have given the clue as to how the bulb each year sinks deeper and deeper into the ground.

It is a pity that this graceful and abundant flower has no good and appropriate common name. It is the earliest of the true lilies, and it has all the grace and charm that belong to this order of flowers. *Erythronium*, its botanical name, is not good, as it is derived from a Greek word that means red, while one species of our flower is yellow and the other is white. How it came to be called adder's-tongue I do

not know; probably from the spotted character of the leaf, which might suggest a snake,
though it in no wise resembles a snake's
tongue.   A fawn is spotted, too, and "fawn-
lily" would be better than adder's-tongue.
Still better is the name "trout-lily," which has
recently been proposed for this plant. It blooms
along the trout streams, and its leaf is as mottled as a trout's back.   The name "dog's-
tooth" may have been suggested by the shape
and color of the bud, but how the "violet"
came to be added is a puzzle, as it has not one
feature of the violet.   It is only another illus-
tration of the haphazard way in which our
wild-flowers, as well as our birds, have been
named.

In my spring rambles I have sometimes come
upon a solitary specimen of this yellow lily
growing beside a mossy stone where the sunshine fell full upon it, and have thought it one
of the most beautiful of our wild-flowers.   Its
two leaves stand up like a fawn's ears, and this
feature, with its re-curved petals, gives it an
alert, wide-awake look.   The white species I
have never seen.   I am told they are very
abundant on the mountains in California.

Another of our common wild-flowers, which
I always look at with an interrogation point in
my mind, is the wild ginger.   Why should this
plant always hide its flower? Its two fuzzy,
heart-shaped green leaves stand up very con-
spicuously amid the rocks or mossy stones, but
its one curious, brown, bell-shaped flower is

always hidden beneath the moss or dry leaves, as if too modest to face the light of the open woods. As a rule, the one thing which a plant is anxious to show and to make much of, and to flaunt before all the world, is its flower. But the wild ginger reverses the rule and blooms in secret. Instead of turning upward toward the light and air, it turns downward toward the darkness and the silence. It has no corolla, but what the botanists call a lurid or brown-purple calyx, which is conspicuous like a corolla. Its root leaves in the mouth a taste precisely like that of ginger.

This plant and the closed gentian are apparent exceptions, in their manner of blooming, to the general habit of the rest of our flowers. The closed gentian does not hide its flower, but the corolla never opens; it always remains a closed bud. It probably never experiences the benefits of insect visits, which Darwin showed us were of such importance in the vegetable world. I once plucked one of the flowers into which a bumble-bee had forced his way, but he had never come out; the flower was his tomb.

There is yet another curious exception which I will mention, namely, the witch-hazel. All our trees and plants bloom in the spring, except this one species; this blooms in the fall. Just as its leaves are fading and falling, its flowers appear, giving out an odor along the bushy lanes and margins of the woods that is to the nose like cool water to the hand. Why it should bloom in the fall instead of in the

spring is a mystery. And it is probably because of this very curious trait that its branches
are used as divining-rods by certain credulous
persons, to point out where springs of water and
precious metals are hidden.

Most young people find botany a dull study.
So it is, as taught from the text-books in the
schools; but study it yourself in the fields and
woods, and you will find it a source of perennial delight. Find your flower and then name
it by the aid of the botany. There is so much
in a name. To find out what a thing is called
is a great help. It is the beginning of knowledge; it is the first step. When we see a
new person who interests us, we wish to know
his or her name. A bird, a flower, a place, —
the first thing we wish to know about it is its
name. Its name helps us to classify it; it
gives us a handle to grasp it by, it sheds a ray
of light where all before was darkness. As
soon as we know the name of a thing, we seem
to have established some sort of relation with it.

The other day, while the train was delayed
by an accident, I wandered a few yards away
from it along the river margin seeking wild-
flowers. Should I find any whose name I did
not know? While thus loitering, a young
English girl also left the train and came in my
direction, plucking the flowers right and left as
she came. But they were all unknown to her;
she did not know the names of one of them,
and she wished to send them home to her
father, too. With what satisfaction she heard

the names; the words seemed to be full of meaning to her, though she had never heard them before in her life. It was what she wanted: it was an introduction to the flowers, and her interest in them increased at once.

"That orange-colored flower which you just plucked from the edge of the water, that is our jewel-weed," I said.

"It looks like a jewel," she replied.

"You have nothing like it in England, or did not have till lately; but I hear it is now appearing along certain English streams, having been brought from this country."

"And what is this?" she inquired, holding up a blue flower with a very bristly leaf and stalk.

"That is viper's-bugloss or blueweed, a plant from your side of the water, one that is making itself thoroughly at home along the Hudson and in the valleys of some of its tributaries among the Catskills. It is a rough, hardy weed, but its flower, with its long, conspicuous purple stamens and blue corolla, as you see, is very pretty."

"Here is another emigrant from across the Atlantic," I said, holding up a cluster of small white flowers, each mounted upon a little inflated brown bag or balloon, — the bladder-campion. "It also runs riot in some of our fields as I am sure you will not see it at home." She went on filling her hands with flowers, and I gave her the names of each, — sweet clover or melilotus, probably a native plant, vervain

(foreign), purple loosestrife (foreign), toad-flax
(foreign), chelone or turtle-head, a native, and
the purple mimulus or monkey-flower, also a
native. It was a likely place for the cardinal-
flower, but I could not find any. I wanted
this hearty English girl to see one of our native
wild-flowers so intense in color that it would
fairly make her eyes water to gaze upon it.

Just then the whistle of the engine sum-
moned us all aboard, and in a moment we were
off.

When one is stranded anywhere in the
country in the season of flowers or birds, if he
feels any interest in these things he always has
something ready at hand to fall back upon.
And if he feels no interest in them he will do
well to cultivate an interest. The tedium of
an eighty-mile drive which I lately took (in
September), cutting through parts of three
counties, was greatly relieved by noting the
various flowers by the roadside. First my
attention was attracted by wild thyme making
purple patches here and there in the meadows
and pastures. I got out of the wagon and
gathered some of it; I found honey-bees working upon it, and remembered that it was a
famous plant for honey in parts of the old
world. It had probably escaped from some
garden; I had never seen it growing wild in
this way before. Along the Schoharie Kill, I
saw acres of blueweed or viper's-bugloss, the
hairy stems of the plants, when looked at
toward the sun, having a frosted appearance.

What is this tall plant by the roadside thickly hung with pendent clusters of long purplish buds or tassels? The stalk is four feet high, the lower leaves are large and lobed, and the whole effect of the plant is striking. The clusters of purple pendents have a very decorative effect. This is a species of nabalus, of the great composite family, and is sometimes called lion's-foot. The flower is cream-colored, but quite inconspicuous. The noticeable thing about it is the drooping or pendulous clusters of what appear to be buds, but which are the involucres, bundles of purple scales, like little staves, out of which the flower emerges.

In another place I caught sight of something intensely blue in a wet, weedy place, and on getting some of it found it to be the closed gentian, a flower to which I have already referred as never opening but always remaining a bud. Four or five of these blue buds, each like the end of your little finger and as long as the first joint, crown the top of the stalk, set in a rosette of green leaves. It is one of our rarer flowers, and a very interesting one, well worth getting out of the wagon to gather. As I drove through a swampy part of Ulster County, my attention was attracted by a climbing plant overrunning the low bushes by the sluggish streams, and covering them thickly with clusters of dull white flowers. I did not remember ever to have seen it before, and on taking it home and examining it found it to be climbing boneset. The flowers are so much like those of boneset that you would suspect their relationship at once.

Without the name any flower is still more or less a stranger to you. The name betrays its family, its relationship to other flowers, and gives the mind something tangible to grasp. It is very difficult for persons who have had no special training to learn the names of the flowers from the botany. The botany is a sealed book to them. The descriptions of the flowers are in a language which they do not understand at all. And the key is no help to them. It is as much a puzzle as the botany itself. They need a key to unlock the key.

One of these days some one will give us a handbook of our wild - flowers, by the aid of which we shall all be able to name those we gather in our walks without the trouble of analyzing them. In this book we shall have a list of all our flowers arranged according to color, as white flowers, blue flowers, yellow flowers, pink flowers, etc., with place of growth and time of blooming. Also lists or sub-lists of fragrant flowers, climbing flowers, marsh flowers, meadow flowers, wood flowers, etc., so that, with flower in hand, by running over these lists we shall be pretty sure to find its name. Having got its name we can turn to Gray or Wood and find a more technical description of it if we choose.

THE HEART OF THE SOUTHERN CATSKILLS

On looking at the Southern and more distant Catskills from the Hudson River on the east, or on looking at them from the west, from some point of vantage in Delaware County, you see, amid the group of mountains, one that looks like the back and shoulders of a gigantic horse. The horse has got his head down grazing; the shoulders are high, and the descent from them down his neck very steep; if he were to lift up his head, one sees that it would be carried far above all other peaks, and that the noble beast might gaze straight to his peers in the Adirondacks or the White Mountains. But the head and neck never come up; some spell or enchantment keeps it down there amid the mighty herd, and the high round shoulders and the smooth strong back of the steed are alone visible. The peak to which I refer is Slide Mountain, the highest of the Catskills by some two hundred feet, and probably the most inaccessible; certainly the hardest to get a view of, it is hedged about so completely by other peaks. The greatest mountain of them all, and apparently the least willing to be seen; only at a distance of thirty or forty miles is it seen to

stand up above all other peaks. It takes its
name from a landslide which occurred many
years ago, down its steep northern side, or
down the neck of the grazing steed. The mane
of spruce and balsam fir was stripped away for
many hundred feet, leaving a long gray streak
visible from afar.

Slide Mountain is the centre and the chief
of the Southern Catskills. Streams flow from
its base and from the base of its subordinates
to all points of the compass: the Rondout and
the Neversink to the south; the Beaverkill to
the west; the Esopus to the north, and several
lesser streams to the east. With its summit as
the centre, a radius of ten miles would include
within the circle described but very little cultivated land; only a few poor, wild farms in some
of the numerous valleys. The soil is poor, a
mixture of gravel and clay, and is subject to
slides. It lies in the valleys in ridges and
small hillocks as if dumped there from a huge
cart. The tops of the Southern Catskills are
all capped with a kind of conglomerate or
"pudden stone" — a rock of cemented quartz
pebbles which underlies the coal measures.
This rock disintegrates under the action of the
elements, and the sand and gravel which result
are carried into the valleys and make up the
most of the soil. From the Northern Catskills,
so far as I know them, this rock has been swept
clean. Low down in the valleys the old red
sandstone crops out, and as you go west into
Delaware County, in many places it alone re-

mains and makes up most of the soil, all the
superincumbent rock having been carried away.

Slide Mountain had been a summons and a
challenge to me for many years. I had fished
every stream that it nourished, and had camped
in the wilderness on all sides of it, and whenever I had caught a glimpse of its summit I
had promised myself to set foot there before
another season had passed. But the seasons
came and went, and my feet got no nimbler
and Slide Mountain no lower, until finally, one
July, seconded by an energetic friend, we
thought to bring Slide to terms by approaching
him through the mountains on the east. With
a farmer's son for guide we struck in by way of
Weaver Hollow, and, after a long and desperate climb, contented ourselves with the Whittenburg, instead of Slide. The view from the
Whittenburg is in many respects more striking,
as you are perched immediately above a broader
and more distant sweep of country, and are
only about two hundred feet lower. You are
here on the eastern brink of the Southern Catskills, and the earth falls away at your feet and
curves down through an immense stretch of
forest till it joins the plain of Shokan, and
thence sweeps away to the Hudson and beyond.
Slide is southwest of you, six or seven miles
distant, but is visible only when you climb
into a treetop. I climbed and saluted him and
promised to call next time.

We passed the night on the Whittenburg,
sleeping on the moss, between two decayed

logs, with balsam boughs thrust into the ground and meeting and forming a canopy over us. In coming off the mountain in the morning we ran upon a huge porcupine, and I learned for the first time that the tail of a porcupine goes with a spring like a trap. It seems to be a set-lock, and you no sooner touch with the weight of a hair one of the quills, than the tail leaps up in a most surprising manner, and the laugh is not on your side. The beast cantered along the path in my front, and I threw myself upon him, shielded by my roll of blankets. He submitted quietly to the indignity, and lay very still under my blankets, with his broad tail pressed close to the ground. This I proceeded to investigate, but had not fairly made a beginning when it went off like a trap, and my hand and wrist were full of quills. This caused me to let up on the creature, when it lumbered away till it tumbled down a precipice. The quills were quickly removed from my hand, when we gave chase. When we came up to him he had wedged himself in between the rocks so that he presented only a back bristling with quills, with the tail lying in ambush below. He had chosen his position well, and seemed to defy us. After amusing ourselves by repeatedly springing his tail and receiving the quills in a rotten stick, we made a slip-noose out of a spruce root, and after much manœuvring got it over his head and led him forth. In what a peevish, injured tone the creature did complain of our unfair tactics.

He protested and protested, and whimpered and scolded like some infirm old man tormented by boys. His game after we led him forth was to keep himself as much as possible in the shape of a ball, but with two sticks and the cord we finally threw him over on his back and exposed his quilless and vulnerable under side, when he fairly surrendered and seemed to say, "Now you may do with me as you like." His great chisel-like teeth, which are quite as formidable as those of the woodchuck, he does not appear to use at all in his defense, but relies entirely upon his quills, and when those fail him he is done for.

After amusing ourselves with him a while longer, we released him and went on our way. The trail to which we had committed ourselves led us down into Woodland Valley, a retreat which so took my eye by its fine trout brook, its superb mountain scenery, and its sweet seclusion, that I marked it for my own and promised myself a return to it at no distant day. This promise I kept and pitched my tent there twice during that season. Both occasions were a sort of laying siege to Slide, but we only skirmished with him at a distance; the actual assault was not undertaken. But the following year, reinforced by two other brave climbers, we determined upon the assault, and upon making it from this the most difficult side. The regular way is by Big Ingin Valley, where the climb is comparatively easy, and where it is often made by women. But from

Woodland Valley only men may essay the ascent. Larkins is the upper inhabitant, and from our camping-ground near his clearing we set out early one June morning.

One would think nothing could be easier to find than a big mountain, especially when one is encamped upon a stream which he knows springs out of its very loins. But for some reason or other we had got an idea that Slide Mountain was a very slippery customer and must be approached cautiously. We had tried from several points in the valley to get a view of it, but were not quite sure we had seen its very head. When on the Whittenburg, a neighboring peak, the year before, I had caught a brief glimpse of it only by climbing a dead tree and craning up for a moment from its topmost branch. It would seem as if the mountain had taken every precaution to shut itself off from a near view. It was a shy mountain, and we were about to stalk it through six or seven miles of primitive woods, and we seemed to have some unreasonable fear that it might elude us. We had been told of parties who had essayed the ascent from this side, and had returned baffled and bewildered. In a tangle of primitive woods, the very bigness of the mountain baffles one. It is all mountain; whichever way you turn — and one turns sometimes in such cases before he knows it — the foot finds a steep and rugged ascent.

The eye is of little service; one must be sure of his bearings and push boldly on and up.

One is not unlike a flea upon a great shaggy beast, looking for the animal's head, or even like a much smaller and much less nimble creature — he may waste his time and steps, and think he has reached the head when he is only upon the rump. Hence I questioned our host, who had several times made the ascent, closely. Larkins laid his old felt hat upon the table, and, placing one hand upon one side and the other upon the other, said: "There Slide lies, between the two forks of the stream, just as my hat lies between my two hands. David will go with you to the forks, and then you will push right on up." But Larkins was not right, though he had traversed all those mountains many times over. The peak we were about to set out for did not lie between the forks, but exactly at the head of one of them; the beginnings of the stream are in the very path of the slide, as we afterward found. We broke camp early in the morning, and with our blankets strapped to our backs and rations in our pockets for two days, set out along an ancient and, in places, an obliterated bark road that followed, and crossed, and recrossed the stream. The morning was bright and warm, but the wind was fitful and petulant, and I predicted rain. What a forest solitude our obstructed and dilapidated wood road led us through: five miles of primitive woods before we came to the forks, three miles before we came to the "burnt shanty," a name merely — no shanty there now for twenty-five years past.

The ravages of the bark peelers were still visible, now in a space thickly strewn with the soft and decayed trunks of hemlock-trees, and overgrown with wild cherry, then in huge mossy logs scattered through the beech and maple woods; some of these logs were so soft and mossy that one could sit or recline upon them as upon a sofa.

But the prettiest thing was the stream soliloquizing in such musical tones there amid the moss-covered rocks and bowlders. How clean it looked, what purity; civilization corrupts the streams as it corrupts the Indian; only in such remote woods can you now see a brook in all its original freshness and beauty. Only the sea and the mountain forest brook are pure; all between is contaminated more or less by the work of man. An ideal trout brook was this, now hurrying, now loitering, now deepening around a great bowlder, now gliding evenly over a pavement of green-gray stone and pebbles; no sediment or stain of any kind, but white and sparkling as snow water, and nearly as cool. Indeed, the water of all this Catskill region is the best in the world. For the first few days one feels as if he could almost live on the water alone; he cannot drink enough of it. In this particular it is indeed the good Bible land, "a land of brooks of water, of fountains and depths that spring out of valleys and hills."

Near the forks we caught, or thought we caught, through an opening, a glimpse of Slide.

Was it Slide, was it the head, or the rump, or the shoulder of the shaggy monster we were in quest of? At the forks there was a bewildering maze of underbrush and great trees, and the way did not seem at all certain, nor was David, who was then at the end of his reckoning, able to reassure us. But in assaulting a mountain, as in assaulting a fort, boldness is the watchword. We pressed forward, following a line of blazed trees for nearly a mile, then turning to the left began the ascent of the mountain. It was steep, hard climbing. We saw numerous marks of both bears and deer; but no birds, save at long intervals the winter wren flitting here and there and darting under logs and rubbish like a mouse. Occasionally its gushing lyrical song would break the silence. After we had climbed an hour or two, the clouds began to gather, and presently the rain began to come down. This was discouraging; but we put our backs up against trees and rocks, and waited for the shower to pass.

"They were wet with the showers of the mountain and embraced the rocks for want of shelter," as they did in Job's time. But the shower was light and brief, and we were soon under way again. Three hours from the forks brought us out on the broad level back of the mountain upon which Slide, considered as an isolated peak, is reared. After a time we entered a dense growth of spruce which covered a slight depression in the table of the mountain. The moss was deep, the ground spongy,

the light dim, the air hushed.   The transition
from the open, leafy woods to this dim, silent,
weird grove was very marked.   It was like the
passage from the street into the temple.   Here
we paused awhile and ate our lunch, and
refreshed ourselves with water gathered from a
little well sunk in the moss.

The quiet and repose of this spruce grove
proved to be the calm that goes before the
storm.   As we passed out of it we came plump
upon the almost perpendicular battlements of
Slide.   The mountain rose like a huge, rock-
bound fortress from this plain-like expanse.   It
was ledge upon ledge, precipice upon precipice,
up which and over which we made our way
slowly and with great labor, now pulling ourselves up by our hands, then cautiously finding
niches for our feet and zigzagging right and left
from shelf to shelf.   This northern side of the
mountain was thickly covered with moss and
lichens, like the north side of a tree.   This
made it soft to the foot and broke many a slip
and fall.   Everywhere a stunted growth of yellow birch, mountain - ash, and spruce and fir
opposed our progress.   The ascent at such an
angle with a roll of blankets on your back is
not unlike climbing a tree; every limb resists
your progress and pushes you back, so that
when we at last reached the summit, after
twelve or fifteen hundred feet of this sort of
work, the fight was about all out of the best of
us.   It was then nearly two o'clock, so that we
had been about seven hours in coming seven
miles.

Here on the top of the mountain we overtook spring, which had been gone from the valley nearly a month. Red clover was opening in the valley below and wild strawberries just ripening; on the summit the yellow birch was just hanging out its catkins, and the claytonia, or spring beauty, was in bloom. The leaf-buds of the trees were just bursting, making a faint mist of green, which, as the eye swept downward, gradually deepened until it became a dense, massive cloud in the valleys. At the foot of the mountain the clintonia, or northern green lily, and the low shad-bush were showing their berries, but long before the top was reached they were found in bloom. I had never before stood amid blooming claytonia, a flower of April, and looked down upon a field that held ripening strawberries. Every thousand feet elevation seemed to make about ten days' difference in the vegetation, so that the season was a month or more later on the top of the mountain than at its base. A very pretty flower which we began to meet with well up on the mountain-side was the painted trillium, the petals white, veined with pink.

The low, stunted growth of spruce and fir which clothes the top of Slide has been cut away over a small space on the highest point, laying open the view on nearly all sides. Here we sat down and enjoyed our triumph. We saw the world as the hawk or the balloonist sees it when he is 3,000 feet in the air. How soft and flowing all the outlines of the hills and mountains beneath us looked. The forests dropped down and undulated away over them, covering them like a carpet. To the east we looked over the near by Whittenburg range to the Hudson and beyond; to the south Peek-o'-Moose, with its sharp crest, and Table Mountain, with its long level top, were the two conspicuous objects; in the west, Mt. Graham and Double Top, about 3,800 feet each, arrested the eye; while in our front to the north we looked over the top of Panther Mountain to the multitudinous peaks of the Northern Catskills. All was mountain and forest on every hand. Civilization seemed to have done little more than to have scratched this rough, shaggy surface of the earth here and there. In any such view, the wild, the aboriginal, the geographical greatly predominate. The works of man dwindle, and the original features of the huge globe come out. Every single object or point is dwarfed; the valley of the Hudson is only a wrinkle in the earth's surface. You discover with a feeling of surprise that the great thing is the earth itself, which stretches away on every hand so far beyond your ken.

The Arabs believe that the mountains steady the earth and hold it together; but they had only to get on the top of a high one to see how insignificant they are, and how adequate the earth looks to get along without them. To the imaginative Oriental people mountains seemed to mean much more than they do to us. They were sacred; they were the abodes of their

divinities.   They offered their sacrifices upon
them.   In the Bible mountains are used as a
symbol of that which is great and holy.   Jeru-
salem is spoken of as a holy mountain.   The
Syrians were beaten by the Children of Israel
because, said they, "Their gods are gods of the
hills; therefore were they stronger than we."
It was on Mount Horeb that God appeared to
Moses in the burning bush, and on Sinai that
he delivered to him the law.   Josephus says
that the Hebrew shepherds never pasture their
flocks on Sinai, believing it to be the abode of
Jehovah.   The solitude of mountain-tops is
peculiarly impressive, and it is certainly easier
to believe the Deity appeared in a burning
bush there than in the valley below.   When
the clouds of heaven, too, come down and en-
velop the top of the mountain — how such a
circumstance must have impressed the old God-
fearing Hebrews.   Moses knew well how to
surround the law with the pomp and circumstance that would inspire the deepest awe and
reverence.

But when the clouds came down and enveloped us on Slide Mountain the grandeur, the
solemnity, was gone in a twinkling; the por-
tentous-looking clouds proved to be nothing
but base fog that wet us and extinguished the
world for us.   How tame, and prosy, and
humdrum the scene instantly became.   But
when the fog lifted, and we looked from under
it as from under a just raised lid, and the eye
plunged again like an escaped bird into those

vast gulfs of space that opened at our feet, the feeling of grandeur and solemnity quickly came back.

The first want we felt on the top of Slide, after we had got some rest, was a want of water. Several of us cast about, right and left, but no sign of water was found. But water must be had, so we all started off deliberately to hunt it up. We had not gone many hundred yards before we chanced upon an ice-cave beneath some rocks — vast masses of ice, with crystal pools of water near. This was good luck indeed, and put a new and brighter face on the situation.

Slide Mountain enjoys a distinction which no other mountain in the State, so far as is known, does — it has a thrush peculiar to itself. This thrush was discovered and described by Eugene Bicknell of New York, in 1880, and has been named Bicknell's thrush. A better name would have been Slide Mountain thrush, as the bird so far has only been found on the mountain. I did not see or hear it upon the Whittenburg, which is only a few miles distant, and only two hundred feet lower. In its appearance to the eye among the trees one would not distinguish it from the gray-cheeked thrush of Baird, or the olive-backed thrush, but its song is totally different. The moment I heard it I said, "There is a new bird, a new thrush," as the quality of all thrush songs is the same. A moment more and I knew it was Bicknell's thrush. The

song is in a minor key, finer, more attenuated,
and more under the breath than that of any
other thrush. It seemed as if the bird was
blowing in a delicate, slender, golden tube, so
fine and yet so flute-like and resonant the song
appeared. At times it was like a musical
whisper of great sweetness and power. The
birds were numerous about the summit, but we
saw them nowhere else. No other thrush was
seen, though a few times during our stay I
caught a mere echo of the hermit's song far
down the mountain-side. A bird I was not
prepared to see or hear was the black poll warbler, a bird usually found much farther north,
but here it was, amid the balsam firs, uttering
its simple, lisping song.

The rocks on the tops of these mountains are
quite sure to attract one's attention, even if he
have no eye for such things. They are masses
of light reddish conglomerate, composed of
round wave-worn quartz pebbles. Every peb-
ble had been shaped and polished upon some
ancient seacoast, probably the Devonian. The
rock disintegrates where it is most exposed to
the weather and forms a loose sandy and pebbly
soil. These rocks form the floor of the coal
formation, but in the Catskill region only the
floor remains; the superstructure has never
existed or has been swept away; hence one
would look for a coal mine here over his head
in the air, rather than under his feet.

This rock did not have to climb up here as
we did; the mountain stooped and took it upon

its back in the bottom of the old seas, and then got lifted up again. This happened so long ago that the memory of the oldest inhabitant of these parts yields no clew to the time.

A pleasant task we had in reflooring and reroofing the log hut with balsam boughs against the night. Plenty of small balsams grew all about, and we soon had a huge pile of their branches in the old hut. What a transformation, this fresh green carpet and our fragrant bed, like the deep-furred robe of some huge animal wrought in that dingy interior! Two or three things disturbed our sleep. A cup of strong beef-tea taken for supper disturbed mine; then the porcupines kept up such a grunting and chattering near our heads, just on the other side of the logs, that sleep was difficult. In my wakeful mood I was a good deal annoyed by a little rabbit that kept whipping in at our dilapidated door and nibbling at our bread and hard-tack. He persisted even after the gray of the morning appeared. Then about four o'clock it began gently to rain. I think I heard the first drop that fell. My companions were all in sound sleep. The rain increased, and gradually the sleepers awoke. It was like the tread of an advancing enemy which every ear had been expecting. The roof over us was of the poorest, and we had no confidence in it. It was made of the thin bark of spruce and balsam, and was full of hollows and depressions. Presently these hollows got full of water, when there was a simultaneous down-

pour of bigger and lesser rills upon the sleepers
beneath. Said sleepers, as one man, sprang
up, each taking his blanket with him; but by
the time some of the party had got themselves
stowed away under the adjacent rock, the rain
ceased. It was little more than the dissolving
of the night-cap of fog which so often hangs
about these heights. With the first appearance of the dawn I had heard the new thrush
in the scattered trees near the hut — a strain
as fine as if blown upon a fairy flute, a sup-
pressed musical whisper from out the tops of
the dark spruces. Probably never did there go
up from the top of a great mountain a smaller
song to greet the day, albeit it was of the pur-
est harmony. It seemed to have in a more
marked degree the quality of interior reverbera-
tion than any other thrush song I had ever
heard. Would the altitude or the situation
account for its minor key? Loudness would
avail little in such a place. Sounds are not far
heard on a mountain-top; they are lost in the
abyss of vacant air. But amid these low,
dense, dark spruces, which make a sort of cano-
pied privacy of every square rod of ground,
what could be more in keeping than this delicate musical whisper? It was but the soft
hum of the balsams, interpreted and embodied
in a bird's voice.

It was the plan of two of our companions to
go from Slide over into the head of the Rondout, and thence out to the railroad at the little
village of Shokan, an unknown way to them,

involving nearly an all-day pull the first day through a pathless wilderness. We ascended to the topmost floor of the tower, and from my knowledge of the topography of the country I pointed out to them their course, and where the valley of the Rondout must lie. The vast stretch of woods, when it came into view from under the foot of Slide, seemed from our point of view very uniform. It swept away to the southeast, rising gently toward the ridge that separates Lone Mountain from Peek o' Moose, and presented a comparatively easy problem. As a clew to the course, the line where the dark belt or saddle-cloth of spruce, which covered the top of the ridge they were to skirt, ended and the deciduous woods began, a sharp, well-defined line was pointed out as the course to be followed. It led straight to the top of the broad level-backed ridge which connected two higher peaks and immediately behind which lay the headwaters of the Rondout. Having studied the map thoroughly and possessed themselves of the points, they rolled up their blankets about nine o'clock and were off, my friend and myself purposing to spend yet another day and night on Slide. As our friends plunged down into that fearful abyss, we shouted to them the old classic caution, "Be bold, be bold, *be not too* bold." It required courage to make such a leap into the unknown as I knew those young men were making, and it required prudence. A faint heart or a bewildered head, and serious consequences might

have resulted. The theory of a thing is so
much easier than the practice. The theory is
in the air, the practice is in the woods; the
eye, the thought, travel easily where the foot
halts and stumbles. However, our friends
made the theory and the fact coincide; they
kept the dividing line between the spruce and
the birches, and passed over the ridge into the
valley safely, but they were torn and bruised
and wet by the showers, and made the last few
miles of their journey on will and pluck alone,
their last pound of positive strength having
been exhausted in making the descent through
the chaos of rocks and logs into the head of the
valley. In such emergencies one overdraws
his account; he travels on the credit of the
strength he expects to gain when he gets his
dinner and some sleep. Unless one has made
such a trip himself (and I have several times
in my life) he can form but a faint idea what
it is like — what a trial it is to the body and
what a trial it is to the mind. You are fighting a battle with an enemy in ambush. How
those miles and leagues which your feet must
compass lie hidden there in that wilderness;
how they seem to multiply themselves; how
they are fortified with logs, and rocks, and
fallen trees; how they take refuge in deep gullies, and skulk behind unexpected eminences!
Your body not only feels the fatigue of the
battle, your mind feels the strain of the under-
taking; you may miss your mark; the mountains may outmanœuvre you. All that day,

whenever I looked down upon that treacherous wilderness, I thought with misgivings of those two friends groping their way there, and would have given something to have known how it fared with them. Their concern was probably less than my own, because they were more ignorant of what was before them. Then there was just a slight shadow of a fear in my mind that I might have been in error about some points of the geography I had pointed out to them. But all was well, and the victory was won according to the campaign which I had planned. When we saluted our friends upon their own doorstep a week afterward, the wounds were nearly all healed and the rents all mended.

When one is on a mountain-top he spends most of the time in looking at the show he has been at such pains to see. About every hour we would ascend the rude lookout to take a fresh observation. With a glass I could see my native hills forty miles away to the north-west. I was now upon the back of the horse, yea, upon the highest point of his shoulders, which had so many times attracted my attention as a boy. We could look along his balsam-covered back to his rump from which the eye glanced away down into the forests of the Neversink, and on the other hand plump down into the gulf where his head was grazing or drinking. During the day there was a grand procession. of thunder-clouds filing along over the Northern Catskills, and letting down veils of rain and enveloping them. From such an elevation one has the same view of the clouds that he does from the prairie or the ocean. They do not seem to rest across and to be upborne by the hills, but they emerge out of the dim west, thin and vague, and grow and stand up as they get nearer and roll by him, on a level but invisible highway, huge chariots of wind and storm.

In the afternoon a thick cloud threatened us, but it proved to be the condensation of vapor that announces a cold wave. There was soon a marked fall in the temperature, and as night drew near it became pretty certain that we were going to have a cold time of it. The wind rose, the vapor above us thickened and came nearer, until it began to drive across the summit in slender wraiths, which curled over the brink and shut out the view. We became very diligent in getting in our night wood, and in gathering more boughs to calk up the openings in the hut. The wood we scraped together was a sorry lot, roots and stumps and branches of decayed spruce, such as we could collect without an axe, and some rags and tags of birch bark. The fire was built in one corner of the shanty, the smoke finding easy egress through large openings on the east side and in the roof over it. We doubled up the bed, making it thicker and more nest-like, and as darkness set in stowed ourselves into it beneath our blankets. The searching wind found out every crevice about our heads and shoulders, and it was icy cold. Yet we fell asleep, and had slept about an hour when my companion sprang up in an unwonted state of excitement for so placid a man. His excitement was occasioned by the sudden discovery that what appeared to be a bar of ice was fast taking the place of his backbone. His teeth chattered and he was convulsed with ague. I advised him to replenish the fire, and to wrap himself in his blanket and cut the liveliest capers he was capable of in so circumscribed a place. This he promptly did, and the thought of his wild and desperate dance there in the dim light, his tall form, his blanket flapping, his teeth chattering, the porcupines outside marking time with their squeals and grunts, still provokes a smile, though it was a serious enough matter at the time. After a while the warmth came back to him, but he dared not trust himself again to the boughs; he fought the cold all night as one might fight a besieging foe. By carefully husbanding the fuel, the beleaguering enemy was kept at bay till morning came, but when morning did come even the huge root he had used as a chair was consumed. Rolled in my blanket beneath a foot or more of balsam boughs, I had got some fairly good sleep, and was most of the time oblivious to the melancholy vigil of my friend. As we had but a few morsels of food left, and had been on rather short rations the day before, hunger was added to his other discomforts. At that time a letter was on the way to him from his wife, which contained this prophetic sentence: "I hope thee is not suffering with cold and hunger on some lone mountain-top."

Mr. Bicknell's thrush struck up again at the first signs of dawn, notwithstanding the cold. I could hear his penetrating and melodious whisper as I lay buried beneath the boughs. Presently I arose and invited my friend to turn in for a brief nap, while I gathered some wood and set the coffee brewing. With a brisk, roaring fire on, I left for the spring to fetch some water and to make my toilet. The leaves of the mountain goldenrod, which everywhere covered the ground in the opening, were covered with frozen particles of vapor, and the scene, shut in by fog, was chill and dreary enough.

We were now not long in squaring an account with Slide, and making ready to leave. Round pellets of snow began to fall, and we came off the mountain on the 10th of June in a November storm and temperature. Our purpose was to return by the same valley we had come. A well-defined trail led off the summit to the north; to this we committed ourselves. In a few minutes we emerged at the head of the slide that had given the mountain its name. This was the path made by visitors to the scene; when it ended the track of the avalanche began, no bigger than your hand apparently had it been at first, but it rapidly grew, until it became several rods in width. It dropped down from our feet straight as an arrow until it was lost in the fog, and looked perilously steep. The dark forms of the spruce were clinging to the edge of it as if reaching out to their fellows to save them. We hesitated on the brink, but finally cautiously began the descent. The rock was quite naked and slippery, and only on the margin of the slide were there any bowlders to stay the foot or bushy growths to aid the hand. As we paused, after some minutes, to select our course, one of the finest surprises of the trip awaited us: the fog in our front was swiftly whirled up by the breeze, like the drop-curtain at the theatre, only much more rapidly, and in a twinkling the vast gulf opened before us. It was so sudden as to be almost bewildering. The world opened like a book and there were the pictures; the spaces were without a film, the forests and mountains looked surprisingly near; in the heart of the Northern Catskills a wild valley was seen flooded with sunlight. Then the curtain ran down again, and nothing was left but the gray strip of rock to which we clung, plunging down into the obscurity. Down and down we made our way. Then the fog lifted again. It was Jack and his bean-stalk renewed; new wonders, new views, awaited us every few moments, till at last the whole valley below us stood in the clear sunshine. We passed down a precipice and there was a rill of water, the beginning of the creek that wound through the valley below; farther on, in a deep depression, lay the remains of an old snow-bank; winter had made his last stand here, and April flowers were springing up almost amid his very bones.

We did not find a palace, and a hungry giant, and a princess, etc., at the end of our beanstalk, but we found a humble roof and the hospitable heart of Mrs. Larkins, which answered our purpose better. And we were in the mood, too, to have undertaken an eating bout with any giant Jack ever discovered.

Of all the retreats I have found amid the Catskills, there is no other that possesses quite so many charms for me as this valley, wherein stands Larkins's humble dwelling; it is so wild, so quiet, and has such superb mountain views. In coming up the valley, you have apparently reached the head of civilization a mile or more lower down; here the rude little houses end, and you turn to the left into the woods. Presently you emerge into a clearing again, and before you rises the rugged and indented crest of Panther Mountain, and near at hand, on a low plateau, rises the humble roof of Larkins, — you get a picture of the Panther and of the homestead at one glance. Above the house hangs a high, bold cliff covered with forest, with a broad fringe of blackened and blasted treetrunks, where the cackling of the great pilated woodpecker may be heard; on the left a dense forest sweeps up to the sharp spruce-covered cone of the Whittenburg, nearly four thousand feet high, while at the head of the valley rises Slide over all. From a meadow just back of Larkins's barn, a view may be had of all these mountains, while the terraced side of Cross Mountain bounds the

view immediately to the east. Running from
the top of Panther toward Slide one sees a
gigantic wall of rock, crowned with a dark line
of fir.   The forest abruptly ends, and in its
stead rises the face of this colossal rocky escarp-
ment, like some barrier built by the mountain
gods.   Eagles might nest here.   It breaks the
monotony of the world of woods very impres-
sively.

I delight in sitting on a rock in one of these
upper fields, and seeing the sun go down behind Panther.   The rapid flowing brook below
me fills all the valley with a soft murmur.
There is no breeze, but the great atmospheric
tide flows slowly in toward the cooling forest;
one can see it by the motes in the air illuminated by the setting sun: presently, as the air
cools a little, the tide turns and flows slowly
out.   The long, winding valley up to the foot
of Slide, five miles of primitive woods, how
wild and cool it looks, its one voice the murmur of the creek.   On the Whittenburg the
sunshine lingers long; now it stands up like an
island in a sea of shadows, then slowly sinks
beneath the wave.   The evening call of a robin
or the thrush at his vespers makes a marked
impression on the silence and the solitude.

The following day my friend and I pitched
our tent in the woods beside the stream where
I had pitched it twice before and passed several
delightful days, with trout in abundance and
wild strawberries at intervals.   Mrs. Larkins's
cream-pot, butter-jar, and bread-box were within

easy reach. Near the camp was an unusually large spring, of icy coldness, which served as our refrigerator. Trout or milk immersed in this spring in a tin pail would keep sweet four or five days. One night some creature, probably a lynx or a raccoon, came and lifted the stone from the pail that held the trout and took out a fine string of them and ate them up on the spot, leaving only the string and one head. In August bears come down to an ancient and now brushy bark peeling near by for blackberries. But the creature that most infests these backwoods is the porcupine. He is as stupid and indifferent as the skunk; his broad, blunt nose points a witless head. They are great gnawers, and will gnaw your house down if you do not look out. Of a summer evening they will walk coolly into your open door if not prevented. The most annoying animal to the camper-out in this region, and the one he needs to be most on the lookout for, is the cow. Backwoods cows and young cattle seem always to be famished for salt, and they will fairly lick the fisherman's clothes off his back, and his tent and equipage out of existence, if you give them a chance. On one occasion some wood-ranging heifers and steers that had been hovering around our camp for some days made a raid upon it when we were absent. The tent was shut and everything snugged up, but they ran their long tongues under the tent, and, tasting something savory, hooked out John Stuart Mill's "Essays on Religion," which one of us had brought along thinking to read in the woods. They mouthed the volume around a good deal, but its logic was too tough for them, and they contented themselves with devouring the paper in which it was wrapped. If the cattle had not been surprised at just that point, it is probable the tent would have gone down before their eager curiosity and thirst for salt.

The raid which Larkins's dog made upon our camp was amusing rather than annoying. He was a very friendly and intelligent shepherd dog, probably a collie. Hardly had we sat down to our first lunch in camp before he called on us. But as he was disposed to be too friendly, and to claim too large a share of the lunch, we rather gave him the cold shoulder. He did not come again; but a few evenings afterward, as we sauntered over to the house on some trifling errand, the dog suddenly conceived a bright little project. He seemed to say to himself, on seeing us, "There come both of them now, just as I have been hoping they would; now while they are away I will run quickly over and know what they have got that a dog can eat." My companion saw the dog get up on our arrival, and go quickly in the direction of our camp, and he said something in the cur's manner suggested to him the object of his hurried departure. He called my attention to the fact, and we hastened back. On cautiously nearing camp, the dog was seen amid the pails in the shallow water of the creek investigating them. He had uncovered the butter, and was about to taste it, when we shouted, and he made quick steps for home, with a very "kill - sheep" look. When we again met him at the house next day he could not look us in the face, but sneaked off, utterly crestfallen. This was a clear case of reasoning on the part of the dog, and afterward a clear case of a sense of guilt from wrong-doing. The dog will probably be a man before any other animal.

"ADMIRE the bird's egg and leave it in its nest" is a wiser forbearance than "Love the wood-rose and leave it on its stalk." We will try to leave these eggs in the nest, and as far as possible show the bird and the nest with them.

The first egg of spring is undoubtedly a hen's egg. The domestic fowls, not being compelled to shift for themselves, and having artificial shelter, are not so mindful of the weather and the seasons as the wild birds. But the hen of the woods and the hen of the prairie, namely, the ruffed and the pinnated grouse, do not usually nest till the season is so far advanced that danger from frost is past.

The first wild egg, in New York and New England, is probably that of an owl, the great horned owl, it is said, laying as early as March. They probably shelter their eggs from the frost and the snow before incubation begins. The little screech-owl waits till April, and seeks the deep snug cavity of an old tree; the heart of a decayed apple-tree suits him well. Begin your search by the middle of April, and before the month is past you will find the four white, round eggs resting upon a little dry grass or a few dry leaves in the bottom of a long cavity. Owls' eggs are inclined to be spherical. You would expect to see a big round-headed, round-eyed creature come out of such an egg.

The passenger pigeon nests before danger from frost is passed; but as it lays but two eggs, probably in two successive days, the risks from this source are not great; though occasionally a heavy April snowstorm breaks them up.

Which is the earliest song-bird's egg? One cannot be quite so certain here, as he can as to which the first wild-flower is, for instance; but I would take my chances on finding that of the phœbe-bird first, and finding it before the close of April, unless the season is very backward. The present season (1883), a pair built their nest under the eaves of my house, and deposited their eggs, the last days of the month. Some English sparrows that had been hanging around, and doubtless watching the phœbes, threw the eggs out and took possession of the nest. How shrewd and quick to take the hint these little feathered John Bulls are. With a handful of rattling pebble-stones I told this couple very plainly that they were not welcome visitors to my premises. They fled precipitately. The next morning they appeared again, but were much shyer. Another discharge of pebbles, and they were off as if bound for the protection of the British flag, and did not return. I notice wherever I go that these birds have got a suspicion in their heads that public opinion has changed with regard to them, and that they are no longer wanted.

The eggs of the phœbe-bird are snow white, and when, in threading the gorge of some mountain trout-brook, or prowling about some high, overhanging ledge, one's eye falls upon this mossy structure planted with such matchless art upon a little shelf of the rocks, with its complement of five or six pearl-like eggs, he is ready to declare it the most pleasing nest in all the range of our bird architecture. It was such a happy thought for the bird to build there, just out of the reach of all four-footed beasts of prey, sheltered from the storms and winds, and, by the use of moss and lichens, blending its nest so perfectly with its surroundings that only the most alert eye can detect it. An egg upon a rock, and thriving there, — the frailest linked to the strongest, as if the geology of the granite mountain had been bent into the service of the bird. I doubt if crows, or jays, or owls ever rob these nests. Phœbe has outwitted them. They never heard of the bird that builded its house upon a rock. "Strong is thy dwelling-place, and thou puttest thy nest in a rock."

The song-sparrow sometimes nests in April, but not commonly in our latitude. Emerson says, in "May-Day:" —

> " The sparrow meek, prophetic-eyed,
> Her nest beside the snow-drift weaves,
> Secure the osier yet will hide
> Her callow brood in mantling leaves."

But the sparrow usually prefers to wait till the snow-drift is gone. I have never found the

nest of one till long after the last drift had
disappeared from the fields, though a late writer
upon New England birds says the sparrow
sometimes lays in April, when snow is yet upon
the ground.

The sparrow is not a beautiful bird except in
our affections and associations, and its eggs are
not beautiful as eggs go, — four or five little
freckled spheres, that, like the bird itself, blend
well with the ground upon which they are
placed.

The eggs of the "chippie," or social sparrow,
are probably the most beautiful of sparrow
eggs, being of a bright bluish green with a ring
of dark purple spots around the larger end.

Generally there is but little relation between
the color of the bird and the color of its egg.
For the most part the eggs of birds that occupy
open, exposed nests are of some tint that har-
monizes well with the surroundings. With the
addition of specks of various hue they are rendered still less conspicuous. The eggs of the
scarlet tanager are greenish blue, with faint
brown or purplish markings. The blackbird
lays a greenish blue egg also, with various
markings. Indeed, the favorite ground tint of
the birds that build open nests is a greenish
blue; sometimes the blue predominates, sometimes the green; while the eggs of birds that
build concealed nests, or lay in dark cavities,
are generally white, as is the case with the
eggs of all our woodpeckers, for instance.
The eggs of the bluebird are bluish white.

Among the flycatchers, the nest of the phœbe is most concealed, at least from above, and her eggs are white, while those of nearly all the other species are more or less tinted and marked. The eggs of the humming-bird are white, but the diminutiveness of their receptacle is a sufficient concealment. Another white egg is that of the kingfisher, deposited upon fish-bones at the end of a hole in the bank eight or nine feet long. The bank swallow also lays white eggs, as does the chimney swallow, the white-bellied swallow, and the purple martin. The eggs of the barn swallow and cliff swallow are more or less speckled. In England the kingfisher (smaller and much more brilliantly colored than ours), woodpeckers, the bank swallow, the swift, the wry-neck (related to the woodpecker), and the dipper, also lay white eggs.

A marked exception to the above rule is furnished by the eggs of the Baltimore oriole, perhaps the most fantastically marked of all our birds' eggs. One would hardly expect a plainly marked egg in such a high-swung, elaborately woven, deeply pouched, aristocratic nest. The threads and strings and horsehairs with which the structure is sewed and bound and stayed are copied in the curious lines and markings of the treasures it holds. After the oriole is through with its nest, it is sometimes taken possession of by the house wren in which to rear its second brood. The long, graceful cavity, with its fine carpet of hair, is filled

with coarse twigs, as if one were to build a log
hut in a palace, and the rusty-colored eggs of
the little busybody deposited there. The wren
would perhaps stick to its bundle of small
fagots in the box or pump tree, and rear its
second brood in the cradle of the first, were it
not that by seeking new lodgings time can be.
saved. The male bird builds and furnishes the
second nest, and the mother bird has begun to
lay in it before the first is empty.

The chatter of a second brood of nearly
fledged wrens is heard now (August 20) in an
oriole's nest suspended from the branch of an
apple-tree near where I write. Earlier in the.
season the parent birds made long and determined attempts to establish themselves in a
cavity that had been occupied by a pair of bluebirds. The original proprietor of the place
was the downy woodpecker. He had excavated
it the autumn before and had passed the winter
there, often to my certain knowledge lying
abed till nine o'clock in the morning. In the
spring he went elsewhere, probably with a
female, to begin the season in new quarters.
The bluebirds early took possession, and in
June their first brood had flown. The wrens
had been hanging around, evidently with an
eye on the place (such little comedies may be
witnessed anywhere), and now very naturally
thought it was their turn. A day or two after
the young bluebirds had flown, I noticed some
fine, dry grass clinging to the entrance to the
cavity; a circumstance which I understood a

few moments later, when the wren rushed by
me into the cover of a small Norway spruce,
hotly pursued by the male bluebird. It was a
brown streak and a blue streak pretty close
together. The wrens had gone to house-clean-
ing, and the bluebird had returned to find his
bed and bedding being pitched out-of-doors,
and had thereupon given the wrens to understand in the most emphatic manner that he had
no intention of vacating the premises so early
in the season. Day after day, for more than
two weeks, the male bluebird had to clear his
premises of these intruders. It occupied much
of his time and not a little of mine, as I sat
with a book in a summer-house near by, laughing at his pretty fury and spiteful onset. On
two occasions the wren rushed under the chair
in which I sat, and a streak of blue lightning
almost flashed in my very face. One day, just
as I had passed the tree in which the cavity
was placed, I heard the wren scream desperately; turning, I saw the little vagabond fall
into the grass with the wrathful bluebird fairly
upon him; the latter had returned just in time
to catch him, and was evidently bent on pun-
ishing him well. But in the squabble in the
grass the wren escaped and took refuge in the
friendly evergreen. The bluebird paused for a
moment with outstretched wings looking for
the fugitive, then flew away. A score of times
during the month of June did I see the wren
taxing every energy to get away from the bluebird. He would dart into the stone wall,

under the floor of the summer-house, into the
weeds — anywhere to hide his diminished head.
The bluebird with his bright coat looked like
an officer in uniform in pursuit of some wicked,
rusty little street gamin. Generally the favorite house of refuge of the wrens was the little
spruce, into which their pursuer made no
attempt to follow them. The female would sit
concealed amid the branches, chattering in a
scolding, fretful way, while the male with his
eye upon his tormentor would perch on the topmost shoot and sing. Why he sang at such
times, whether in triumph and derision, or to
keep his courage up and reassure his mate, I
could not make out. When his song was suddenly cut short and I glanced to see him dart
down into the spruce, my eye usually caught
a twinkle of blue wings hovering near. The
wrens finally gave up the fight, and their enemies reared their second brood in peace.

That the wren should use such coarse, refrac-
tory materials, especially since it builds in holes
where twigs are so awkward to carry and ad-
just, is curious enough. All its congeners, the
marsh wrens, the Carolina wren, the winter
wren, build of soft flexible materials. The
nest of the winter wren, and of the English
"Jenny Wren," is mainly of moss, and is a
marvel of softness and warmth.

One day a swarm of honey-bees went into
my chimney, and I mounted the stack to see
into which flue they had gone. As I craned
my neck above the sooty vent, with the bees

humming about my ears, the first thing my eye
rested upon in the black interior was two long
white pearls upon a little shelf of twigs, the
nest of the chimney swallow, or swift, —
honey, soot, and birds' eggs closely associated.
The bees, though in an unused flue, soon found
the gas of anthracite that hovered about the top
of the chimney too much for them, and they
left. But the swallows are not repelled by
smoke. They seem to have entirely abandoned
their former nesting-places in hollow trees and
stumps and to frequent only chimneys. A
tireless bird, never perching, all day upon' the
wing and probably capable of flying one thousand miles in twenty-four hours; they do not
even stop to gather materials for their nests,
but snap off the small dry twigs from the treetops as they fly by. Confine one of these swallows to a room and it will not perch, but after
flying till it becomes bewildered and exhausted,
it clings to the side of the wall till it dies. I
once found one in my room on returning, after
several days' absence, in which life seemed
nearly extinct; its feet grasped my finger as I
removed it from the wall, but its eyes closed
and it seemed about on the point of joining its
companion which lay dead upon the floor.
Tossing it into the air, however, seemed to
awaken its wonderful powers of flight, and
away it went straight toward the clouds. On
the wing the chimney swallow looks like an
athlete stripped for the race. There is the
least appearance of quill and plumage of any of

our birds, and, with all its speed and marvelous evolutions, the effect of its flight is stiff and
wiry. There appears to be but one joint in
the wing, and that next the body. This peculiar inflexible motion of the wings, as if they
were little sickles of sheet iron, seems to be
owing to the length and development of the
primary quills and the smallness of the secondary. The wing appears to hinge only at the
wrist. The barn swallow lines its rude ma-
sonry with feathers, but the swift begins life on
bare twigs, glued together by a glue of home
manufacture as adhesive as Spaulding's.

I have wondered if Emerson referred to any
particular bird in these lines from "The Problem."

"Know'st thou what wove yon wood-bird's nest
Of leaves, and feathers from her breast?"

Probably not, but simply availed himself of
the general belief that certain birds or fowls
lined their nests with their own feathers. This
is notably true of the eider duck, and in a
measure of our domestic fowls, but so far as I
know is not true of any of our small birds.
The barn swallow and house wren feather their
nests at the expense of the hens and geese.
The winter wren picks up the feathers of the
ruffed grouse. The chickadee, Emerson's
favorite bird, uses a few feathers in its uphol-
stering, but not its own. In England, I
noticed that the little willow warbler makes a
free use of feathers from the poultry yard.
Many of our birds use hair in their nests, and

the kingbird and cedar-bird like wool. I have found a single feather of the bird's own in the nest of the phœbe. Such a circumstance would perhaps justify the poet.

About the first of June there is a nest in the woods upon the ground with four creamy white eggs in it spotted with brown or lilac, chiefly about the larger ends, that always gives the walker, who is so lucky as to find it, a thrill of pleasure. It is like a ground-sparrow's nest with a roof or canopy to it. The little brown or olive backed bird starts away from your feet and runs swiftly and almost silently over the dry leaves, and then turns her speckled breast to see if you are following. She walks very prettily, by far the prettiest pedestrian in the woods. But if she thinks you have discovered her secret, she feigns lameness and disability of both legs and wing, to decoy you into the pursuit of her. This is the golden-crowned thrush, or accentor, a strictly wood-bird, about the size of a song-sparrow, with the dullest of gold upon his crown, but the brightest of songs in his heart. The last nest of this bird I found was while in quest of the pink cypripedium. We suddenly spied a couple of the flowers a few steps from the path along which we were walking and had stooped to admire them, when out sprang the bird from beside them, doubtless thinking she was the subject of observation instead of the flowers that swung their purple bells but a foot or two above her. But we never should have seen her had she kept her place. She had found a rent in the matted carpet of dry leaves and pine needles that covered the ground, and into this had insinuated her nest, the leaves and needles forming a canopy above it, sloping to the south and west, the source of the more frequent summer rains.

At about the same time one finds the nest above described, if he were to explore the woods very thoroughly, he might chance upon two curious eggs lying upon the leaves as if dropped there by chance. They are elliptical, both ends of a size, about an inch and a quarter long, of a creamy white spotted with lavender. These are the eggs of the whippoorwill, a bird that has absolutely no architectural instincts or gifts. Perhaps its wide, awkward mouth and short beak are ill-adapted to carrying nest materials. It is awkward upon the ground and awkward upon the tree, being unable to perch upon a limb, except lengthwise of it.

The song and game birds lay pointed eggs, but the night birds lay round or elliptical eggs.

The egg collector sometimes stimulates a bird to lay an unusual number of eggs. A youth, whose truthfulness I do not doubt, told me he once induced a highhole to lay twenty-nine eggs, by robbing her of an egg each day. The eggs became smaller and smaller, till the twenty-ninth one was only the size of a chippie's egg. At this point the bird gave up the contest.

There is a last egg of summer as well as a

first egg of spring, but one cannot name either with much confidence. Both the robin and the chippie sometimes rear a third brood in August, but the birds that delay their nesting till midsummer are the goldfinch and the cedar-bird, the former waiting for the thistle to ripen its seeds, and the latter probably for the appearance of certain insects which it takes on the wing. Often the cedar-bird does not build till August, and will line its nest with wool if it can get it, even in this sultry month. The eggs are marked and colored, as if a white egg were to be spotted with brown, then colored a pale blue, then again sharply dotted or blotched with blackish or purplish spots.

But the most common August nest with me — early August — is that of the goldfinch, — a deep, snug, compact nest, with no loose ends hanging, placed in the fork of a small limb of an apple-tree, peach-tree, or ornamental shade-tree. The eggs are a faint bluish white.

While the female is sitting, the male feeds her regularly. She calls to him on his approach, or when she hears his voice passing by, in the most affectionate, feminine, childlike tones, the only case I know of where the sitting bird makes any sound while in the act of incubation. When a rival male invades the tree, or approaches too near, the male whose nest it holds pursues and reasons or expostulates with him in the same bright, amicable, confiding tones. Indeed, most birds make use of their sweetest notes in war. The song of love is the

song of battle too. The male yellow-birds flit
about from point to point, apparently assuring
each other of the highest sentiments of esteem
and consideration, at the same time that one
intimates to the other that he is carrying his
joke a little too far. It has the effect of saying
with mild and good-humored surprise, "Why,
my dear sir, this is my territory; you surely do
not mean to trespass; permit me to salute you,
and to escort you over the line." Yet the
intruder does not always take the hint. Occasionally the couple have a brief sparring match
in the air, and mount up and up, beak to beak,
to a considerable height, but rarely do they
actually come to blows.

The yellow-bird becomes active and conspicuous after the other birds have nearly all withdrawn from the stage and become silent, their
broods reared and flown. August is his month,
his festive season. It is his turn now. The
thistles are ripening their seeds, and his nest is
undisturbed by jay-bird or crow. He is the first
bird I hear in the morning, circling and swinging through the air in that peculiar undulating
flight and calling out on the downward curve
of each stroke, "Here we go, here we go!"
Every hour in the day he indulges in his circling, billowy flight. It is a part of his musical performance. His course at such times is
a deeply undulating line, like the long gentle
roll of the summer sea, the distance from crest
to crest or from valley to valley being probably
thirty feet; this distance is made with but one

brief beating of the wings on the downward curve. As he quickly opens them they give him a strong upward impulse and he describes the long arc with them closely folded. Thus falling and recovering, rising and sinking like dolphins in the sea, he courses through the summer air. In marked contrast to this feat is his manner of flying when he indulges in a brief outburst of song in the air. Now he flies level, with broad expanded wings nearly as round and as concave as two shells, which beat the air slowly. The song is the chief matter now, and the wings are used only to keep him afloat while delivering it. In the other case the flight is the main concern, and the voice merely punctuates it.

I know no autumn egg but a hen's egg, though a certain old farmer tells me he finds a quail's nest full of eggs nearly every September; but fall progeny of any kind has a belated start in life, and the chances are against it.

BIRD COURTSHIP

THERE is something about the matchmaking of birds that is not easily penetrated. The jealousies and rivalries of the males and of the females is easily understood — it is quite human; but those sudden rushes of several males, some of them already mated, after one female, with squeals and screams and a great clatter of wings — what does it mean? There is nothing human about that, unless it be illustrative of a trait that has at times cropped out in the earlier races and which is still seen among the Esquimaux, where the male carries off the female by force. But in these sudden sallies among the birds the female, so far as I have observed, is never carried off. One may see half a dozen English sparrows engaged in what at first glance appears to be a general mêlée in the gutter or on the sidewalk, but if you look more closely you will see a single female in the midst of the mass, beating off the males who, with plumage puffed out and screaming and chattering, are all making a set at her. She strikes right and left, and seems to be equally displeased with them all. But her anger may be all put on, and she may be giving the wink all the time to her favorite.

The Esquimaux maiden is said by Doctor Nan-
sen to resist stoutly being carried off even by
the man she is desperately in love with.

In the latter half of April we pass through
what I call the "robin racket"—trains of
three or four birds rushing pell-mell over the
lawn and fetching up in a tree or bush, or
occasionally upon the ground, all piping and
screaming at the top of their voices, but
whether in mirth or anger it is hard to tell.
The nucleus of the train is a female. One
cannot see that the males in pursuit of her are
rivals; it seems rather as if they had united to
hustle her out of the place. But somehow the
matches are no doubt made and sealed during
these mad rushes. Maybe the female shouts
out to her suitors, "Who touches me first
wins," and away she scurries like an arrow.
The males shout out, "Agreed!" and away
they go in pursuit, each trying to outdo the
other. The game is a brief one. Before one
can get the clew to it the party has dipersed.

Earlier in the season the pretty sparring of
the males is the chief feature. You may see
two robins apparently taking a walk or a run
together over the sward or along the road; only
first one bird runs, and then the other. They
keep a few feet apart, stand very erect, and the
course of each describes the segment of an arc
about the other, thus:—

How courtly and deferential their manners

toward each other are; often they pipe a shrill, fine strain, audible only a few yards away. Then, in a twinkling, one makes a spring and they are beak to beak and claw to claw as they rise up a few feet into the air. But usually no blow is delivered; not a feather is ruffled; each, I suppose, finds the guard of the other perfect. Then they settle down upon the ground again and go through with the same running challenge as before. How their breasts glow in the strong April sunlight; how perk and military the bearing of each! Often they will run about each other in this way for many rods. After a week or so the males seem to have fought all their duels, when the rush and racket I have already described begins.

The bluebird wins his mate by the ardor of his attentions and the sincerity of his compliments, and by finding a house ready built which cannot be surpassed. The male bluebird is usually here several days before the female, and he sounds forth his note as loudly and eloquently as he can till she appears. On her appearance he flies at once to the box or tree cavity upon which he has had his eye, and as he looks into it calls and warbles in his most persuasive tones. The female at such times is always shy and backward, and the contrast in the manners of the two birds is as striking as the contrast in their colors. The male is brilliant and ardent; the female is dim and retiring, not to say indifferent. She may take a hasty peep into the hole in the box or tree and then fly away, uttering a lonesome, homesick note. Only by a wooing of many days is she to be fully won.

The past April I was witness one Sunday morning to the jealousies that may rage in these little brown breasts. A pair of bluebirds had apparently mated and decided to occupy a woodpecker's lodge in the limb of an old apple-tree near my study. But that morning another male appeared on the scene and was bent on cutting the first male out, and carrying off his bride. I happened to be near by when the two birds came into collision. They fell to the grass and kept their grip upon each other for half a minute. Then they separated and the first up flew to the hole and called fondly to the female. This was too much for the other male and they clinched again and fell to the ground as before. There they lay upon the grass, blue and brown intermingled. But not a feather was tweaked out or even disturbed, that I could see. They simply held each other down. Then they separated again, and again rushed upon each other. The battle raged for about fifteen minutes, when one of the males, which one, of course, I could not tell, withdrew and flew to a box under the eaves of the study and exerted all the eloquence he possessed to induce the female to come to him there. How he warbled and called and lifted his wings and flew to the entrance to the box and called again! The female was evidently strongly attracted; she would respond

and fly about halfway to an apple-tree and look
toward him. The other male in the mean time
did his best to persuade her to cast her lot with
him. He followed her to the tree toward his
rival, and then flew back to the nest and spread
his plumage and called and warbled, oh, so con-
fidently, so fondly, so reassuringly! When the
female would return and peep into the hole in
the tree what fine, joyous notes he would utter;
then he would look in and twinkle his wings
and say something his rival could not hear.
This vocal and pantomimic contest went on for
a long time. The female was evidently greatly
shaken in her allegiance to the male in the old
apple-tree. In less than an hour another
female responded to the male who had sought
the eaves of the study, and flew with him to
the box. Whether this was their first meeting
or not I do not know, but it was clear enough
that the heart of the male was fixed upon the
bride of his rival. He would devote himself a
moment to the new-comer and then turn toward
the old apple-tree, and call and lift his wings.
Then, apparently admonished by the bird near
him, would turn again to her and induce her to
look into the box and warble fondly. Then
up on a higher branch again, with his attention
directed toward his first love, between whom
and himself salutations seemed constantly passing. This little play went on for some time,
when the two females came into collision, and
fell to the ground tweaking each other spitefully. Then the four birds drifted away from

me down into the vineyard, where the males closed with each other again and fell to the ploughed ground and lay there a surprisingly long time, nearly two minutes, as we calculated. Their wings were outspread, and their forms were indistinguishable. They tugged at each other most doggedly, one or the other brown breast was generally turned up, partly overlaid by a blue coat. They were determined to make a finish of it this time, but which got the better of the fight I could not tell. But it was the last battle; they finally separated, neither, apparently, any the worse for the encounter. The females fought two more rounds, the males looking on and warbling approvingly when they separated, and the two pairs drifted away in different directions. The next day they were about the box and tree again, and seemed to have definitely settled matters. Who won and who lost I do not know, but two pairs of bluebirds have since been very busy and very happy about the two nesting places. One of the males I recognize as a bird that appeared early in March; I recognize him from one peculiar note in the midst of his warble, a note that suggests a whistle.

The matchmaking of the highholes, which often comes under my observation, is in marked contrast to that of the robins and bluebirds. There does not appear to be any anger or any blows. The male or two males will alight on a limb in front of the female, and go through with a series of bowings and scrapings that are

truly comical. He spreads his tail, he puffs
out his breast, he throws back his head, and
then bends his body to the right and to the
left, uttering all the while a curious musical
hiccough. The female confronts him unmoved,
but whether her attitude is critical or defensive I
cannot tell. Presently she flies away, followed
by her suitor or suitors, and the little comedy is
enacted on another stump or tree. Among all
the woodpeckers the drum plays an important
part in the matchmaking. The male takes
up his stand on a dry, resonant limb, or on the
ridgeboard of a building, and beats the loudest
call he is capable of. The downy woodpecker
usually has a particular branch to which he
resorts for advertising his matrimonial wants.
A favorite drum of the highholes about me is
a hollow wooden tube, a section of a pump
which stands as a bird box upon my summer-
house. It is a good instrument; its tone is
sharp and clear. A highhole alights upon it
and sends forth a rattle that can be heard a
long way off. Then he lifts up his head and
utters that long April call, Wick, wick, wick,
wick. Then he drums again. If the female
does not find him it is not because he does not
make noise enough. But his sounds are all
welcome to the ear. They are simple and
primitive and voice well a certain sentiment of
the April days. As I write these lines I hear
through the half-open door his call come up
from a distant field. Then I hear the steady
hammering of one that has been for three days

trying to penetrate the weather boarding of the big icehouse by the river and reach the sawdust filling for a nesting place.

Among our familiar birds the matchmaking of none other is quite so pretty as that of the goldfinch. The goldfinches stay with us in lorn flocks and clad in a dull olive suit throughout the winter. In May the males begin to put on their bright summer plumage. This is the result of a kind of superficial moulting. Their feathers are not shed, but their dusky covering or overalls are cast off. When the process is only partly completed the bird has a smutty, unpresentable appearance. But we seldom see them at such times. They seem to retire from society. When the change is complete and the males have got their bright uniforms of yellow and black the courting begins. All the goldfinches of a neighborhood collect together and hold a sort of a musical festival. To the number of many dozens they may be seen in some large tree, all singing and calling in the most joyous and vivacious manner. The males sing, and the females chirp and call. Whether there is actual competition on a trial of musical abilities of the males before the females or not I do not know. The best of feeling seems to pervade the company; there is no sign of quarreling or fighting; "all goes merry as a marriage bell," and the matches seem actually to be made during these musical picnics. Before May is passed the birds are seen in couples, and in June housekeeping usually begins. This I call the ideal of love-making among birds, and is in striking contrast to the squabbles and jealousies of most of our songsters.

I have known the goldfinches to keep up this musical and lovemaking festival through three consecutive days of a cold northeast rain-storm. Bedraggled, but ardent and happy, the birds were not to be dispersed by wind or weather.

All the woodpeckers, so far as I have observed, drum up their mates; the male advertises his wants by hammering upon a dry, resonant limb, when in due time the female approaches and is duly courted and won. The drumming of the ruffed grouse is for the same purpose; the female hears, concludes to take a walk that way, approaches timidly, is seen and admired, and the match is made. That the male accepts the first female that offers herself is probable. Among all the birds the choice, the selection, seems to belong to the female. The males court promiscuously; the females choose discreetly. The grouse, unlike the woodpecker, always carries his drum with him, which is his own proud breast; yet, if undisturbed, he selects some particular log or rock in the woods from which to sound forth his willingness to wed. What determines the choice of the female it would be hard to say. Among song-birds it is probably the best songster, or the one whose voice suits her taste best. Among birds of bright plumage it is probably the gayest dress; among the drummers she is doubtless drawn by some quality of the sound. Our ears and eyes are too coarse to note any differences in these things, but doubtless the birds themselves note differences.

Birds show many more human traits than do quadrupeds. That they actually fall in love admits of no doubt; that there is a period of courtship, during which the male uses all the arts he is capable of to win his mate, is equally certain; that there are jealousies and rivalries, and that the peace of families is often rudely disturbed by outside males or females is a common observation. The females, when they come to blows, fight much more spitefully and recklessly than do the males. One species of bird has been known to care for the young of another species which had been made orphans. The male turkey will sometimes cover the eggs of his mate and hatch and rear the brood alone. Altogether, birds often present some marked resemblances in their actions to men, when love is the motive.

Mrs. Martin, in her "Home Life on an Ostrich Farm," relates this curious incident: —

"One undutiful hen — having apparently imbibed advanced notions — absolutely refused to sit at all, and the poor husband, determined not to be disappointed of his little family, did all the work himself, sitting bravely and patiently day and night, though nearly dead with exhaustion, till the chicks were hatched out. The next time this pair of birds had a nest the cock's mind was firmly made up that he would stand no more nonsense. He fought the hen [kicked her], giving her so severe a thrashing that she was all but killed, and this Petruchio-like treatment had the desired effect, for the wife never again rebelled, but sat submissively."

In the case of another pair of ostriches of which Mrs. Martin tells, the female was accidentally killed, when the male mourned her loss for over two years and would not look at another female. He wandered up and down, up and down, the length of his camp, utterly disconsolate. At last he mated again with a most magnificent hen, who ruled him tyrannically; he became the most hen-pecked, or, rather, hen-kicked of husbands.

NOTES FROM THE PRAIRIE

THE best lesson I have had for a long time in the benefits of contentment and of the value of one's own nook or corner of the world, however circumscribed it may be, as a point from which to observe nature and life, comes to me from a prairie correspondent, an invalid lady, confined to her room year in and year out, and yet who sees more and appreciates more than many of us who have the freedom of a whole continent. Having her permission, why should I not share these letters with my readers, especially since there are other house-bound or bed-bound invalids whom they may reach and who may derive some cheer or suggestion from them? Words uttered in a popular magazine like "The Century" are like the vapors that go up from the ground and the streams: they are sure to be carried far and wide, and to fall again as rain or dew, and one little knows what thirsty plant or flower they may reach and nourish. I am thinking of another fine spirit, couch-bound in one of the northern New England States, who lives in a town that bears the same name as that in which my Western correspondent resides, and into whose chamber my slight and desultory papers have also brought

something of the breath of the fields and woods,
and who in return has given me many glimpses
of nature through eyes purified by suffering.

Women are about the best lovers of nature,
after all; at least of nature in her milder and
more familiar forms.   The feminine character,
the feminine perceptions, intuitions, delicacy,
sympathy, quickness, etc., are more responsive
to natural forms and influences than is the masculine mind.

My Western correspondent sees existence as
from an altitude, and sees where the comple-
ments and compensations come in.   She lives
upon the prairie, and she says it is as the ocean
to her, upon which she is adrift, and always
expects to be, until she reaches the other shore.
Her house is the ship which she never leaves.
"What is visible from my window is the sea,
changing only from winter to summer as the
sea changes from storm to sunshine.   But there
is one advantage, — messages can come to me
continually from all the wide world."

One summer she wrote she had been hoping
to be well enough to renew her acquaintance
with the birds, the flowers, the woods, but
instead was confined to her room more closely
than ever.

"It is a disappointment to me, but I decided
long ago that the wisest plan is to make the
best of things; to take what is given you, and
make the most of it.   To gather up the fragments that nothing may be lost, applies to
one's life as well as to other things.   Though

I cannot walk, I can think and read and write;
probably I get my share of pleasure from
sources that well people are apt to neglect. I
have learned that the way to be happy is to
keep so busy that thoughts of self are forced
out of sight; and to live for others, not for ourselves.

"Sometimes, when I think over the matter,
I am half sorry for well people, because, you
see, I have so much better company than they
can have, for I have so much more time to go
all over the world and meet all the best and
wisest people in it. Some of them died long
ago to the most of people, but to me they are
just as much alive as they ever were; they give
me their best and wisest thoughts without the
disagreeable accompaniments others must endure. Other people use their eyes and ears
and pens for me; all I have to do is to sit still
and enjoy the results. Dear friends I have
everywhere, though I am unknown to them;
what right have I to wish for more privileges
than I have?"

There is philosophy for you — philosophy
which looks fate out of countenance. It seems
that if we only have the fortitude to take the
ills of life cheerfully and say to fortune, "Thy
worst is good enough for me," behold the worst
is already repentant and fast changing to the
best. Love softens the heart of the inevitable.
The magic phrase which turns the evil spirits
into good angels is, "I am contented." Happiness is always at one's elbow, it seems, in

one disguise or another; all one has to do is to
stop seeking it afar, or stop *seeking* it at all,
and say to this unwelcome attendant, "Be thou
my friend," when, lo, the mask falls, and the
angel is disclosed. Certain rare spirits in this
world have accepted poverty with such love
and pride that riches at once became contempti-
ble.

My correspondent has the gift of observation.
In renouncing self she has opened the door for
many other things to enter. In cultivating the
present moment, she cultivates the present incident. The power to see things comes of
that mental attitude which is directed to the
now and the here: keen, alert perceptions,
those faculties that lead the mind and take the
incident as it flies. Most people fail to see
things because the print is too small for their
vision; they read only the large-lettered events
like the newspaper headings, and are apt to
miss a part of these, unless they see in some
way their own initials there.

The small type of the lives of bird and beast
about her is easily read by this cheerful invalid.
"To understand that the sky is everywhere
blue," says Goethe, "we need not go around
the world;" and it would seem that this
woman has got all the good and pleasure there
is in natural history from the pets in her room,
and the birds that build before her window. I
had been for a long time trying to determine
whether or not the blue-jay hoarded up nuts
for winter use, but had not been able to settle

the point. I applied to her, and, sitting by her window, she discovered that jays do indeed hoard food in a tentative, childish kind of way, but not with the cunning and provident foresight of the squirrels and native mice. She saw a jay fly to the ground with what proved to be a peanut in its beak and carefully cover it up with leaves and grass. "The next fall, looking out of my own window, I saw two jays hiding chestnuts with the same blind instinct. They brought them from a near tree and covered them up in the grass, putting but one in a place. Subsequently, in another locality, I saw jays similarly employed. It appears to be simply the crow instinct to steal, or to carry away and hide any superfluous morsel of food." The jays were really planting chestnuts instead of hoarding them. There was no possibility of such supplies being available in winter, and in spring a young tree might spring from each nut. This fact doubtless furnishes a key to the problem why a forest of pine is usually succeeded by a forest of oak. The acorns are planted by the jays. Their instinct for hiding things prompts them to seek the more dark and secluded pine woods with their booty, and the thick layer of needles furnishes an admirable material with which to cover the nut. The germ sprouts and remains a low slender shoot for years, or until the pine woods are cut away, when it rapidly becomes a tree.

My correspondent thinks the birds possess some of the frailties of human beings; among

other things, ficklemindedness. "I believe
they build nests just for the fun of it, to pass
away the time, to have something to chatter
about and dispute over." (I myself have seen
a robin play at nest building late in October,
and have seen two young bluebirds ensconce
themselves in an old thrush's nest in the fall
and appear to amuse themselves like children,
while the wind made the branch sway to and
fro.) "Now my wrens' nest is so situated
that nothing can disturb them, and where I
can see it at any time. They have often made
a nest and left it. A year ago, during the
latter part of May, they built a nest, and in a
few days they kicked everything out of the box
and did the work all over again, repeating the
operation all July, then left the country without accomplishing anything further. This
season they reared one brood, built another
nest, and, I think, laid one or more eggs, idled
around a few weeks, and then went away."
(This last was probably a "cock-nest," built by
the male as a roosting place.) "I have noticed,
too, that blue-jays build their apology for a
nest, and abandon it for another place in the
same tree." Her jays and wrens do not live
together on the most amiable terms. "I had
much amusement while the jay was on the
nest, watching the actions of the wrens whose
nest was under the porch close by the oak.
Perched on a limb over the jay, the male wren
sat flirting his tail and scolding, evidently saying all the insulting things he could think of;

for after enduring it for some time, the jay would fly off its nest in a rage, and, with the evident intention of impaling Mr. Wren with his bill, strike down vengefully and — find his bill fast in the bark, while his enemy was somewhere else, squeaking · in derision. They kept that up day after day, but the wren is too lively to be caught by a large bird.

"I have never had the opportunity to discover whether there was any difference in the dispositions of birds of the same species; it would take a very close and extended observation to determine that; but I do know there is as much difference between animals as between human beings in that respect. Horses, cats, dogs, squirrels, — all have their own individuality. I have had five gray squirrels for pets, and even their features were unlike. Fred and Sally were mates, who were kept shut up in their cages all the time. Fred was wonderfully brave, would strut and scold until there was something to be afraid of, then would crouch down behind Sally and let her defend him, the sneak! He abused her shamefully, but she never resented it. Being the larger, she could have whipped him and not half tried; but she probably labored under the impression, which is shared by some people, that it is a wife's duty to submit to whatever abuse the husband chooses to inflict. Their characters reminded me so strongly of some people I have seen that I used to take Fred out and whip him regularly, as a sort of vicarious punishment of those who deserved it. Chip was a gentle, pretty squirrel, fond of being petted, spent most of her time in my pocket or around my neck, but she died young; probably she was too good to live.

"Dick, lazy and a glutton, also died young, from over-eating. Chuck, the present pet, has Satan's own temper — very ugly — but so intelligent that she is the plague of our lives, though at the same time she is a constant source of amusement. It is impossible to remain long angry with her, however atrocious her crimes are. We are obliged to let her run loose through the house, for when shut up she squeals and chatters and rattles her cage so we can't endure it. From one piece of mischief to another as fast as she can go, she requires constant watching. She knows what is forbidden very well, for if I chance to look at her after she has been up to mischief, she quickly drops down flat, spreads her tail over her back, looking all the time so very innocent that she betrays herself. If I go towards her, she springs on my back, where I cannot reach her to whip her. She never bites *me*, but if others tease her she is very vicious. When I tease her she relieves her feelings by biting any one else who happens to be in the room; and it is no slight matter being bitten by a squirrel's sharp teeth. Knowing that the other members of the family are afraid of her, she amuses herself by putting nuts in their shoes, down their necks, or in their hair, then standing guard, so that if they remove the nuts she flies at them.

"Chuck will remember an injury for months, and take revenge whenever opportunity offers. She claims all the nuts and candy that come into the house, searching Mr. B——'s pockets *on Sundays,* never on other days. I don't see how she distinguishes, unless from the fact that he comes home early on that day. Once when she caught one of the girls eating some of her nuts, she flew at her, bit her, and began carrying off the nuts to hide as fast as she could. For months afterward she would slip slyly up and bite the girl. She particularly despises my brother, he teases her so, and gives her no chance to bite; so she gets even with him by tearing up everything of his she can find, — his books, his gloves, etc. ; and if she can get into the closet where I keep the soiled clothing, she will select such articles as belong to him, and tear them up! And she has a wonderful memory, never forgets where she puts things; people whom she has not seen for several years she remembers.

"She had the misfortune to have about two inches of her tail cut off, by being caught in the door, which made it too short to be used for wiping her face; it would slip out of her hands, making her stamp her feet and chatter her teeth with anger. By experimenting, she found by backing up in a corner it was prevented from slipping out of her reach. Have had her five years; wonder how long their lives nsually are? One of my neighbors got a young squirrel, so young that it required milk; so they got a small nursing-bottle for it. Until that squirrel was over a year old, whenever he got hungry, he would get his bottle and sit and hold it up as if he thought that quite the proper way for a squirrel to obtain his nourishment. It was utterly comical to see him. We have no black squirrels; a few red ones and a great many gray ones of different kinds."

I was much interested in her pet squirrel, and made frequent inquiries about it. A year later she writes: "My squirrel still lives and rules the house. She has an enemy that causes her much trouble, — a rat that comes into the wood-shed. I had noticed that whenever she went out there, she investigated the dark corners with care before she ventured to play, but did not understand it till I chanced to be sitting in the kichen door once, as she was digging up a nut she had buried. Just as she got it up, a great rat sprung on her back; there ensued a trial of agility and strength to see which should have that nut. Neither seemed to be angry, for they did not attempt to bite, but raced around the shed, cuffing each other at every opportunity; sometimes one had the nut, sometimes the other. I regret to say my squirrel, whenever she grew tired, took a base advantage of the rat by coming and sitting at my feet, gnawing the nut, and plainly showing by her motions her exultation over her foe. Finally the rat became so exasperated that he forgot prudence and forced her to climb up on my shoulder.

"In an extract from a London paper I see it asserted that birds and snakes cannot taste. As to the snakes I cannot say, but I know birds can taste, from observing my canary when I give him something new to eat. He will edge up to it carefully, take a bit, back off to meditate; then if he decides he likes it, he walks up boldly and eats his fill. But if there is anything disagreeable in what I offer him, acid, for instance, there is such a fuss! He scrapes his bill, raises and lowers the feathers on the top of his head, giving one the impression that he is making a wry face. He cannot be induced to touch it a second time.

"I have taught him to think I am afraid of him, and how he tyrannizes over me, chasing me from place to place, pecking and squeaking! He delights in pulling out my hair. When knitting or crocheting, he tries to prevent my pulling the yarn by standing on it; when that fails, he takes hold with his bill and pulls with all his little might."

Some persons have a special gift or quality that enables them to sustain more intimate relations with wild creatures than others. Women, as a rule, are ridiculously afraid of cattle and horses turned loose in a field, but my correspondent, when a young girl, had many a lark with the prairie colts. "Is it not strange," she says, "that a horse will rarely hurt a child, or any person that is fond of

NOTES FROM THE PRAIRIE

them? To see a drove of a hundred or even a hundred and fifty unbroken colts branded and turned out to grow up was a common occurrence then [in her childhood]. I could go among them, catch them, climb on their backs, and they never offered to hurt me; they seemed to consider it *fun*. They would come up and touch me with their noses and prance off around and around me; but just let a man come near them, and they were off like the wind."

All her reminiscences of her early life in Iowa, thirty years ago, are deeply interesting to me. Her parents, a Boston family, moved to that part of the State in advance of the railroads, making the journey from the Mississippi in a wagon. "My father had been fortunate enough to find a farm with a frame house upon it (the houses were mostly log ones) built by an Englishman whose homesickness had driven him back to England. It stood upon a slight elevation in the midst of a prairie, though not a very level one. To the east and to the west of us, about four miles away, were the woods along the banks of the streams. It was in the month of June when we came, and the prairie was tinted pink with wild roses. From early spring till late in the fall the ground used to be so covered with some kinds of flowers that it had almost as decided a color as the sky itself, and the air would be fragrant with their perfume. First it is white with 'dog-toes' [probably an orchid], then a cold blue from being covered with some kind of light blue

flower; next come the roses; in July and
August it is pink with the 'prairie pink,'
dotted with scarlet lilies; as autumn comes on
it is vivid with orange-colored flowers.   I
never knew their names; they have woody
stalks; one kind that grows about a foot high
has a feathery spray of little blossoms [golden-
rod?].   There are several kinds of tall ones;
the blossom has yellow leaves and brown vel-
vety centres [cone-flower, or rudbeckia, probably, now common in the East].   We young-
sters used to gather the gum that exuded from
the stalk.   Every one was poor in those days,
and no one was ashamed of it.   Plenty to eat,
such as it was.   We introduced some innova-
tions in that line that shocked the people here.
We used *corn meal;* they said it was only fit
for hogs.   Worse than that, we ate 'greens'
— weeds, they called them.   It does not seem
possible, but it is a fact, that with all those
fertile acres around them waiting for cultivation, and to be had almost for the asking, those
people (they were mainly Hoosiers) lived on
fried salt pork, swimming in fat, and hot bis-
cuit all the year round; no variety, no vegeta-
bles, no. butter saved for winter use, no milk
after cold weather began, for it was too much
trouble to milk the cows — *such* a shiftless set!
And the hogs they raised — you should have
seen them! 'Prairie sharks' and 'razor-
backs were the local names for them, and
either name fitted them; long noses, long legs,
bodies about five inches thick, and no amount

of food would make them fat. They were allowed to run wild to save the trouble of caring for them, and when the pork-barrel was empty they *shot* one.

"Everybody drove oxen and used lumber-wagons with a board across the box for a seat. How did we ever endure it, riding over the roadless prairies! Then, any one who owned a horse was considered an aristocrat and despised accordingly. One yoke of oxen that we had were not to be sneezed at as a fast team. They were trained to trot, and would make good time too." [I love to hear oxen praised. An old Michigan farmer, an early settler, told me of a famous pair of oxen he once had; he spoke of them with great affection. They would draw any log he hitched them to. When they had felt of the log and found they had their match, he said they would nudge each other, give their tails a kink, lift up their heads, and say *eh-h-h-h!* then something had to come.]

"One phrase you used in your last letter — ' the start from the stump ' · — shows how locality governs the illustrations we use. The start was not from the *stump* here, quite the reverse. Nature made the land ready for man's hand, and there were no obstacles in the shape of stumps and stones to overcome. Probably in the East a pine-stump fence is not regarded as either particularly attractive or odd; but to me, when I first saw one in York State, it was both. I had never even heard of the stumps being utilized in that way. Seen for the first time, there is something grotesque in the appearance of those long arms forever reaching out after something they never find, like a petrified octopus. Those fences are an evidence of Eastern thrift — making an enemy serve as a friend. I think they would frighten our horses and cattle, used as they are to the almost invisible wire fence. ' Worm ' fences were the fashion at first. But they soon learned the necessity of economizing wood. The people were extravagant, too, in the outlay of power in tilling the soil, sixteen yoke of oxen being thought absolutely necessary to run a breaking-plough; and I have seen twenty yoke used, requiring three men to drive and attend the great clumsy plough. Every summer you might see them in any direction, looking like ' thousand - legged worms.' They found out after a while that two yoke answered quite as well. There is something very queer about the bowlders that are supposed to have been brought down from northern regions during the glacial period; like Banquo's ghost, they refuse to stay down. Other stones beside them gradually become buried, but the bowlders are always on top of the ground. Is there something repellent about them, that the earth refuses to cover them? They seem to be of no use, for they cannot be worked as other stone; they have to be broken open with heat in some way, though I did see a building made of them once. The bowlders had been broken and put in big squares and little squares, oblong pieces and triangles. The effect was curious, if not fine.

"In those days there were such quantities of game-birds, it was the sportsman's paradise, and during the summer a great many gunners from the cities came there. Prairie-chickens without number, as great a nuisance as the crows in the East, only we could eat them to pay for the grain they ate; also geese, turkeys, ducks, quail, and pigeons. Did you ever hear the prairie-chickens during the spring? I never felt sure spring had come to stay till, in the early morning, there came the boom of the chickens, *Poor old booff.* It is an indescribable sound, as if there were a thousand saying the same thing and keeping perfect time. No trouble then getting a child up early in the morning, for it is time for hunting prairie-chickens' nests. In the most unexpected places in the wild grass the nests would be found, with about sixteen eggs in them, looking somewhat like a guinea-hen's egg. Of course an omelet made out of them tasted ever so much better than if made out of home-laid eggs; now I should not like the taste so well, probably, for there is a wild flavor to the egg, as there is to the flesh of the bird. Many a time I've stepped right into the nest, so well was it hidden. After a prairie fire is a good time to go egging, the nests being in plain sight, and the eggs already roasted. I have tried again and again to raise the chickens by setting the eggs under the tame hens, but it cannot be done; they seem to inherit a shyness that makes them refuse to eat, and at the first opportunity they slip off in the grass and are gone. Every kind of food, even to live insects, they will refuse, and will starve to death rather than eat in captivity. There are but few chickens here now; they have taken Horace Greeley's advice and gone West. As to four-footed game, there were any number of the little prairie-wolves and some big gray ones. Could see the little wolves running across the prairie any time a day, and at night their continual *yap, yap* was almost unendurable. They developed a taste for barn-yard fowl that made it necessary for hens to roost high. They are cowards in the daytime, but brave enough to come close to the house at night. If people had only had foxhounds, they would have afforded an opportunity for some sport. I have seen people try to run them down on horseback, but never knew them to succeed.

"One of my standard amusements was to go every little while to a den the wolves had, where the rocks cropped out of the ground, and poke in there with a stick, to see a wolf pop out scared almost to death. As to the big wolves, it was dangerous sport to meddle with them. I had an experience with them one winter that would have begotten a desire to keep a proper distance from them, had I not felt it before. An intensely cold night three

of us were riding in an open wagon on one
seat. The road ran for about a mile through
the woods, and as we entered it four or five
gray wolves sprang out at us; the horse needed
no urging, you may be sure, but to me it
seemed an age before we got out into the
moonlight on the prairie; then the wolves
slunk back into the woods. Every leap they
made it seemed as if they would jump into the
wagon. I could hear them strike against the
back of it and hear their teeth *click* together as
they barely missed my hand where I held on to
the seat to keep from being thrown out. My
most prominent desire about that time was to
sit in the middle and let some one else have the
outside seat.

"Grandfather was very fond of trapping,
and used to catch a great many wolves for their
skins and the bounty; also minks and muskrats. I always had to help skin them, which
I considered dreadful, especially skinning the
muskrats; but as that was the only condition
under which I was allowed to go along, of
course I submitted, for I would n't miss the
excitement of seeing whether we had succeeded
in outwitting and catching the sly creatures for
any consideration. The beautiful minks, with
their slender satiny bodies, it seemed a pity to
catch them. Muskrats I had no sympathy for,
they looked so ratty, and had so unpleasant a
smell. The gophers were one of the greatest
plagues the farmers had. The ground would
be dotted with their mounds, so round and

regular, the black dirt pulverized so finely. I always wondered how they could make them of such a perfect shape, and wished I could see way down into their houses. They have more than one entrance to them, because I've tried to drown them out, and soon I would see what I took to be my gopher, that I thought I had covered so nicely, skipping off. They took so much corn out of the hills after it was planted that it was customary to mix corn soaked with strychnine with the seed corn. Do they have pocket gophers in the East? [No.] They are the cutest little animals, with their pockets on each side of their necks, lined with fur; when they get them stuffed full they look as broad as they are long, and so saucy. I have met them and had them show fight, because I wouldn't turn out of their path — the little impudent things!

"One nuisance that goes along with civilization we escaped until the railroad was built, and that was *rats*. The railroads brought other nuisances too, the weeds; they soon crowded out the native plants. I don't want to be understood as calling *all* weeds nuisances; the beautiful flowers some of them bear save their reputations — the dandelion, for instance; I approve of the dandelion, whatever others may think. I shall never forget the first one I found in the West; it was like meeting an old friend. It grew alongside of an emigrant road, about five miles from my home; here I spied the golden treasure in the grass. Some of the many 'prairie schooners' that had passed that way had probably dropped the one seed. Mother dug it up and planted it in our flower-bed, and in two years the neighborhood was yellow with them — all from that one root. The prairies are gone now, and the wild-flowers, those that have not been civilized to death like the Indians, have taken refuge in the fence-corners."

I had asked her what she knew about cranes, and she replied as follows: —

"During the first few years after we came West, cranes, especially the sand-hill variety, were very plentiful. Any day in the summer you might see a triangle of them flying over, with their long legs dragging behind them; or if you had sharp eyes, could see them stalking along the sloughs sometimes found on the prairie. In the books I see them described as being brown in color. Now I should not call them brown, for they are more of a yellow. They are just the color of a gosling, should it get its down somewhat soiled, and they look much like overgrown goslings set up on stilts. I have often found their nests, and always in the shallow water in the slough, built out of sticks, much as the children build cob-houses, about a foot high, with two large flat eggs in them. I have often tried to catch them on their nests, so as to see how they disposed of their long legs, but never quite succeeded. They are very shy, and their nests are always so situated as to enable them to see in every direction. I had a great desire to possess a pet crane, but every attempt to raise one resulted in failure, all on account of those same slender legs.

"The egg I placed under a 'sitting hen' (one was as much as a hen could conveniently manage); it would hatch out all right, and I had no difficulty in feeding the young crane, for it would eat anything, and showed no shyness — quite different from a young prairie-chicken; in fact, their tameness was the cause of their death, for, like Mary's little lamb, they insisted on going everywhere I went. When they followed me into the house, and stepped upon the smooth floor, one leg would go in one direction and the other in the opposite, breaking one or both of them. They seemed to be unable to walk upon any smooth surface. Such ridiculous looking things they were! I have seen a few pure white ones, but only on the wing. They seem more shy than the yellow ones.

"Once I saw a curious sight; I saw seven or eight cranes dance a cotillon, or something very much like it. I have since read of wild fowl performing in that way, but then I had never heard of it. They were in a meadow about half a mile from the house; I did not at all understand what they were doing, and proceeded to investigate. After walking as near as I could without frightening them; I crept through the tall grass until I was within a rod of the cranes, and then lay and watched them.

It was the most comical sight to see them waltz around, sidle up to each other and back again, their long necks and legs making the most clumsy motions. With a little stretch of the imagination one might see a smirk on their faces, and suspect them of caricaturing human beings. There seemed to be a regular method in their movements, for the changes were repeated. How long they kept it up I do not know, for I tired of it and went back to the house, but they had danced until the grass was trampled down hard and smooth. I always had a mania for trying experiments, so I coaxed my mother to cook one the men had shot, though I had never heard of any one's eating crane. It was not very good, tasted somewhat peculiar, and the thought that maybe it was poison struck me with horror. I was badly scared, for I reflected that I had no proof that it was *not* poison, and I had been told so many times that I was bound to come to grief, sooner or later, from trying to find out things."

I am always glad to have the views of a sensible person, outside of the literary circles, upon my favorite authors, especially when the views are spontaneous. "Speaking of Thoreau," says my correspondent, "I am willing to allow most that is said in his praise, but *I do not like him*, all the same. Do you know I feel that he was not altogether human. There is something uncanny about him. I guess that instead of having a human soul, his body was inhabited by some sylvan deity that flourished in Grecian times; he seemed out of place among human beings."

Of Carlyle, too, she has an independent opinion. "It is a mystery to me why men so universally admire Carlyle; women do not, or if there is occasionally one who does, she does not *like* him. A woman's first thought about him would be, 'I pity his wife!' Do you remember what he said in answer to Mrs. Welsh's proposal to come and live with them and help support them? He said they could only live pleasantly together on the condition that she looked up to him, not he to her. Here is what he says: 'Now, think, Liebchen, whether your mother will consent to forget her riches and our poverty, and uncertain, more probably scanty, income, and consent in the spirit of Christian meekness to make me her guardian and director, and be a second wife to her daughter's husband?' Now, isn't that insufferable conceit for you? To expect that a woman old enough to be his mother would lay aside her self-respect and individuality to accept him, a comparatively young and inexperienced man, as her master? The cheekiness of it! Here you have the key-note of his character — 'great I and little u.'

"I have tried faithfully to like him, for it seemed as if the fault must be in me because I did not; I have labored wearily through nearly all his works, stumbling over his superlatives (why, he is an adjective factory; his pages look like the alphabet struck by a cyclone.

You call it picturesqueness; I call it grotesqueness). But it was of no use; it makes me tired all over to think of it. All the time I said to myself, 'Oh, do stop your scolding; you are not so much better than the rest of us.' One is willing to be led to a higher life, but who wants to be pushed and cuffed along? How can people place him and our own Emerson, the dear guide and friend of so many of us, on the same level? It may be that the world had need of him, just as it needs lightning and rain and cold and pain, but must we *like* these things?" [1]

[1] My correspondent was Mrs. Beardslee of Manchester, Iowa. She died in October, 1885.

EYE–BEAMS

My most interesting note of the season of 1893
relates to a weasel. One day in early November
my boy and I were sitting on a rock at the
edge of a tamarack swamp in the woods hoping
to get a glimpse of some grouse which we knew
were in the habit of feeding in the swamp.
We had not sat there very long before we
heard a slight rustling in the leaves below us
which we at once fancied was made by the
cautious tread of a grouse. (We had no gun.)
Presently through the thick brushy growth, we
caught sight of a small animal running along,
that we at first took for a red squirrel. A
moment more, and it came into full view but a
few yards from us, and we saw that it was a
weasel. A second glance showed that it carried something in its mouth, which, as it drew
near, we saw was a mouse, or a mole of some
sort. The weasel ran nimbly along, now the
length of a decayed log, then over stones and
branches, pausing a moment every three or four
yards, and passed within twenty feet of us, and
disappeared behind some rocks on the bank at
the edge of the swamp. "He is carrying food

into his den," I said; "let us watch him."
In four or five minutes he reappeared, coming
back over the course along which he had just
passed, running over and under the same stones
and down the same decayed log, and was soon
out of sight in the swamp. We had not
moved, and evidently he had not noticed us.
After about six minutes we heard the same
rustle as at first, and in a moment saw the
weasel coming back with another mouse in his
mouth. He kept to his former route as if
chained to it, making the same pauses and
gestures, and repeating exactly his former
movements. He disappeared on our left as
before, and after a few moments' delay, re-
emerged and took his course down into the
swamp again. We waited about the same
length of time as before, when back he came
with another mouse. He evidently had a big
crop of mice down there amid the bogs and
bushes, and he was gathering his harvest in
very industriously. We became curious to see
exactly where his den was, and so walked
around where he had seemed to disappear each
time, and waited. He was as punctual as
usual, and was back with his game exactly on
time. It happened that we had stopped within
two paces of his hole, so that, as he approached
it, he evidently discovered us. He paused,
looked steadily at us, and then without any
sign of fear entered his den. The entrance
was not under the rocks as we had expected,
but was in the bank a few feet beyond them.

We remained motionless for some time, but he did not reappear. Our presence had made him suspicious, and he was going to wait awhile. Then I removed some dry leaves and exposed his doorway, a small, round hole, hardly as large as the chipmunk makes, going straight down into the ground. We had a lively curiosity to get a peep into his larder. If he had been carrying in mice at this rate very long his cellars must be packed with them. With a sharp stick I began digging into the red clayey soil, but soon encountered so many roots from near trees that I gave it up, deciding to return next day with a mattock. So I repaired the damages I had done as well as I could, replaced the leaves, and we moved off.

The next day, which was mild and still as usual, I came back armed, as I thought, to unearth the weasel and his treasures. I sat down where we had sat the day before and awaited developments. I was curious to know if the weasel was still carrying in his harvest. I had sat but a few minutes when I heard again the rustle in the dry leaves, and saw the weasel coming home with another mouse. I observed him till he had made three trips; about every six or seven minutes, I calculated, he brought in a mouse. Then I went and stood near his hole. This time he had a fat meadow-mouse. He laid it down near the entrance, went in and turned around, and reached out and drew the mouse in after him. That store of mice I am bound to see, I thought, and then fell to with the heavy mattock. I followed the hole down about two feet, when it turned to the north. I kept the clue by thrusting into the passage slender twigs; these it was easy to follow. Two or three feet more and the hole branched, one part going west, the other northeast. I followed the west one a few feet till it branched. Then I turned to the easterly tunnel, and pursued it till it branched. I followed one of these ways till it divided. I began to be embarrassed and hindered by the accumulations of loose soil. Evidently this weasel had foreseen just such an assault upon his castle as I was making, and had planned it accordingly. He was not to be caught napping. I found several enlargements in the various tunnels, breathing spaces, or spaces to turn around in, or to meet and chat with a companion, but nothing that looked like a terminus, a permanent living-room. I tried removing the soil a couple of paces away with the mattock, but found it slow work. I was getting warm and tired, and my task was apparently only just begun. The farther I dug the more numerous and intricate became the passages. I concluded to stop, and come again the next day, armed with a shovel in addition to the mattock.

Accordingly, I came back on the morrow, and fell to work vigorously. I soon had quite a large excavation; I found the bank a labyrinth of passages, with here and there a large chamber. One of the latter I struck only six inches under the surface, by making a fresh breach a few feet away.

While I was leaning upon my shovel-handle and recovering my breath, I heard some light-footed creature tripping over the leaves above me just out of view, which I fancied might be a squirrel. Presently I heard the bay of a hound and the yelp of a cur, and then knew that a rabbit had passed near me. The dogs came hurrying after, with a great rumpus, and then presently the hunters followed. The dogs remained barking not many rods south of me on the edge of the swamp, and I knew the rabbit had run to hole. For half an hour or more I heard the hunters at work there, digging their game out; then they came along and discovered me at my work. (An old trapper and woodsman and his son.) I told them what I was in quest of. "A mountain weasel," said the old man. "Seven or eight years ago I used to set dead falls for rabbits just over there, and the game was always partly eaten up. It must have been this weasel that visited my traps." So my game was evidently an old resident of the place. This swamp, maybe, had been his hunting ground for many years, and he had added another hall to his dwelling each year. After further digging, I struck at least one of his banqueting halls, a cavity about the size of one's hat, arched over by a network of fine tree-roots. The occupant evidently lodged, or rested here also. There was a warm, dry nest, made of leaves and the fur of

mice and moles. I took out two or three handfuls. In finding this chamber, I had followed
one of the tunnels around till it brought me
within a foot of the original entrance. A few
inches to one side of this cavity there was
what I took to be a back alley where the weasel
threw his waste; there were large masses of
wet, decaying fur here, and fur pellets such as
are regurgitated by hawks and owls. In the
nest there was the tail of a flying squirrel,
showing that the weasel sometimes had a flying
squirrel for supper or dinner.

I continued my digging with renewed energy; I should yet find the grand depot where
all these passages centred; but the farther I
excavated, the more complex and baffling the
problem became; the ground was honeycombed
with passages. What enemy has this weasel,
I said to myself, that he should provide so
many ways of escape, that he should have a
back door at every turn? To corner him
would be impossible; to be lost in his fortress
were like being lost in Mammoth Cave. How
he could bewilder his pursuer by appearing
now at this door, now at that; now mocking
him from the attic, now defying him from the
cellar. So far, I had discovered but one entrance; but some of the chambers were so near
the surface that it looked as if the planner had
calculated upon an emergency when he might
want to reach daylight quickly in a new place.

Finally I paused, rested upon my shovel
awhile, eased my aching back upon the ground,

and then gave it up, feeling as I never had
before the force of the old saying, that you
cannot catch a weasel asleep. I had made an
ugly hole in the bank, had handled over two or
three times a ton or more of earth, and was
apparently no nearer the weasel and his store
of mice than when I began.

Then I regretted that I had broken into his
castle at all; that I had not contented myself
with coming day after day and counting his mice
as he carried them in, and continued my observation upon him each succeeding year. Now
the rent in his fortress could not be repaired,
and he would doubtless move away, as he most
certainly did, for his doors, which I had closed
with soil, remained unopened after winter had
set in.

But little seems known about the intimate
private lives of any of our lesser wild creatures.
It was news to me that any of the weasels
lived in dens in this way, and that they stored
up provision against a day of need. This
species was probably the little ermine, eight or
nine inches long, with tail about five inches.
It was still in its summer dress of dark chest-
nut-brown above and whitish below.

It was a mystery where the creature had put
the earth which it must have removed in digging its den; not a grain was to be seen anywhere, and yet a bushel or more must have been
taken out. Externally, there was not the
slightest sign of that curious habitation there
under the ground. The entrance was hidden

beneath dry leaves, and was surrounded by little passages and flourishes between the leaves and the ground. If any of my readers find a weasel's den, I hope they will be wiser than I was, and observe his goings and comings without disturbing his habitation.

II. KEEN PERCEPTIONS

Success in observing nature, as in so many other things, depends upon alertness of mind and quickness to take a hint. One's perceptive faculties must be like a trap lightly and delicately set; a touch must suffice to spring it. But how many people have I walked with, whose perceptions were rusty and unpracticed — nothing less than a bear would spring their trap. All the finer play of nature, all the small deer they miss. The little dramas and tragedies that are being enacted by the wild creatures in the fields and woods are more or less veiled and withdrawn; and the actors all stop when a spectator appears upon the scene. One must be able to interpret the signs, to penetrate the scenes, to put this and that together.

Then nature speaks a different language from our own; the successful observer translates this language into human speech. He knows the meaning of every sound, movement, gesture, and gives the human equivalent. Careless or hasty observers, on the other hand, make the mistake of reading their own thoughts or mental and emotional processes into nature; plans

and purposes are attributed to the wild creatures
which are quite beyond them. Some people in
town saw an English sparrow tangled up in a
horsehair, and suspended from a tree, with
other sparrows fluttering and chattering about
it They concluded at once that the sparrows
had executed one of their number, doubtless
for some crime. I have several times seen
sparrows suspended in this way about their
nesting and roosting places. Accidents happen
to birds as well as to other folks. But they
do not yet imitate us in the matter of capital
punishment.

One day I saw a little bush sparrow fluttering along in the grass, disabled in some way,
and a large number of its mates flitting and
calling about it. I captured the bird, and in
doing so, its struggles in my hand broke the
bond that held it — some kind of web or silken
insect thread that tied together the quills of
one wing. When I let it fly away all its mates
followed it as if wondering at the miracle that
had been wrought. They no doubt experienced some sort of emotion. Birds sympathize
with each other in their distress, and will make
common cause against an enemy. Crows will
pursue and fight a tame crow. They seem to
look upon him as an alien and an enemy. He
is never so shapely and bright and polished as
his wild brother. He is more or less demoral-
ized, and has lost caste. Probably a pack of
wolves would in the same way destroy a tame
wolf, should such an one appear in their midst.

The wild creatures are human — with a difference, a wide difference. They have the keenest powers of perception; what observers they are! how quickly they take a hint! but they have little or no powers of reflection. The crows do not meet in parliaments and caucuses, as has been fancied, and try offenders, and discuss the tariff, or consider ways and means. They are gregarious and social, and probably in the fall have something like a reunion of the tribe. At least their vast assemblages upon the hills at this season have a decidedly festive appearance.

The crow has fine manners. He always has the walk and air of a lord of the soil. One morning I put out some fresh meat upon the snow near my study window. Presently a crow came and carried it off, and alighted with it upon the ground in the vineyard. While he was eating of it, another crow came, and, alighting a few yards away, slowly walked up to within a few feet of this fellow and stopped. I expected to see a struggle over the food, as would have been the case with domestic fowls or animals. Nothing of the kind. The feeding crow stopped eating, regarded the other for a moment, made a gesture or two, and flew away. Then the second crow went up to the food, and proceeded to take his share. Presently the first crow came back, when each seized a portion of the food and flew away with it. Their mutual respect and good-will seemed perfect. Whether it really was so in our hu-

man sense, or whether it was simply an illus-
tration of the instinct of mutual support which
seems to prevail among gregarious birds, I
know not. Birds that are solitary in their
habits, like hawks or woodpeckers, behave
quite differently toward each other in the presence of their food.

The lives of the wild creatures revolve about
two facts or emotions, appetite and fear.
Their keenness in discovering food and in discovering danger are alike remarkable. But
man can nearly always outwit them, because
while his perceptions are not as sharp, his
power of reflection is so much greater. His
cunning carries a great deal farther. The crow
will quickly discover anything that looks like
a trap or snare set to catch him, but it takes
him a long time to see through the simplest
contrivance. As I have above stated, I sometimes place meat on the snow in front of my
study window to attract him. On one occasion,
after a couple of crows had come to expect
something there daily, I suspended a piece of
meat by a string from a branch of the tree just
over the spot where I usually placed the food.
A crow soon discovered it, and came into the
tree to see what it meant. His suspicions
were aroused. There was some design in that
suspended meat evidently. It was a trap to
catch him. He surveyed it from every near
branch. He pecked and pried, and was bent
on penetrating the mystery. He flew to the
ground, and walked about and surveyed it from

all sides. Then he took a long walk down about
the vineyard as if in hope of hitting upon
some clue. Then he came to the tree again,
and tried first one eye, then the other, upon
it; then to the ground beneath; then he went
away and came back; then his fellow came
and they both squinted and investigated and
then disappeared. Chickadees and woodpeckers
would alight upon the meat and peck it swinging in the wind, but the crows were fearful.
Does this show reflection? Perhaps it does,
but I look upon it rather as that instinct of
fear and cunning so characteristic of the crow.
Two days passed thus: every morning the
crows came and surveyed the suspended meat
from all points in the tree, and then went
away. The third day, I placed a large bone
on the snow beneath the suspended morsel.
Presently one of the crows appeared in the
tree, and bent his eye upon the tempting bone.
"The mystery deepens," he seemed to say to
himself. But after half an hour's investigation, and after approaching several times within
a few feet of the food upon the ground, he
seemed to conclude there was no connection
between it and the piece hanging by the string.
So he finally walked up to it and fell to pecking it, flipping his wings all the time, as a sign
of his watchfulness. He also turned up his
eye, momentarily, to the piece in the air above,
as if it might be some disguised sword of
Damocles, ready to fall upon him. Soon his
mate came and alighted on a low branch of the

tree. The feeding crow regarded him a moment, and then flew up to his side, as if to give him a turn at the meat. But he refused to run the risk. He evidently looked upon the whole thing as a delusion and a snare, and presently went away, and his mate followed him. Then I placed the bone in one of the main forks of the tree, but the crows kept at a safe distance from it. Then I put it back to the ground, but they grew more and more suspicious; some evil intent in it all, they thought. Finally, a dog carried off the bone, and the crows ceased to visit the tree.

III. A SPARROW'S MISTAKE

If one has always built one's nest upon the ground, and if one comes of a race of ground-builders, it is a risky experiment to build in a tree. The conditions are ⋅ vastly different. One of my near neighbors, a little song-sparrow, learned this lesson the past season. She grew ambitious; she departed from the traditions of her race, and placed her nest in a tree. Such a pretty spot she chose, too — the pendent cradle formed by the interlaced sprays of two parallel branches of a Norway spruce. These branches shoot out almost horizontally; indeed, the lower ones become quite so in spring, and the side shoots with which they are clothed droop down, forming the slopes of miniature ridges; where the slopes of two branches join, a little valley is formed which often looks more stable than it really is. My sparrow selected one of these little valleys about six feet from the ground and quite near the walls of the house. Here, she has thought, I will build my nest, and pass the heat of June in a miniature Norway. This tree is the fir-clad mountain, and this little vale on its side I select for my own. She carried up a great quantity of coarse grass and straws for the foundation, just as she would have done upon the ground. On the top of this mass there gradually came into shape the delicate structure of her nest, compacting and refining till its delicate carpet of hairs and threads was reached. So sly as the little bird was about it too — every moment on her guard lest you discover her secret! Five eggs were laid, and incubation was far advanced, when the storms and winds came. The cradle indeed did rock. The boughs did not break, but they swayed and separated as you would part your two interlocked hands. The ground of the little valley fairly gave way, the nest tilted over till its contents fell into the chasm. It was like an earthquake that destroys a hamlet.

No born tree-builder would have placed its nest in such a situation. Birds that build at the end of the branch, like the oriole, tie the nest fast; others, like the robin, build against the main trunk; still others build securely in the fork. The sparrow, in her ignorance, rested her house upon the spray of two branches, and when the tempest came the branches parted company and the nest was engulfed.

Another sparrow friend of mine met with a curious mishap the past season. It was the little social sparrow, or chippie. She built her nest on the arm of a grapevine in the vineyard, a favorite place with chippie. It had a fine canopy of leaves, and was firmly and securely placed. Just above it hung a bunch of young grapes, which in the warm July days grew very rapidly. The little bird had not foreseen the calamity that threatened her. The grapes grew down into her nest and completely filled it, so that when I put my hand in, there were the eggs sat upon by the grapes. The bird was crowded out, and had perforce abandoned her nest, ejected by a bunch of grapes. How long she held her ground I do not know; probably till the fruit began to press heavily upon her.

IV. A POOR FOUNDATION

It is a curious habit the wood-thrush has of starting its nest with a fragment of newspaper or other paper. Except in remote woods, I think it nearly always puts a piece of paper in the foundation of its nest. Last spring I chanced to be sitting near a tree in which a wood-thrush had concluded to build. She came with a piece of paper nearly as large as my hand, placed it upon the branch, stood upon it a moment, and then flew down to the ground. A little puff of wind caused the paper to leave the branch a moment afterward. The thrush watched it eddy slowly down to the ground, when she seized it and carried it back. She placed it in position as before, stood upon it again for a moment, and then flew away. Again the paper left the branch, and sailed away slowly to the ground. The bird seized it again, jerking it about rather spitefully, I thought; she turned it around two or three times, then labored back to the branch with it, upon which she shifted it about as if to hit upon some position in which it would lie more securely. This time she sat down upon it for a moment, and then went away, doubtless with the thought in her head that she would bring something to hold it down. The perverse paper followed her in a few seconds. She seized it again, and hustled it about more than before. As she rose with it toward the nest, it in some way impeded her flight, and she was compelled to return to the ground with it. But she kept her temper remarkably well. She turned the paper over and took it up in her beak several times before she was satisfied with her hold, and then carried it back to the branch, where, however, it would not stay. I saw her make six trials of it when I was called away. I think she finally abandoned the restless fragment, probably a scrap that held some "breezy" piece of writing, for later in the season I examined the nest and found no paper in it.

In walking through the woods one day in early winter, we read upon the newly fallen snow the record of a mink's fright the night before. The mink had been traveling through the woods post-haste, not along the water-courses where one sees them by day, but over ridges and across valleys. We followed his track some distance to see what adventures he had met with. We tracked him through a bushy swamp, saw where he had left it to explore a pile of rocks, then where he had taken to the swamp again, then to the more open woods. Presently the track turned sharply about, and doubled upon itself in long hurried strides. What had caused the mink to change its mind so suddenly? We explored a few paces ahead, and came upon a fox track. The mink had seen the fox stalking stealthily through the woods, and the sight had probably brought his heart into his mouth. I think he climbed a tree, and waited till the fox passed. His track disappeared amid a clump of hemlocks, and then reappeared again a little beyond them. It described a big loop around, and then crossed the fox track only a few yards from the point where its course was interrupted. Then it followed a little watercourse, went under a rude bridge in a wood-road, then mingled with squirrel tracks in a denser part of the thicket. If the mink met a muskrat or a rabbit in his travels, or came upon a grouse,

or quail, or a farmer's hen-roost, he had the
supper he was in quest of.

VI. A LEGLESS CLIMBER

The eye always sees what it wants to see,
and the ear hears what it wants to hear. If I
am intent upon birds' nests in my walk, I find
birds' nests everywhere. Some people see
four-leaved clovers wherever they look in the
grass. A friend of mine picks up Indian relics
all about the fields; he has Indian relics in his
eye. I have seen him turn out of the path at
right angles, as a dog will when he scents something, and walk straight away several rods, and
pick up an Indian pounding-stone. He saw it
out of the corner of his eye. I find that without conscious effort I see and hear birds with
like ease. Eye and ear are always on the
alert.

One day in early June I was walking with
some friends along a secluded wood-road.
Above the hum of the conversation I caught
the distressed cry of a pair of blue-jays. My
companions heard it also, but did not heed it.

But to my ear the cry was peculiar. It was
uttered in a tone of anguish and alarm. I
said, "Let us see what is the trouble with
these jays." I presently saw a nest twenty-
five or thirty feet from the ground in a small
hemlock which I at once concluded belonged
to the jays. The birds were but a few yards
away hopping about amid the neighboring

branches, uttering now and then their despairing note.   Looking more intently at the nest, I became aware in the dim light of the tree of something looped about it, or else there was a dark, very crooked limb that partly held it. Suspecting the true nature of the case, I threw a stone up through the branches, and then another and another, when the dark loops and folds upon one side of the nest began to disappear, and the head and neck of a black snake to slowly slide out on a horizontal branch on the other; in a moment the snake had cleared the nest, and stretched himself along the branch.

Another rock-fragment jarred his perch when he slid cautiously along toward the branch of a large pine-tree which came out and mingled its spray with that of the hemlock.   It was soon apparent that the snake was going to take refuge in the pine.   As he made the passage from one tree to the other we sought to dislodge him by a shower of sticks and stones, but without success; he was soon upon a large branch of the pine, and, stretched out on top of the limb, thought himself quite hidden. And so he was; but we knew his hiding-place, and the stones and clubs we hurled soon made him uneasy.   Presently a club struck the branch with such force that he was fairly dislodged, but saved himself by quickly wrapping his tail about the limb.   In this position he hung for some moments, but the intervening branches shielded him pretty well from our missiles, and he soon recovered himself and gained a still higher branch that reached out over the road and nearly made a bridge to the trees on the other side.

Seeing the monster was likely to escape us, unless we assailed him at closer quarters, I determined to climb the tree. A smaller tree growing near helped me up to the first branches, where the ascent was not very difficult. I finally reached the branch upon which the snake was carefully poised, and began shaking it. But he did not come down; he wrapped his tail about it, and defied me. My own position was precarious, and I was obliged to move with great circumspection.

After much manœuvring I succeeded in arming myself with a dry branch eight or ten feet long, where I had the serpent at a disadvantage. He kept his hold well. I clubbed him about from branch to branch while my friends, with cautions and directions, looked on from beneath. Neither man nor snake will indulge in very lively antics in a treetop thirty or forty feet from the ground. But at last I dislodged him, and swinging and looping like a piece of rubber hose he went to the ground, where my friends pounced upon him savagely and quickly made an end of him.

I worked my way carefully down the tree, and was about to drop upon the ground from the lower branches, when I saw another black snake coiled up at the foot of the tree, as if lying in wait for me. Had he started to his mate's rescue, and, seeing the battle over, was he now waiting to avenge himself upon the victor? But the odds were against him; my friends soon had him stretched beside his comrade.

The first snake killed had swallowed two young jays just beginning to feather out.

How the serpent discovered the nest would be very interesting to know. What led him to search in this particular tree amid all these hundreds of trees that surrounded it? It is probable that the snake watches like a cat, or, having seen the parent birds about this tree, explored it. Nests upon the ground and in low boughs are frequently rifled by black snakes, but I have never before known one to climb to such a height in a forest tree.

It would also be interesting to know if the other snake was in the secret of this nest, and was waiting near to share in its contents. One rarely has the patience to let these little dramas or tragedies be played to the end; one cannot look quietly on, and see a snake devour anything. Not even when it is snake eat snake. Only a few days later my little boy called me to the garden to see a black snake in the act of swallowing a garter snake. The little snake was holding back with all his might and main, hooking his tail about the blackberry bushes, and pulling desperately; still his black enemy was slowly engulfing him, and had accomplished about eight or ten inches of him, when he suddenly grew alarmed at some motion of ours, and ejected the little snake from him with unexpected ease and quickness, and tried to escape. The little snake's head was bleeding, but he did not seem otherwise to have suffered from the adventure.

Still a few days later, the man who was mowing the lawn called to me to come and witness a similar tragedy, but on a smaller scale — a garter snake swallowing a little green snake. Half the length of the green snake had disappeared from sight, and it was quite dead. The process had been a slow one, as the garter snake was only two or three inches longer than his victim. There seems to be a sort of poetic justice in snake swallowing snake, shark eating shark, and one can look on with more composure than when a bird or frog is the victim. It is said that in the deep sea there is a fish that will swallow another fish eight or ten times its own size. It seizes its victim by the tail and slowly sucks it in, stretching and expanding itself at the same time, and probably digesting the big fish by inches, till after many days it is completely engulfed. Would it be hard to find something analogous to this in life, especially in American politics?

A YOUNG MARSH HAWK

MOST country boys, I fancy, know the marsh hawk. It is he you see flying low over the fields, beating about bushes and marshes and dipping over the fences, with his attention directed to the ground beneath him. He is a cat on wings. He keeps so low that the birds and mice do not see him till he is fairly upon them. The hen-hawk swoops down upon the meadow-mouse from his position high in air, or from the top of a dead tree; but the marsh-hawk stalks him and comes suddenly upon him from over the fence, or from behind a low bush or tuft of grass. He is nearly as large as the hen-hawk, but has a much longer tail. When I was a boy I used to call him the long-tailed hawk. The male is a bluish slate-color; the female a reddish brown like the hen-hawk, with a white rump.

Unlike the other hawks, they nest on the ground in low, thick marshy places. For several seasons a pair have nested in a bushy marsh a few miles back of me, near the house of a farmer friend of mine, who has a keen eye for the wild life about him. Two years ago he found the nest, but when I got over to see it the next week, it had been robbed, probably

by some boys in the neighborhood. The past
season, in April or May, by watching the
mother bird, he found the nest again. It was
in a marshy place, several acres in extent, in
the bottom of a valley, and thickly grown with
hardhack, prickly ash, smilax, and other low
thorny bushes. My friend brought me to the
brink of a low hill, and pointed out to me in
the marsh below us, as nearly as he could, just
where the nest was located. Then we crossed
the pasture, entered upon the marsh, and made
our way cautiously toward it. The wild thorny
growths, waist high, had to be carefully dealt
with. As we neared the spot I used my eyes
the best I could, but I did not see the hawk
till she sprang into the air not ten yards away
from us. She went screaming upward, and
was soon sailing in a circle far above us.
There, on a coarse matting of twigs and weeds,
lay five snow-white eggs, a little more than
half as large as hen's eggs. My companion
said the male hawk would probably soon appear and join the female, but he did not. She
kept drifting away to the east, and was soon
gone from our sight.

We soon withdrew and secreted ourselves
behind the stone wall, in hopes of seeing the
mother hawk return. She appeared in the distance, but seemed to know she was being
watched, and kept away. About ten days later
we made another visit to the nest. An adventurous young Chicago lady also wanted to see
a hawk's nest, and so accompanied us. This

time three of the eggs were hatched, and as the mother hawk sprang up, either by accident or intentionally, she threw two of the young hawks some feet from the nest. She rose up and screamed angrily. Then, turning toward us, she came like an arrow straight at the young lady, a bright plume in whose hat probably drew her fire. The damsel gathered up her skirts about her and beat a hasty retreat. Hawks were not so pretty as she thought they were. A large hawk launched at one's face from high in the air is calculated to make one a little nervous. It is such a fearful incline down which the bird comes, and she is aiming exactly toward your eye. When within about thirty feet of you she turns upward with a rushing sound, and mounting higher falls toward you again. She is only firing blank cartridges, as it were; but it usually has the desired effect, and beats the enemy off.

After we had inspected the young hawks, a neighbor of my friend offered to conduct us to a quail's nest. Anything in the shape of a nest is always welcome, it is such a mystery, such a centre of interest and affection, and, if upon the ground, is usually something so dainty and exquisite amid the natural wreckage and confusion. A ground nest seems so exposed, too, that it always gives a little thrill of pleasurable surprise to see the group of frail eggs resting there behind so slight a·barrier. I will walk a long distance any day just to see a song-sparrow's nest amid the stubble or under

a tuft of grass.   It is a jewel in a rosette of
jewels, with a frill of weeds or turf.   A quail's
nest I had never seen, and to be shown one
within the hunting-ground of this murderous
hawk would be a double pleasure.   Such a
quiet, secluded, grass-grown highway as we
moved along was itself a rare treat.   Seques-
tered was the word that the little valley suggested, and peace the feeling the road evoked.
The farmer, whose fields lay about us, half
grown with weeds and bushes, evidently did
not make stir or noise enough to disturb anything.   Beside this rustic highway, bounded
by old mossy stone walls, and within a stone's
throw of the farmer's barn, the quail had made
her nest.   It was just under the edge of a pros-
trate thorn-bush.

"The nest is right there," said the farmer,
pausing within ten feet of it, and pointing to
the spot with his stick.

In a moment or two we could make out the
mottled brown plumage of the sitting bird.
Then we approached her cautiously till we bent
above her.

She never moved a feather.

Then I put my cane down in the brush behind her.   We wanted to see the eggs, yet did
not want rudely to disturb the sitting hen.

She would not move.

Then I put down my hand within a few
inches of her; still she kept her place.   Should
we have to lift her off bodily?

Then the young lady put down her hand,

probably the prettiest and the whitest hand the
quail had ever seen.   At least it startled her,
and off she sprang, uncovering such a crowded
nest of eggs as I had never before beheld.
Twenty-one of them! a ring or disk of white
like a china tea-saucer. You could not help saying how pretty, how cunning, like baby hen's
eggs, as if the bird was playing at sitting as
children play at housekeeping.

If I had known how crowded her nest was,
I should not have dared disturb her, for fear
she would break some of them. But not an egg
suffered harm by her sudden flight; and no
harm came to the nest afterward. Every egg
hatched, I was told, and the little chicks,
hardly bigger than bumblebees, were led away
by the mother into the fields.

In about a week I paid another visit to the
hawk's nest. The eggs were all hatched, and
the mother bird was hovering near. I shall
never forget the curious expression of those
young hawks sitting there on the ground. The
expression was not one of youth, but of extreme age. Such an ancient, infirm look as
they had — the sharp, dark, and shrunken look
about the face and eyes, and their feeble, tot-
tering motions! They sat upon their elbows
and the hind part of their bodies, and their
pale, withered legs and feet extended before
them in the most helpless fashion. Their
angular bodies were covered with a pale yellowish down, like that of a chicken; their
heads had a plucked, seedy appearance; and

their long, strong, naked wings hung down by
their sides till they touched the ground: power
and ferocity in the first rude draught, shorn of
everything but its sinister ugliness. Another
curious thing was the gradation of the young in
size; they tapered down regularly from the first
to the fifth, as if there had been, as probably
there was, an interval of a day or two between
the hatching of each.

The two older ones showed some signs of
fear on our approach, and one of them threw
himself upon his back, and put up his impotent
legs, and glared at us with open beak. The
two smaller ones regarded us not at all.

Neither of the parent birds appeared during
our stay.

When I visited the nest again, eight or ten
days later, the birds were much grown, but of
as marked a difference in size as before, and
with the same look of extreme old age — old
age in men of the aquiline type, nose and chin
coming together, and eyes large and sunken.
They now glared upon us with a wild, savage
look, and opened their beaks threateningly.

The next week, when my friend visited the
nest, the larger of the hawks fought him savagely. But one of the brood, probably the
last to hatch, had made but little growth. It
appeared to be on the point of starvation. The
mother hawk (for the male seemed to have disappeared) had doubtless found her family too
large for her, and was deliberately allowing one
of the number to perish; or did the larger and

stronger young devour all the food before the weaker member could obtain any? Probably this was the case.

Arthur brought the feeble nestling away, and the same day my little boy got it and brought it home, wrapped in a woolen rag. It was clearly a starved bantling. It cried feebly, but would not lift up its head.

We first poured some warm milk down its throat, which soon revived it, so that it would swallow small bits of flesh. In a day or two we had it eating ravenously, and its growth became noticeable. Its voice had the sharp whistling character of that of its parents, and was stilled only when the bird was asleep. We made a pen for it, about a yard square, in one end of the study, covering the floor with several thicknesses of newspapers; and here, upon a bit of brown woolen blanket for a nest, the hawk waxed strong day by day. An uglier-looking pet, tested by all the rules we usually apply to such things, would have been hard to find. There he would sit upon his elbows, his helpless feet out in front of him, his great featherless wings touching the floor, and shrilly cry for more food. For a time we gave him water daily from a stylograph-pen filler, but the water he evidently did not need or relish. Fresh meat, and plenty of it, was his demand. And we soon discovered that he liked game, such as mice, squirrels, birds, much better than butcher's meat.

Then began a lively campaign on the part of

my little boy against all the vermin and small
game in the neighborhood to keep the hawk
supplied.   He trapped and he hunted, he en-
listed his mates in his service, he even robbed
the cats to feed the hawk.   His usefulness as
a boy of all work was seriously impaired.
"Where is J——?"   "Gone after a squirrel
for his hawk."   And often the day would be
half gone before his hunt was successful.   The
premises were very soon cleared of mice, and
the vicinity of chipmunks and squirrels.
Farther and farther he was compelled to hunt
the surrounding farms and woods to keep up
with the demands of the hawk.   By the time
the hawk was ready to fly he had consumed
twenty-one chipmunks, fourteen red squirrels,
sixteen mice, and twelve English sparrows, besides a lot of butcher's meat.

His plumage very soon began to show itself,
crowding off tufts of the down.   The quills on
his great wings sprouted and grew apace.

What a ragged, uncanny appearance he presented! but his look of extreme age gradually
became modified.   What a lover of the sunlight he was!   We would put him out upon
the grass in the full blaze of the morning sun,
and he would spread his wings and bask in it
with the most intense enjoyment.   In the nest
the young must be exposed to the full power of
the midday sun during our first heated terms in
June and July, the thermometer often going up
to 93 or 95 degrees, so that sunshine seemed to
be a need of his nature.   He liked the rain

equally well, and when put out in a shower would sit down and take it as if every drop did him good.

His legs developed nearly as slowly as his wings. He could not stand steadily upon them till about ten days before he was ready to fly. The talons were limp and feeble. When we came with food he would hobble along toward us like the worst kind of a cripple, dropping and moving his wings, and treading upon his legs from the foot back to the elbow, the foot remaining closed and useless. Like a baby learning to stand, he made many trials before he succeeded. He would rise up on his trembling legs only to fall back again.

One day, in the summer-house, I saw him for the first time stand for a moment squarely upon his legs with the feet fully spread beneath them. He looked about him as if the world suddenly wore a new aspect.

His plumage now grew quite rapidly. One red squirrel per day, chopped fine with an axe, was his ration. He began to hold his game with his foot while he tore it. The study was full of his shed down. His dark brown mottled plumage began to grow beautiful. The wings drooped a little, but gradually he got control of them and held them in place.

It was now the 20th of July, and the hawk was about five weeks old. In a day or two he was walking or jumping about the ground. He chose a position under the edge of a Norway spruce, where he would sit for hours dozing, or

looking out upon the landscape. When we
brought him game he would advance to meet us
with wings slightly lifted, and uttering a shrill
cry. Toss him a mouse or sparrow, and he
would seize it with one foot and hop off to his
cover, where he would bend above it, spread
his plumage, look this way and that, uttering
all the time the most exultant and satisfied
chuckle.

About this time he began to practice striking
with his talons, as an Indian boy might begin
practicing with his bow and arrow. He would
strike at a dry leaf in the grass, or at a fallen
apple, or at some imaginary object. He was
learning the use of his weapons. His wings
also — he seemed to feel them sprouting from
his shoulder. He would lift them straight up
and hold them expanded, and they would seem
to quiver with excitement. Every hour in the
day he would do this. The pressure was beginning to centre there. Then he would strike
playfully at a leaf or a bit of wood, and keep
his wings lifted.

The next step was to spring into the air and
beat his wings. He seemed now to be thinking
entirely of his wings. They itched to be put
to use.

A day or two later he would leap and fly
several feet. A pile of brush ten or twelve feet
below the bank was easily reached. Here he
would perch in true hawk fashion, to the be-
wilderment and scandal of all the robins and
catbirds in the vicinity. Here he would dart

his eye in all directions, turning his head over and glancing it up into the sky.

He was now a lovely creature, fully fledged, and as tame as a kitten. But he was not a bit like a kitten in one respect — he could not bear to have you stroke or even touch his plumage. He had a horror of your hand, as if it would hopelessly defile him. But he would perch upon it, and allow you to carry him about.

If a dog or cat appeared, he was ready to give battle instantly. He rushed up to a little dog one day, and struck him with his foot savagely. He was afraid of strangers, and of any unusual object.

The last week in July he began to fly quite freely, and it was necessary to clip one of his wings. As the clipping embraced only the ends of his primaries, he soon overcame the difficulty, and by carrying his broad, long tail more on that side, flew with considerable ease. He made longer and longer excursions into the surrounding fields and vineyards, and did not always return. On such occasions we would go find him and fetch him back.

Late one rainy afternoon he flew away into the vineyard, and when, an hour later, I went after him, he could not be found, and we never saw him again.

We hoped hunger would soon drive him back, but we have had no clue to him from that day to this.

THE CHIPMUNK

THE first chipmunk in March is as sure a token of the spring as the first bluebird or the first robin; and it is quite as welcome. Some genial influence has found him out there in his burrow, deep under the ground, and waked him up and enticed him forth into the light of day. The red squirrel has been more or less active all winter; his track has dotted the surface of every new fallen snow throughout the season. But the chipmunk retired from view early in December and has passed the rigorous months in his nest, beside his hoard of nuts, some feet underground, and hence, when he emerges in March and is seen upon his little journeys along the fences, or perched upon a log or rock near his hole in the woods, it is another sign that spring is at hand. His store of nuts may or may not be all consumed; it is certain that he is no sluggard, to sleep away these first bright warm days.

Before the first crocus is out of the ground, you may look for the first chipmunk. When I hear the little downy woodpecker begin his spring drumming, then I know the chipmunk is due. He cannot sleep after that challenge of the woodpecker reaches his ear.

Apparently the first thing he does on coming forth, as soon as he is sure of himself, is to go courting. So far as I have observed, the love-making of the chipmunk occurs in March. A single female will attract all the males in the vicinity. One early March day I was at work for several hours near a stone fence where a female had apparently taken up her quarters. What a train of suitors she had that day! how they hurried up and down, often giving each other a spiteful slap or bite as they passed. The young are born in May, four or five at a birth.

The chipmunk is quite a solitary creature; I have never known more than one to occupy the same den. Apparently no two can agree to live together. What a clean, pert, dapper, nervous little fellow he is! How fast his heart beats, as he stands up on the wall by the roadside, and with hands spread out upon his breast regards you intently! A movement of your arm, and he darts into the wall with a saucy *chip-r-r*, which has the effect of slamming the door behind him.

On some still day in autumn, the nutty days, the woods will often be pervaded by an under-tone of sound, produced by their multitudinous clucking, as they sit near their dens. It is one of the characteristic sounds of fall.

The chipmunk has many enemies, such as cats, weasels, black snakes, hawks, and owls. One season one had his den in the side of the bank near my study. As I stood regarding his

goings and comings, one October morning, I
saw him, when a few yards away from his hole,
turn and retreat with all speed. As he darted
beneath the sod, a shrike swooped down and
hovered a moment on the wing just over the
hole where he had disappeared. I doubt if the
shrike could have killed him, but it certainly
gave him a good fright.

It was amusing to watch this chipmunk carry
nuts and other food into his den. He had
made a well-defined path from his door out
through the weeds and dry leaves, into the territory where his feeding ground lay. The
path was a crooked one; it dipped under weeds,
under some large loosely piled stones, under a
pile of chestnut posts, and then followed the
remains of an old wall. Going and coming,
his motions were like clockwork. He always
went by spurts and sudden sallies. He was
never for one moment off his guard. He
would appear at the mouth of his den, look
quickly about, take a few leaps to a tussock of
grass, pause a breath with one foot raised, slip
quickly a few yards over some dry leaves, pause
again by a stump beside a path, rush across the
path to the pile of loose stones, go under the
first and over the second, gain the pile of posts,
make his way through that, survey his course a
half moment from the other side of it, and then
dart on to some other cover, and presently beyond my range, where I think he gathered
acorns, as there were no other nut-bearing trees
than oaks near. In four or five minutes I

would see him coming back, always keeping rigidly to the course he took going out, pausing at the same spots, darting over or under the same objects, clearing at a bound the same pile of leaves. There was no variation in his manner of proceeding all the time I observed him.

He was alert, cautious, and exceedingly methodical. He had found safety in a certain course, and he did not at any time deviate a hair's breadth from it. Something seemed to say to him all the time, "Beware, beware!" The nervous, impetuous ways of these creatures are no doubt the result of the life of fear which they lead.

My chipmunk had no companion. He lived all by himself in true hermit fashion, as is usually the case with this squirrel. Provident creature that he is, one would think that he would long ago have discovered that heat, and therefore food, is economized by two or three nesting together.

One day in early spring a chipmunk that lived near me met with a terrible adventure, the memory of which will probably be handed down through many generations of its family. I was sitting in the summer-house with Nig the cat upon my knee, when the chipmunk came out of its den a few feet away, and ran quickly to a pile of chestnut posts about twenty yards from where I sat. Nig saw it and was off my lap upon the floor in an instant. I spoke sharply to the cat, when she sat down and folded her paws under her, and regarded the squirrel, as I

thought, with only a dreamy kind of interest.
I fancied she thought it a hopeless case there
amid that pile of posts. "That is not your
game, Nig," I said, "so spare yourself any
anxiety." Just then I was called to the house,
where I was detained about five minutes. As
I returned I met Nig coming to the house with
the chipmunk in her mouth. She had the air
of one who had won a wager. She carried the
chipmunk by the throat, and its body hung
limp from her mouth. I quickly took the
squirrel from her and reproved her sharply. It
lay in my hand as if dead, though I saw no
marks of the cat's teeth upon it. Presently it
gasped for its breath, then again and again. I
saw that the cat had simply choked it. Quickly
the film passed off its eyes, its heart began
visibly to beat, and slowly the breathing became
regular. I carried it back and laid it down in
the door of its den. In a moment it crawled or
kicked itself in. In the afternoon I placed a
handful of corn there, to express my sympathy,
and as far as possible make amends for Nig's
cruel treatment.

Not till four or five days had passed did my
little neighbor emerge again from its den and
then only for a moment. That terrible black
monster with the large green-yellow eyes — it
might be still lurking near. How the black
monster had captured the alert and restless
squirrel so quickly, under the circumstances,
was a great mystery to me. Was not its eye
as sharp as the cat's and its movements as quick?

Yet cats do have the secret of catching squirrels, and birds, and mice, but I have never yet had the luck to see it done.

It was not very long before the chipmunk was going to and from her den as usual, though the dread cf the black monster seemed ever before her, and gave speed and extra alertness to all her movements. In early summer four young chipmunks emerged from the den, and ran freely about. There was nothing to disturb them, for alas, Nig herself was now dead.

One summer day I watched a cat for nearly a half hour trying her arts upon a chipmunk that sat upon a pile of stone. Evidently her game was to stalk him. She had cleared half the distance, or about twelve feet, that separated the chipmunk from a dense Norway spruce when I chanced to become a spectator of the little drama. There sat the cat crouched low on the grass, her big, yellow eyes fixed upon the chipmunk, and there sat the chipmunk at the mouth of his den motionless with his eye fixed upon the cat. For a long time neither moved. "Will the cat bind him with her fatal spell?" I thought. Sometimes her head slowly lowered and her eyes seemed to dilate, and I fancied she was about to spring. But she did not. The distance was too great to be successfully cleared in one bound. Then the squirrel moved nervously, but kept his eye upon the enemy. Then the cat evidently grew tired and relaxed a little and looked behind her. Then she crouched again and riveted her gaze upon the squirrel. But the latter would not be hypnotized; it shifted its position a few times and finally quickly entered its den, when the cat soon slunk away.

In digging his hole it is evident that the chipmunk carries away the loose soil. Never a grain of it is seen in front of his door. Those pockets of his probably stand him in good stead on such occasions. Only in one instance have I seen a pile of earth before the entrance to a chipmunk's den, and that was where the builder had begun his house late in November and was probably too much hurried to remove this ugly mark from before his door. I used to pass his place every morning in my walk, and my eye always fell upon that little pile of red, freshly dug soil. A little later I used frequently to surprise the squirrel furnishing his house, carrying in dry leaves of the maple and plane-tree. He would seize a large leaf and with both hands stuff it into his cheek pockets, and then carry it into his den. I saw him on several different days occupied in this way. I trust he had secured his winter stores, though I am a little doubtful. He was hurriedly making himself a new home, and the cold of December was upon us while he was yet at work. It may be that he had moved the stores from his old quarters, wherever they were, and again it may be that he had been dispossessed of both his house and provender by some other chipmunk.

When nuts or grain are not to be had, these

thrifty little creatures will find some substitute to help them over the winter.   Two chipmunks near my study were occupied many days in carrying in cherry pits which they gathered beneath a large cherry-tree that stood ten or twelve rods away.   As Nig was no longer about to molest them, they grew very fearless, and used to spin up and down the garden path to and from their source of supplies in a way quite unusual with these timid creatures.   After they had got enough cherry pits, they gathered the seed of a sugar maple that stood near.   Many of the keys remained upon the tree after the leaves had fallen and these the squirrels harvested.   They would run swiftly out upon the ends of the small branches, reach out for the maple keys, snip off the wings and deftly slip the nut or samara into their cheek pockets. Day after day in late autumn I used to see them thus occupied.

As I have said, I have no evidence that more than one chipmunk occupy the same den.   One March morning after a light fall of snow I saw where one had come up out of his hole, which was in the side of our path to the vineyard, and after a moment's survey of the surroundings had started off on his travels.   I followed the track to see where he had gone.   He had passed through my woodpile, then under the beehives, then around the study and under some spruces and along the slope to the hole of a friend of his, about sixty yards from his own. Apparently he had gone in here, and then his

friend had come forth with him, for there were
two tracks leading from this doorway. I followed them to a third humble entrance, not far
off, where the tracks were so numerous that I
lost the trail. It was pleasing to see the evidence of their morning sociability written there
upon the new snow.

One of the enemies of the chipmunk, as I
discovered lately, is the weasel. I was sitting
in the woods one autumn day when I heard a
small cry, and a rustling amid the branches of
a tree a few rods beyond me. Looking thither
I saw a chipmunk fall through the air, and
catch on a limb twenty or more feet from the
ground. He appeared to have dropped from
near the top of the tree.

He secured his hold upon the small branch
that had luckily intercepted his fall, and sat
perfectly still. In a moment more I saw a
weasel — one of the smaller red varieties —
come down the trunk of the tree, and begin
exploring the branches on a level with the
chipmunk.

I saw in a moment what had happened. The
weasel had driven the squirrel from his retreat
in the rocks and stones beneath, and had pressed
him so closely that he had taken refuge in the
top of a tree. But weasels can climb trees too,
and this one had tracked the frightened chipmunk to the topmost branch, where he had tried
to seize him. Then the squirrel had, in horror,
let go his hold, screamed, and fallen through
the air, till he struck the branch as just described.

Now his bloodthirsty enemy was looking for him again, apparently relying entirely upon his sense of smell to guide him to the game.

How did the weasel know the squirrel had not fallen clear to the ground? He certainly did know, for when he reached the same tier of branches, he began exploring them. The chipmunk sat transfixed with fear, frozen with terror, not twelve feet away, and yet the weasel saw him not.

Round and round, up and down he went on the branches, exploring them over and over. How he hurried, lest the trail get cold! How subtle and cruel and fiendish he looked! His snakelike movements, his tenacity, his speed!

He seemed baffled; he knew his game was near, but he could not strike the spot. The branch, upon the extreme end of which the squirrel sat, ran out and up from the tree seven or eight feet, and then, turning a sharp elbow, swept down and out at right angles with its first course.

The weasel would pause each time at this elbow and turn back. It seemed as if he knew that particular branch held his prey, and yet its crookedness each time threw him out. He would not give it up, but went over his course again and again.

One can fancy the feelings of the chipmunk, sitting there in plain view a few feet away, watching its deadly enemy hunting for the clue. How its little heart must have fairly stood still each time the fatal branch was struck. Prob-

ably as a last resort it would again have let go
its hold and fallen to the ground, where it
might have eluded its enemy a while longer.

In the course of five or six minutes, the
weasel gave over the search, and ran hurriedly
down the tree to the ground.

The chipmunk remained motionless for a long
time; then he stirred a little as if hope was reviving. Then he looked nervously about him;
then he had recovered himself so far as to
change his position.

Presently he began to move cautiously along
the branch to the bole of the tree; then, after
a few moments' delay, he plucked up courage
to descend to the ground, where I hope no
weasel has disturbed him since.

For ten or more years past I have been in the habit of jotting down, among other things in my note-book, observations upon the seasons as they passed, — the complexion of the day, the aspects of nature, the arrival of the birds, the opening of the flowers, or any characteristic feature of the passing moment or hour which the great open-air panorama presented. Some of these notes and observations touching the opening and the progress of the spring season follow herewith.

I need hardly say they are off-hand and informal; what they have to recommend them to the general reader is mainly their fidelity to actual fact. The sun always crosses the line on time, but the seasons which he makes are by no means so punctual; they loiter or they hasten, and the spring tokens are three or four weeks earlier or later some seasons than others. The ice often breaks up on the river early in March, but I have crossed upon it as late as the 10th of April. My journal presents many samples of both early and late springs.

But before I give these extracts let me say a word or two in favor of the habit of keeping a journal of one's thoughts and days. To a

countryman, especially of a meditative turn,
who likes to preserve the flavor of the passing
moment, or to a person of leisure anywhere,
who wants to make the most of life, a journal
will be found a great help. It is a sort of deposit account wherein one saves up bits and fragments of his life that would otherwise be lost to
him.

What seemed so insignificant in the passing,
or as it lay in embryo in his mind, becomes a
valuable part of his experiences when it is fully
unfolded and recorded in black and white. The
process of writing develops it; the bud becomes
the leaf or flower; the one is disentangled from
the many and takes definite form and hue. I
remember that Thoreau says in a letter to a
friend after his return from a climb to the top
of Monadnock, that it is not till he gets home
that he really goes over the mountain; that is,
I suppose, sees what the climb meant to him
when he comes to write an account of it to his
friend. Every one's experience is probably
much the same; when we try to tell what we
saw and felt, even to our journals, we discover
more and deeper meanings in things than we
had suspected.

The pleasure and value of every walk or
journey we take may be doubled to us by carefully noting down the impressions it makes
upon us. How much of the flavor of Maine
birch I should have missed had I not compelled
that vague, unconscious being within me, who
absorbs so much, and says so little, to unbosom

himself at the point of the pen. It was not till after I got home that I really went to Maine, or to the Adirondacks, or to Canada. Out of the chaotic and nebulous impressions which these expeditions gave me, I evolved the real experience. There is hardly anything that does not become much more in the telling than in the thinking, or in the feeling.

I see the fishermen floating up and down the river above their nets, which are suspended far out of sight in the water beneath them. They do not know what fish they have got, if any, till after a while they lift the nets up and examine them. In all of us there is a region of sub-consciousness above which our ostensible lives go forward, and in which much comes to us or is slowly developed, of which we are quite ignorant, until we lift up our nets and inspect them.

Then the charm and significance of a day are so subtle and fleeting! Before we know it, it is gone past all recovery. I find that each spring, that each summer, and fall, and winter of my life has a hue and quality of its own, given by some prevailing mood, a train of thought, an event, an experience, — a color or quality of which I am quite unconscious at the time, being too near to it, and too completely enveloped by it. But afterward, some mood or circumstance, an odor, or fragment of a tune brings it back as by a flash; for one brief second the adamantine door of the past swings open and gives me a glimpse of my former life.

One's journal dashed off without any secondary motive may often preserve and renew the past for him in this way.

These leaves from my own journal are not very good samples of this sort of thing, but they preserve for me the image of many a day which memory alone could never have kept.

March 3, 1879. The sun is getting strong, but winter still holds his own. No hint of spring in the earth or air. No sparrow or sparrow song yet. But on the 5th there was a hint of spring. The day warm and the snow melting. The first bluebird note this morning. How sweetly it dropped down from the blue overhead!

March 10. A real spring day at last, and a rouser! Thermometer between 50° and 60° in the coolest spot; bees very lively about the hive and working on the sawdust in the wood yard; how they dig and wallow in the woody meal, apparently squeezing it as if forcing it to yield up something to them! Here they get their first substitute for pollen. The sawdust of hickory and maple is preferred. The inner milky substance between the bark and the wood, called the cambium layer, is probably the source of their supplies.

In the growing tree it is in this layer or secretion that the vital processes are the most active and potent. It has been found by experiment that this tender, milky substance is capable of exerting a very great force; a growing tree exerts a lifting and pushing force of more than thirty pounds to the square inch, and the force is thought to reside in the soft fragile cells that make up the cambium layer. It is like the strength of Samson residing in his hair. Saw one bee enter the hive with pollen on his back, which he must have got from some open greenhouse; or had he found the skunk cabbage in bloom ahead of me?

The bluebirds! It seemed as if they must have been waiting somewhere close by for the first warm day, like actors behind the scenes, for they were here in numbers early in the morning; they rushed upon the stage very promptly when their parts were called. No robins yet. Sap runs, but not briskly. It is too warm and still; it wants a brisk day for sap, with a certain sharpness in the air, a certain crispness and tension.

March 12. A change to more crispness and coolness, but a delicious spring morning. Hundreds of snowbirds with a sprinkling of song and Canada sparrows are all about the house, chirping and lisping and chattering in a very animated manner. The air is full of bird voices; through this maze of fine sounds comes the strong note and warble of the robin, and the soft call of the bluebird. A few days ago, not a bird, not a sound; everything rigid and severe; then in a day the barriers of winter give way, and spring comes like an inundation. In a twinkling all is changed.

Under date of February 27, 1881, I find this note: "Warm; saw the male bluebird warbling and calling cheerily. The male bluebird spreads his tail as he flits about at this season, in a way to make him look very gay and dressy. It adds to his expression considerably, and makes him look alert and beau-like, and every inch a male. The grass is green under the snow and has grown perceptibly. The warmth of the air seems to go readily through a covering of ice and snow. Note how quickly the ice lets go of the door-stones, though completely covered, when the day becomes warm."

The farmers say a deep snow draws the frost out of the ground. It is certain that the frost goes out when the ground is deeply covered for some time, though it is of course the warmth rising up from the depths of the ground that does it. A winter of deep snows is apt to prove fatal to the peach buds. The frost leaves the ground, the soil often becomes so warm that angle-worms rise to near the surface, the sap in the trees probably stirs a little; then there comes a cold wave, the mercury goes down to ten or fifteen below zero, and the peach buds are killed. It is not the cold alone that does it; it is the warmth at one end and the extreme cold at the other. When the snow is removed so that the frost can get at the roots also, peach buds will stand fourteen or fifteen degrees below zero.

March 7, 1881. A perfect spring day at last, — still, warm, and without a cloud. Tapped two trees; the sap runs, the snow runs, everything runs. Bluebirds the only birds yet.

Thermometer 42° in the shade. A perfect sap day. A perfect sap day is a crystalline day; the night must have a keen edge of frost, and the day a keen edge of air and sun, with wind north or northwest. The least film, the least breath from the south, the least suggestion of growth, and the day is marred as a sap day. Maple sap is maple frost melted by the sun. (9 P. M.) A soft, large-starred night; the moon in her second quarter; perfectly still and freezing; Venus throbbing low in the west. A crystalline night.

March 21, 1884. The top of a high barometric wave, a day like a crest, lifted up, sightly, sparkling. A cold snap without storm issuing in this clear, dazzling, sharp, northern day. How light, as if illuminated by more than the sun; the sky is full of light; light seems to be streaming up all around the horizon. The leafless trees make no shadows; the woods are flooded with light; everything shines; a day large and imposing, breathing strong masculine breaths out of the north; a day without a speck or film, winnowed through and through, all the windows and doors of the sky open. Day of crumpled rivers and lakes, of crested waves, of bellying sails, high-domed and lustrous day. The only typical March day of the bright heroic sort we have yet had.

March 24, 1884. Damp, still morning, much fog on the river. All the branches and twigs of the trees strung with drops of water. The grass and weeds beaded with fog drops.

Two lines of ducks go up the river, one a few
feet beneath the other. On second glance the
under line proves to be the reflection of the
other in the still water. As the ducks cross a
large field of ice, the lower line is suddenly
blotted out, as if the birds had dived beneath
the ice. A train of cars across the river, — the
train sunk beneath a solid stratum of fog, its
plume of smoke and vapor unrolling above it
and slanting away in the distance; a liquid
morning; the turf buzzes as you walk over it.

Skunk cabbage on Saturday the 22d, probably in bloom several days. This plant always
gets ahead of me. It seems to come up like a
mushroom in a single night. Water newts just
out, and probably piping before the frogs,
though not certain about this.

March 25. One of the rare days that go before a storm; the flower of a series of days in-
creasingly fair. To-morrow, probably, the flower
falls, and days of rain and cold prepare the way
for another fair day or days. The barometer
must be high to-day; the birds fly high. I feed
my bees on a rock and sit long and watch them
covering the combs, and rejoice in the multitudinous humming. The river is a great mirror
dotted here and there by small cakes of ice.
The first sloop comes lazily up on the flood tide,
like the first butterfly of spring; the little
steamer, our river omnibus, makes her first trip,
and wakes the echoes with her salutatory whistle, her flags dancing in the sun.

April 1. Welcome to April, my natal

month; the month of the swelling buds, the
springing grass, the first nests, the first plant-
ings, the first flowers, and, last but not least,
the first shad! The door of the seasons first
stands ajar this month, and gives us a peep beyond. The month in which to begin the world,
in which to begin your house, in which to begin
your courtship, in which to enter upon any new
enterprise. The bees usually get their first pollen this month and their first honey. All hibernating creatures are out before April is past.
The coon, the chipmunk, the bear, the turtles,
the frogs, the snakes, come forth beneath April
skies.

April 8. A day of great brightness and
clearness, — a crystalline April day that precedes
snow. In this sharp crisp air the flakes are
forming. As in a warm streaming south wind
one can almost smell the swelling buds, so a
wind from the opposite quarter at this season
as often suggests the crystalline snow. I go up
in the sugar bush (this was up among the Catskills) and linger for an hour among the old
trees. The air is still and has the property of
being "hollow," as the farmers say; that is, it
is heavy, motionless, and transmits sounds well.
Every warble of a bluebird, or robin, or caw of
crow, or bark of dog, or bleat of sheep, or
cackle of geese, or call of boy or man, within
the landscape, comes distinctly to the ear. The
smoke from the chimney goes straight up.

I walk through the bare fields; the shore
larks run or flit before me; I hear their shuf-

fling, gurgling, lisping, half inarticulate song.
Only of late years have I noticed the shore larks
in this section. Now they breed and pass the
summer on these hills, and I am told that they
are gradually becoming permanent residents in
other parts of the State. They are nearly as
large as the English skylark, with conspicuous
black markings about the head and throat; shy
birds squatting in the sear grass, and probably
taken by most country people who see them to
be sparrows.

Their flight and manner in song is much like
that of the skylark. The bird mounts up and
up on ecstatic wing, till it becomes a mere speck
against the sky, where it drifts to and fro, and
utters at intervals its crude song, a mere fraction
or rudiment of the skylark's song, a few sharp,
lisping, unmelodious notes, as if the bird had a
bad cold and could only now and then make any
sound, — heard a long distance, but insignificant,
a mere germ of the true lark's song; as it were
the first rude attempt of nature in this direction.
After due trial and waiting, she develops the
lark's song itself. But if the law of evolution
applies to bird-songs as well as to other things,
the shore lark should in time become a fine
songster. I know of no bird-song that seems
so obviously struggling to free itself and reach a
fuller expression. As the bird seems more and
more inclined to abide permanently amid cultivated fields, and to forsake the wild and savage
north, let me hope that its song is also under-
going a favorable change.

How conspicuous the crows in the brown fields, or against the lingering snowbanks, or in the clear sky. How still the air! One could carry a lighted candle over the hills. The light is very strong, and the effect of the wall of white mountains rising up all around from the checkered landscape, and holding up the blue dome of the sky, is strange indeed.

April 14. A delicious day, warm as May. This to me is the most bewitching part of the whole year. One's relish is so keen, and the morsels are so few, and so tender. How the fields of winter rye stand out! They call up visions of England. A perfect day in April far excels a perfect day in June, because it provokes and stimulates while the latter sates and cloys. Such days have all the peace and geniality of summer without any of its satiety or enervating heat.

April 15. Not much cloud this morning, but much vapor in the air. A cool south wind with streaks of a pungent vegetable odor, probably from the willows. When I make too dead a set at it I miss it; but when I let my nose have its own way, and take in the air slowly, I get it, an odor as of a myriad swelling buds. The long-drawn call of the highhole comes up from the fields, then the tender rapid trill of the bush or russet sparrow, then the piercing note of the meadow-lark, a flying shaft of sound.

April 21. The enchanting days continue without a break. One's senses are not large enough to take them all in. Maple buds just bursting, apple-trees full of infantile leaves. How the poplars and willows stand out! A moist, warm, brooding haze over all the earth. All day my little rustic sparrow sings and trills divinely. The most prominent bird music in April is from the sparrows.

The yellow-birds (goldfinches) are just getting on their yellow coats. I saw some yesterday that had a smutty, unwashed look, because of the new yellow shining through the old drab-colored webs of the feathers. These birds do not shed their feathers in the spring, as careless observers are apt to think they do, but merely shed the outer webs of their feathers and quills, which peel off like a glove from the hand.

All the groves and woods lightly touched with new foliage. Looks like May; violets and dandelions in bloom. Sparrow's nest with two eggs. Maples hanging out their delicate fringe-like bloom. First swallows may be looked for any day after April 20.

This period may be called the vernal equipoise, and corresponds to the October calm called the Indian summer.

April 2, 1890. The second of the April days, clear as a bell. The eye of the heavens wide open at last. A sparrow day; how they sang! And the robins, too, before I was up in the morning. Now and then I could hear the rat-tat-tat of the downy at his drum. How many times I paused at my work to drink in the beauty of the day.

How I like to walk out after supper these days! I stroll over the lawn and stand on the brink of the hill. The sun is down, the robins pipe and call, and as the dusk comes on they indulge in that loud chiding note or scream, whether in anger or in fun I never can tell. Up the road in the distance the multitudinous voice of the little peepers, — a thicket or screen of sound. An April twilight is unlike any other.

April 12. Lovely, bright day. We plough the ground under the hill for the new vine-yard. In opening the furrow for the young vines I guide the team by walking in their front. How I soaked up the sunshine to-day. At night I glowed all over; my whole being had had an earth bath; such a feeling of freshly ploughed land in every cell of my brain. The furrow had struck in; the sunshine had photo-graphed it upon my soul.

April 13. A warm, even hot April day. The air full of haze; the sunshine golden. In the afternoon J. and I walk out over the country north of town. Everybody is out, all the paths and byways are full of boys and young fellows. We sit on a wall a long time by a meadow and orchard, and drink in the scene. April to perfection, such a sentiment of spring everywhere. The sky is partly overcast, the air moist, just enough so to bring out the odors, — a sweet perfume of bursting growing things. One could almost eat the turf like a horse. All about the robins sang. In the trees the crow-blackbird cackled and jingled. Athwart these sounds came every half minute the clear, strong note of the meadow-lark. The larks were very numerous and were lovemaking. Then the highhole called and the bush sparrow trilled. Arbutus days these, everybody wants to go to the woods for arbutus; it fairly calls one. The soil calls for the plough, too, the garden calls for the spade, the vineyard calls for the hoe. From all about the farm voices call, Come and do this, or do that. At night how the "peepers" pile up the sound.

How I delight to see the plough at work such mornings; the earth is ripe for it, fairly lusts for it, and the freshly turned soil looks good enough to eat. Plucked my first bloodroot this morning, — a full-blown flower with a young one folded up in a leaf beneath it, only just the bud emerging like the head of a pappoose protruding from its mother's blanket, — a very pretty sight. The bloodroot always comes up with the leaf shielding the flower-bud, as one shields the flame of the candle in the open air with his hand half closed about it.

These days the song of the toad — tr-r-r-r-r-r-r-r-r-r-r-r-r-r-r-r-r-r — is heard in the land. At nearly all hours I hear it, and it is as welcome to me as the song of any bird. It is a kind of gossamer of sound drifting in the air. Mother toad is in the pools and puddles now depositing that long chain or raveling of eggs, while her dapper little mate rides upon her back and fertilizes them as they are laid. As

I look toward the fields where the first brown thrasher is singing, I see emerald patches of rye. The unctuous confident strain of the bird seems to make the fields grow greener hour by hour.

May 4. The perfection of early May weather. How green the grass, how happy the birds, how placid the river, how busy the bees, how soft the air! — that kind of weather when there seems to be dew in the air all day, — the day a kind of prolonged morning, — so fresh, so wooing, so caressing! The baby leaves on the apple-trees have doubled in size since last night.

March 12, 1891. Had positive proof this morning that at least one song-sparrow has come back to his haunts of a year ago. One year ago to-day my attention was attracted, while walking over to the post-office, by an unfamiliar bird-song. It caught my ear while I was a long way off. I followed it up and found that it proceeded from a song-sparrow. Its chief feature was one long, clear high note, very strong, sweet, and plaintive. It sprang out of the trills and quavers of the first part of the bird-song, like a long arc or parabola of sound. To my mental vision it rose far up against the blue, and turned sharply downward again and finished in more trills and quavers. I had never before heard anything like it. It was the usual long, silvery note in the sparrow's song greatly increased; indeed, the whole breath and force of the bird put in this note, so that you caught little else than this silver loop of sound. The

bird remained in one locality — the bushy
corner of a field — the whole season. He indulged in the ordinary sparrow song also. I
had repeatedly had my eye upon him when he
changed from one to the other.

And now here he is again, just a year after,
in the same place, singing the same remarkable
song, capturing my ear with the same exquisite
lasso of sound. What would I not give to
know just where he passed the winter, and what
adventures by flood and field befell him.

(I will add that the bird continued in song
the whole season, apparently confining his wanderings to a few acres of ground. But the following spring he did not return, and I have
never heard him since, and if any of his progeny inherited this peculiar song I have not
heard them.)

I

Any glimpse of the wild and savage in nature, especially after long confinement indoors or in town, always gives a little fillip to my mind. Thus, when in my walk from the city the other day I paused, after a half hour, in a thick clump of red cedars crowning a little hill that arose amid a marshy and bushy bit of landscape, and found myself in the banqueting-hall of a hawk, something more than my natural history tastes stirred within me.

No hawk was there then, but the marks of his nightly presence were very obvious. The branch of a cedar about fifteen feet from the ground was his perch. It was worn smooth, with a feather or two adhering to it. The ground beneath was covered with large pellets and wads of mouse-hair; the leaves were white with his droppings, while the dried entrails of his victims clung here and there to the bushes. The bird evidently came here nightly to devour and digest its prey. This was its den, its retreat; all about lay its feeding-grounds. It revealed to me a new trait in the hawk, — its local attachments and habits; that it, too, had a home, and did not wander about like a vagabond. It had its domain, which it no doubt assiduously cultivated. Here it came to dine and meditate, and a most attractive spot it had chosen, a kind of pillared cave amid the cedars. It was such a spot as the pedestrian would be sure to direct his steps to, and, having reached it, would be equally sure to tarry and eat his own lunch there.

The winged creatures are probably quite as local as the four-footed. Sitting one night on a broad, gently rising hill, to see the darkness close in upon the landscape, my attention was attracted by a marsh hawk industriously working the fields about me. Time after time he made the circuit, varying but little in his course each time; dropping into the grass here and there, beating low over the bogs and bushes, and then disappearing in the distance. This was his domain, his preserve, and doubtless he had his favorite perch not far off.

All our permanent residents among the birds, both large and small, are comparatively limited in their ranges. The crow is nearly as local as the woodchuck. He goes farther from home in quest of food, but his territory is well defined, both winter and summer. His place of roosting remains the same year after year. Once, while spending a few days at a mountain lake nearly surrounded by deep woods, my attention was attracted each night, just at sundown, by an osprey that always came from the same direction, dipped into the lake as he passed over it for a sip of its pure water, and disappeared in the woods beyond. The routine of his life was probably as marked as that of any of ours. He fished the waters of the Delaware all day, probably never going beyond a certain limit, and returned each night at sundown, as punctual as a day-laborer, to his retreat in the forest. The sip of water, too, from the lake he never failed to take.

All the facts we possess in regard to the habits of the song-birds in this respect point to the conclusion that the same individuals return to the same localities year after year, to nest and to rear their young. I am convinced that the same woodpecker occupies the same cavity in a tree winter after winter, and drums upon the same dry limb spring after spring. I like to think of all these creatures as capable of local attachments, and not insensible to the sentiment of home.

But I set out to give some glimpses of the wild life which one gets about the farm. Not of a startling nature are they, certainly, but very welcome for all that. The domestic animals require their lick of salt every week or so, and the farmer, I think, is equally glad to get a taste now and then of the wild life that has so nearly disappeared from the older and more thickly settled parts of the country.

Last winter a couple of bears, an old one and a young one, passed through our neighborhood. Their tracks were seen upon the snow in the woods, and the news created great excitement among the Nimrods. It was like the commotion in the water along shore after a steamer had passed. The bears were probably safely in the Catskills by the time the hunters got dogs and guns ready and set forth. Country people are as eager to accept any rumor of a strange and dangerous creature in the woods as they are to believe in a ghost story. They want it to be true; it gives them something to think about and talk about. It is to their minds like strong drink to their palates. It gives a new interest to the woods, as the ghost story gives a new interest to the old house.

A few years ago the belief became current in our neighborhood that a dangerous wild animal lurked in the woods about, now here, now there. It had been seen in the dusk. Some big dogs had encountered it in the night, and one of them was nearly killed. Then a calf and a sheep were reported killed and partly devoured. Women and children became afraid to go through the woods, and men avoided them after sundown. One day as I passed an Irishman's shanty that stood in an opening in the woods, his wife came out with a pail, and begged leave to accompany me as far as the spring, which lay beside the road some distance into the woods. She was afraid to go alone for water on account of the "wild baste." Then, to cap the climax of wild rumors, a horse was killed. One of my neighbors, an intelligent man and a good observer, went up to see the horse. He reported that a great gash had been eaten in the top of the horse's neck, that its back was bitten and scratched, and that he was convinced it was the work of some wild animal like a panther which had landed upon the horse's back and fairly devoured it alive. The horse had run up and down the field trying to escape, and finally, in its desperation, had plunged headlong off a high stone wall by the barn and been killed. I was compelled to accept his story, but I pooh-poohed the conclusions. It was impossible that we should have a panther in the midst of us, or, if we had, that it would attack and kill a horse. But how eagerly the people believed it! It tasted good. It tasted good to me too, but I could not believe it. It soon turned out that the horse was killed by another horse, a vicious beast that had fits of murderous hatred toward its kind. The sheep and calf were probably not killed at all, and the big dogs had had a fight among themselves. So the panther legend faded out, and our woods became as tame and humdrum as before. We cannot get up anything exciting that will hold, and have to make the most of such small deer as coons, foxes, and woodchucks. Glimpses of these and of the birds are all I have to report.

II

The day on which I have any adventure with a wild creature, no matter how trivial, has a little different flavor from the rest; as when, one morning in early summer, I put my head out of the back window and returned the challenge of a quail that sent forth his clear call from a fence-rail one hundred yards away. Instantly he came sailing over the field of raspberries straight toward me. When about fifteen yards away he dropped into the cover and repeated his challenge. I responded, when in an instant he was almost within reach of me. He alighted under the window, and looked quickly around for his rival. How his eyes shone, how his form dilated, how dapper and polished and brisk he looked! He turned his eye up to me and seemed to say, "Is it you, then, who are mocking me?" and ran quickly around the corner of the house. Here he lingered some time amid the rosebushes, half persuaded that the call, which I still repeated, came from his rival. Ah, I thought, if with his mate and young he would only make my field his home! The call of the quail is a country sound that is becoming all too infrequent.

So fond am I of seeing Nature reassert herself that I even found some compensation in the loss of my chickens that bright November night when some wild creature, coon or fox, swept two of them out of the evergreens, and their squawking as they were hurried across the lawn called me from my bed to shout good-by after them. It gave a new interest to the hen-roost, this sudden incursion of wild nature. I feel bound to caution the boys about disturbing the wild rabbits that in summer breed in my currant-patch, and in autumn seek refuge under

my study floor.   The occasional glimpses I get
of them about the lawn in the dusk, their cotton
tails twinkling in the dimness, afford me a genuine pleasure.   I have seen the time when I
would go a good way to shoot a partridge, but
I would not have killed, if I could, the one
that started out of the vines that cover my rustic porch, as I approached that side of the
house one autumn morning.   How much of the
woods, and of the untamable spirit of wild
nature, she brought to my very door!   It was
tonic and exhilarating to see her whirl away
toward the vineyard.   I also owe a moment's
pleasure to the gray squirrel that, finding my
summer-house in the line of his travels one
summer day, ran through it and almost over my
feet as I sat idling with a book.

I am sure my power of digestion was im-
proved that cold winter morning when, just as
we were sitting down to breakfast about sunrise, a red fox loped along in front of the window, looking neither to the right nor to the
left, and disappeared amid the currant-bushes.
What of the wild and the cunning did he not
bring!   His graceful form and motion were in
my mind's eye all day.   When you have seen
a fox loping along in that way you have seen
the poetry there is in the canine tribe.   It is
to the eye what a flowing measure is to the
mind, so easy, so buoyant; the furry creature
drifting along like a large red thistledown, or
like a plume borne by the wind.   It is something to remember with pleasure, that a muskrat

sought my door one December night when a
cold wave was swooping down upon us. Was
he seeking shelter, or had he lost his reckoning? The dogs cornered him in the very doorway, and set up a great hubbub. In the darkness, thinking it was a cat, I put my hand
down to feel it. The creature skipped to the
other corner of the doorway, hitting my hand
with its cold, rope-like tail. Lighting a match,
I had a glimpse of him sitting up on his
haunches like a woodchuck, confronting his
enemies. I rushed in for the lantern, with the
hope of capturing him alive, but before I returned the dogs, growing bold, had finished
him.

I have had but one call from a coon, that I
am aware of, and I fear we did not treat him
with due hospitality. He took up his quarters
for the day in a Norway spruce, the branches
of which nearly brushed the house. I had
noticed that the dog was very curious about
that tree all the forenoon. After dinner his
curiosity culminated in repeated loud and confident barking. Then I began an investigation,
expecting to find a strange cat, or at most a red
squirrel. But a moment's scrutiny revealed
his coonship. Then how to capture him became the problem. A long pole was procured,
and I sought to dislodge him from his hold.
The skill with which he maintained himself
amid the branches excited our admiration.
But after a time he dropped lightly to the
ground, not in the least disconcerted, and at

once on his guard against both man and beast. The dog was a coward, and dared not face him. When the coon's attention was diverted the dog would rush in; then one of us would attempt to seize the coon's tail, but he faced about so quickly, his black eyes gleaming, that the hand was timid about seizing him. But finally in his skirmishing with the dog I caught him by the tail, and bore him safely to an open flour barrel, and he was our prisoner. Much amusement my little boy and I anticipated with him. He partook of food that same day, and on the second day would eat the chestnuts in our presence. Never did he show the slightest fear of us or of anything, but he was unwearied in his efforts to regain his freedom. After a few days we put a strap upon his neck and kept him tethered by a chain. But in the night, by dint of some hocus-pocus, he got the chain unsnapped and made off, and is now, I trust, a patriarch of his tribe, wearing a leather necktie.

The skunk visits every farm sooner or later. One night I came near shaking hands with one on my very door-stone. I thought it was the cat, and put down my hand to stroke it, when the creature, probably appreciating my mistake, moved off up the bank, revealing to me the white stripe on its body and the kind of cat I had saluted. The skunk is not easily ruffled, and seems to employ excellent judgment in the use of its terrible weapon.

Several times I have had calls from wood-

chucks. One looked in at the open door of my
study one day, and, after sniffing a while, and
not liking the smell of such clover as I was
compelled to nibble there, moved on to better
pastures. Another one invaded the kitchen
door while we were at dinner. The dogs
promptly challenged him, and there was a lively
scrimmage upon the door-stone. I thought the
dogs were fighting, and rushed to part them.
The incident broke in upon the drowsy summer
noon, as did the appearance of the muskrat upon
the frigid December night. The woodchuck
episode that afforded us the most amusement
occurred last summer. We were at work in a
newly-planted vineyard, when the man with
the cultivator saw, a few yards in front of him,
some large gray object that at first puzzled him.
He approached it, and found it to be an old
woodchuck with a young one in its mouth.
She was carrying her kitten as does a cat, by
the nape of the neck. Evidently she was moving her family to pastures new. As the man
was in the line of her march, she stopped and
considered what was to be done. He called to
me, and I approached slowly. As the mother
saw me closing in on her flank, she was suddenly seized with a panic, and, dropping her
young, fled precipitately for the cover of a large
pile of grape-posts some ten or twelve rods distant. We pursued hotly, and overhauled her
as she was within one jump of the house of
refuge. Taking her by the tail, I carried her
back to her baby; but she heeded it not. It

was only her own bacon now that she was solicitous about. The young one remained where
it had been dropped, keeping up a brave, reas-
suring whistle that was in ludicrous contrast to
its exposed and helpless condition. It was the
smallest woodchuck I had ever seen, not much
larger than a large rat. Its head and shoulders
were so large in proportion to the body as to
give it a comical look. It could not walk about
yet, and had never before been above ground.
Every moment or two it would whistle cheerily,
as the old one does when safe in its den and the
farm dog is fiercely baying outside. We took
the youngster home, and my little boy was delighted over the prospect of a tame woodchuck.
Not till the next day would it eat. Then, getting a taste of the milk, it clutched the spoon
that held it with great eagerness, and sucked
away like a little pig. We were all immensely
diverted by it. It ate eagerly, grew rapidly,
and was soon able to run about. As the old
one had been killed, we became curious as to
the fate of the rest of her family, for no doubt
there were more. Had she moved them, or
had we intercepted her on her first trip? We
knew where the old den was, but not the new.
So we would keep a lookout. Near the end of
the week, on passing by the old den, there were
three young ones creeping about a few feet from
its mouth. They were starved out, and had
come forth to see what could be found. We
captured them all, and the young family was
again united. How these poor, half-famished

creatures did lay hold of the spoon when they got a taste of the milk! One could not help laughing. Their little shining black paws were so handy and so smooth; they seemed as if incased in kid gloves. They throve well upon milk, and then upon milk and clover. But after the novelty of the thing had worn off, the boy found he had encumbered himself with serious duties in assuming the position of foster-mother to this large family; so he gave them all away but one, the first one captured, which had outstripped all the others in growth. This soon became a very amusing pet, but it always protested when handled, and always objected to confinement. I should mention that the cat had a kitten about the age of the chuck, and as she had more milk than the kitten could dispose of, the chuck, when we first got him, was often placed in the nest with the kitten, and was regarded by the cat as tenderly as her own, and allowed to nurse freely. Thus a friendship sprang up between the kitten and the woodchuck, which lasted as long as the latter lived. They would play together precisely like two kittens: clinch and tumble about and roll upon the grass in a very amusing way. Finally the woodchuck took up his abode under the floor of the kitchen, and gradually relapsed into a half-wild state. He would permit no familiarities from any one save the kitten, but each day they would have a turn or two at their old games of rough-and-tumble. The chuck was now over half grown, and procured his own living. One day the dog, who had all along looked upon him with a jealous eye, encountered him too far from cover, and his career ended then and there.

In July the woodchuck was forgotten in our interest in a little gray rabbit which we found nearly famished. It was so small that it could sit in the hollow of one's hand. Some accident had probably befallen its mother. The tiny creature looked spiritless and forlorn. We had to force the milk into its mouth. But in a day or two it began to revive, and would lap the milk eagerly. Soon it took to grass and clover, and then to nibbling sweet apples and early pears. It grew rapidly, and was one of the softest and most harmless-looking pets I had ever seen. For a month or more the little rabbit was the only company I had, and it helped to beguile the time immensely. In coming in from the field or from my work, I seldom failed to bring it a handful of red clover blossoms, of which it became very fond. One day it fell slyly to licking my hand, and I discovered it wanted salt. I would then moisten my fingers, dip them into the salt, and offer them to the rabbit. How rapidly the delicate little tongue would play upon them, darting out to the right and left of the large front incisors, the slender paws being pressed against my hand as if to detain it! But the rabbit proved really untamable; its wild nature could not be overcome. In its large box-cage or prison, where it could see nothing but the tree above it, it

was tame, and would at times frisk playfully
about my hand and strike it gently with its fore-
feet; but the moment it was liberated in a room
or let down in the grass with a string about its
neck, all its wild nature came forth. In the
room it would run and hide; in the open it
would make desperate efforts to escape, and leap
and bound as you drew in the string that held
it. At night, too, it never failed to try to
make its escape from the cage, and finally,
when two thirds grown, succeeded, and we saw
it no more.

III

How completely the life of a bird revolves
about its nest, its home! In the case of the
wood-thrush, its life and joy seem to mount
higher and higher as the nest prospers. The
male becomes a fountain of melody; his happiness waxes day by day; he makes little trium-
phal tours about the neighborhood, and pours
out his pride and gladness in the ears of all.
How sweet, how well-bred, is his demonstra-
tion! But let any accident befall that precious
nest, and what a sudden silence falls upon him!
Last summer a pair of wood-thrushes built
their nest within a few rods of my house, and
when the enterprise was fairly launched and the
mother bird was sitting upon her four blue eggs,
the male was in the height of his song. How
he poured forth his rich melody, never in the
immediate vicinity of the nest, but always

within easy hearing distance! Every morning,
as promptly as the morning came, between five
and six, he would sing for half an hour from
the top of a locust-tree that shaded my roof. I
came to expect him as much as I expected my
breakfast, and I was not disappointed till one
morning I seemed to miss something. What
was it? Oh, the thrush has not sung this
morning. Something is the matter; and recol-
lecting that yesterday I had seen a red squirrel
in the trees not far from the nest, I at once
inferred that the nest had been harried. Going to the spot, I found my fears were well
grounded; every egg was gone. The joy of
the thrush was laid low. No more songs from
the treetop, and no more songs from any point,
till nearly a week had elapsed, when I heard
him again under the hill, where the pair had
started a new nest, cautiously tuning up, and
apparently with his recent bitter experience
still weighing upon him.

After a pair of birds have been broken up
once or twice during the season, they become
almost desperate, and will make great efforts to
outwit their enemies. The past season my attention was attracted by a pair of brown thrashers. They first built their nest in a pasture-
field under a low, scrubby apple-tree which the
cattle had browsed down till it spread a thick,
wide mass of thorny twigs only a few inches
above the ground. Some blackberry briers had
also grown there, so that the screen was perfect.
My dog first started the bird, as I was passing

by. By stooping low and peering intently, I could make out the nest and eggs. Two or three times a week, as I passed by, I would pause to see how the nest was prospering. The mother bird would keep her place, her yellow eyes never blinking. One morning as I looked into her tent I found the nest empty. Some night-prowler, probably a skunk or fox, or maybe a black snake or red squirrel by day, had plundered it. It would seem as if it was too well screened: it was in such a spot as any depredator would be apt to explore. "Surely," he would say, "this is a likely place for a nest." The birds then moved over the hill a hundred rods or more, much nearer the house, and in some rather open bushes tried again. But again they came to grief. Then, after some delay, the mother bird made a bold stroke. She seemed to reason with herself thus: "Since I have fared so disastrously in seeking seclusion for my nest, I will now adopt the opposite tactics, and come out fairly in the open. What hides me hides my enemies: let us try greater publicity." So she came out and built her nest by a few small shoots that grew beside the path that divides the two vineyards, and where we passed to and fro many times daily. I discovered her by chance early in the morning as I proceeded to my work. She started up at my feet and flitted quickly along above the ploughed ground, almost as red as the soil. I admired her audacity. Surely no prowler by night or day would suspect a nest in this open and exposed place. There was no cover by which they could approach, and no concealment anywhere. The nest was a hasty affair, as if the birds' patience at nest-building had been about exhausted. Presently an egg appeared, and then the next day another, and on the fourth day a third. No doubt the bird would have succeeded this time had not man interfered. In cultivating the vineyards the horse and cultivator had to pass over this very spot. Upon this the bird had not calculated. I determined to assist her. I called my man, and told him there was one spot in that vineyard, no bigger than his hand, where the horse's foot must not be allowed to fall, nor tooth of cultivator to touch. Then I showed him the nest, and charged him to avoid it. Probably if I had kept the secret to myself and let the bird run her own risk, the nest would have escaped. But the result was that the man, in elaborately trying to avoid the nest, overdid the matter; the horse plunged, and set his foot squarely upon it. Such a little spot, the chances were few that the horse's foot would fall exactly there; and yet it did, and the birds' hopes were again dashed. The pair then disappeared from my vicinity, and I saw them no more.

The summer just gone I passed at a farmhouse on the skirts of the Northern Catskills. How could I help but see what no one else of all the people about seemed to notice, — a little bob-tailed song-sparrow building her nest in a pile of dry brush very near the kitchen door.

It was late in July, and she had doubtless
reared one brood in the earlier season.   Her
toilet was decidedly the worse for wear.   I
noted her day after day very busy about the
fence and quince bushes between the house and
milk house with her beak full of coarse straw
and hay.   To a casual observer she seemed flitting about aimlessly, carrying straws from place
to place just to amuse herself.   When I came
to watch her closely to learn the place of her
nest, she seemed to suspect my intention and
made many little feints and movements calculated to put me off the track.   But I would not
be misled, and presently had her secret.   The
male did not assist her at all, but sang much of
the time in an apple-tree or upon the fence, on
the other side of the house.   Those artists who
paint pictures of devoted male birds singing
from the branch that holds the nest, or in its
immediate vicinity, do not give the birds credit
for all the wit they possess.   They do not ad-
vertise the place where their treasures are hid
in this way.   See yonder indigo-bird shaking
out its happy song from the topmost twig of the
maple or oak; its nest is many yards away in
a low bush not more than three feet from the
ground.

And so with nearly all the birds.   The one
thing to which they bend all their wits is the
concealment of their nests.   When you come
upon the sitting bird, she will almost let you
touch her rather than to start up before you and
thus betray her secret.   The bobolink begins

to scold and to circle about you as soon as you
enter the meadow where his nest is so well hidden.   He does not wait to show his anxiety till
you are almost upon it.   By no action of his
can you get a clue as to its exact whereabouts.

The song-sparrow nearly always builds upon
the ground, but my little neighbor of last July
laid the foundations of her domicile a foot or
more above the soil.   And what a mass of
straws and twigs she did collect together!
How coarse and careless and aimless at first; a
mere lot of rubbish dropped upon the tangle of
dry limbs, but presently how it began to refine
and come into shape in the centre! till there
was the most exquisite hair-lined cup set about
by a chaos of coarse straws and branches.
What a process of evolution!   The completed
nest was foreshadowed by the first stiff straw,
but how far off is yet that dainty casket with
its complement of speckled eggs!   The nest was
so placed that it had for canopy a large broad,
drooping leaf of yellow dock.   This formed a
perfect shield against both sun and rain, while it
served to conceal it from any curious eyes from
above, — from the cat, for instance, prowling
along the top of the wall.   Before the eggs had
hatched the docken leaf wilted and dried and
fell down upon the nest.   But the mother bird
managed to insinuate herself beneath it, and
went on with her brooding all the same.

Then I arranged an artificial cover of leaves
and branches which shielded her charge till they
had flown away.   A mere trifle was this little

bob-tailed bird with her arts and her secrets, and the male with his song, and yet the pair gave a touch of something to those days and to that place which I would not willingly have missed.

I have spoken of nature as a stage whereon the play, more or less interrupted and indirect, constantly goes on. One amusing actor upon that stage one season, upon my own premises, was a certain male bluebird. To the spectator it was a comedy, but to the actor himself I imagine it was quite serious business. The bird and his mate had a nest in a box upon an outhouse. In this outhouse was a window with one pane broken out. At almost any hour in the day from spring to early summer, the male bird could be seen fluttering and pecking against this window from the outside. Did he want to get within? Apparently so, and yet he would now and then pause in his demonstrations, alight in the frame of the broken pane, look intently within, and after a moment resume his assault upon the window. The people who saw the actions of the bird were at a loss how to interpret them. But I could see at once what was the matter. The bird saw its image in the mirror of the glass (the dark interior helped the reflection) and was making war as he supposed upon a rival. Only the unyielding glass kept him from tweaking out every saucy blue feather upon the spot! Then he would peep in through the vacant pane and try to determine where his rival had so suddenly disappeared. How it must have puzzled his little poll! And he learned nothing from experience. Hundreds of times did he perch in the broken pane and sharply eye the interior. And for two months there did not seem to be an hour when he was not assaulting the window. He never lost faith in the reality of the bird within, and he never abated one jot his enmity toward him. If the glass had been a rough surface he would certainly have worn his beak and claws and wings to mere stubs. The incident shows the pugnacious disposition of the bluebird, and it shows how shallow a bird's wit is when new problems or conditions confront it. I have known a cock-robin to assault an imaginary rival in a garret window, in the same manner, and keep up the warfare for weeks.

On still another occasion similar antics of a male bluebird greatly disturbed the sleep of my hired man in the early morning. The bird with its mate had a nest in a box near by the house, and after the manner of the bluebirds was very inquisitive and saucy about windows; one morning it chanced to discover its reflected image in the windows of the hired man's room. The shade, of some dark stuff, was down on the inside, which aided in making a kind of looking-glass of the window. Instantly the bird began an assault upon his supposed rival in the window, and made such a clattering that there was no more sleep inside that room. Morning after morning the bird kept this up till the tired ploughman complained bitterly and

declared his intention to kill the bird. In an
unlucky moment I suggested that he leave the
shade up and try the effect. He did so, and
his morning sleep was thenceforth undisturbed.

A Western correspondent writes me that she
once put a looking-glass down on the floor in
front of the canary bird's cage The poor canary had not had any communion with his own
kind for years. "He used often to watch the
ugly sparrows — the little plebeians — from his
aristocratic gilded palace. I opened his cage
and he walked up to the looking-glass and it
was not long before he made up his mind. He
collected dead leaves, twigs, bits of paper, and
all sorts of stray bits, and began a nest right off.
Several days after in his lonely cage he would
take bits of straw and arrange them when they
were given him."

A LIFE OF FEAR

As I sat looking from my window the other morning upon a red squirrel gathering hickory nuts from a small hickory, and storing them up in his den in the bank, I was forcibly reminded of the state of constant fear and apprehension in which the wild creatures live, and I tried to picture to myself what life would be to me, or to any of us, hedged about by so many dangers, real or imaginary.

The squirrel would shoot up the tree, making only a brown streak from the bottom to the top; would seize his nut and rush down again in the most precipitate manner. Half way to his den, which was not over three rods distant, he would rush up the trunk of another tree for a few yards to make an observation. No danger being near, he would dive into his den and reappear again in a twinkling.

Returning for another nut, he would mount the second tree again for another observation. Satisfied that the coast was clear, he would spin along the top of the ground to the tree that bore the nuts, shoot up it as before, seize the fruit, and then back again to his retreat.

Never did he fail during the half hour or more that I watched him to take an observation on his way both to and from his nest. It was "snatch and run" with him. Something seemed to say to him all the time: "Look out! look out!" "The cat!" "The hawk!" "The owl!" "The boy with the gun!"

It was a bleak December morning; the first fine flakes of a cold, driving snowstorm were just beginning to sift down, and the squirrel was eager to finish harvesting his nuts in time. It was quite touching to see how hurried and anxious and nervous he was. I felt like going out and lending a hand. The nuts were small, poor pig-nuts, and I thought of all the gnawing he would have to do to get at the scanty meat they held. My little boy once took pity on a squirrel that lived in the wall near the gate and cracked the nuts for him and put them upon a small board shelf in the tree where he could sit and eat them at his ease.

The red squirrel is not so provident as the chipmunk. He lays up stores irregularly, by fits and starts; he never has enough put up to carry him over the winter; hence he is more or less active all the season. Long before the December snow the chipmunk has for days been making hourly trips to his den with full pockets of nuts or corn or buckwheat, till his bin holds enough to carry him through to April. He need not, and I believe does not, set foot out of doors during the whole winter. But the red squirrel trusts more to luck.

As alert and watchful as the red squirrel is, he is frequently caught by the cat. My Nig,

as black as ebony, knows well the taste of his
flesh. I have known him to be caught by the
black snake and successfully swallowed. The
snake, no doubt, lay in ambush for him.

This fear, this ever present source of danger
of the wild creatures, we know little about.
Probably the only person in the civilized coun-
tries who is no better off than the animals in
this respect is the Czar of Russia. He would
not even dare gather nuts as openly as my
squirrel. A blacker and more terrible cat than
Nig would be lying in wait for him and would
make a meal of him. The early settlers in
this country must have experienced something of
this dread of apprehension from the Indians.
Many African tribes now live in the same state
of constant fear of the slave-catchers or of other
hostile tribes. Our ancestors, back in pre-his-
toric times, or back of that in geologic times,
must have known fear as a constant feeling.
Hence the prominence of fear in infants and
children when compared with the youth or the
grown person. Babies are nearly always afraid
of strangers.

In the domestic animals also, fear is much
more active in the young than in the old.
Nearly every farm boy has seen a calf but a day
or two old, which its mother has secreted in the
woods or in a remote field, charge upon him fu-
riously with a wild bleat, when first discovered.
After this first ebullition of fear, it usually set-
tles down into the tame humdrum of its bovine
elders.

Eternal vigilance is the price of life with most of the wild creatures. There is only one among them whose wildness I cannot understand, and that is the common water turtle. Why is this creature so fearful? What are its enemies? I know of nothing that preys upon it. Yet see how watchful and suspicious these turtles are as they sun themselves upon a log or a rock. Before you are fairly in gunshot of them, they slide down into the water and are gone.

The land turtle, or terrapin, on the other hand, shows scarcely a trace of fear. He will indeed pause in his walk when you are very near him, but he will not retreat into his shell till you have poked him with your foot or your cane. He appears to have no enemies; but the little spotted water turtle is as shy as if he was the delicate tidbit that every creature was searching for. I did once find one which a fox had dug out of the mud in winter, and carried a few rods and dropped on the snow, as if he had found he had no use for it.

One can understand the fearlessness of the skunk. Nearly every creature but the farm dog yields to him the right of way. All dread his terrible weapon. If you meet one in your walk in the twilight fields, the chances are that you will turn out for him, not he for you. He may even pursue you, just for the fun of seeing you run. He comes waltzing toward you, apparently in the most hilarious spirits.

The coon is probably the most courageous

creature among our familiar wild animals. Who ever saw a coon show the white feather? He will face any odds with perfect composure. I have seen a coon upon the ground, beset by four men and two dogs, and never for a moment lose his presence of mind, or show a sign of fear. The raccoon is clear grit.

The fox is a very wild and suspicious crea- ture, but curiously enough, when you suddenly come face to face with him, when he is held by a trap, or driven by the hound, his expression is not that of fear, but of shame and guilt. He seems to diminish in size and to be over- whelmed with humiliation. Does he know himself to be an old thief, and is that the reason of his embarrassment? The fox has no enemies but man, and when he is fairly outwitted, he looks the shame he evidently feels.

In the heart of the rabbit fear constantly abides. How her eyes protrude! She can see back and front and on all sides as well as a bird. The fox is after her, the owls are after her, the gunners are after her, and she has no defense but her speed. She always keeps well to cover. The Northern hare keeps in the thickest brush. If the hare or rabbit crosses a broad open exposure it does so hurriedly, like a mouse when it crosses the road. The mouse is in danger of being pounced upon by a hawk, and the hare or rabbit by the snowy owl, or else the great horned owl.

A friend of mine was following one morning a fresh rabbit track through an open field.

Suddenly the track came to an end, as if the creature had taken wings — as it had after an unpleasant fashion. There, on either side of its last foot imprint, were several parallel lines in the snow, made by the wings of the great owl that had swooped down and carried it off. What a little tragedy was seen written there upon the white, even surface of the field!

The rabbit has not much wit. I once, when a boy, saw one that had been recently caught, liberated in an open field in the presence of a dog that was being held a few yards away. But the poor thing lost all presence of mind and was quickly caught by the clumsy dog.

A hunter once saw a hare running upon the ice along the shore of one of the Rangely lakes. Presently a lynx appeared in hot pursuit; as soon as the hare found it was being pursued, it began to circle, foolish thing. This gave the lynx greatly the advantage, as it could follow in a much smaller circle. Soon the hare was run down and seized.

I saw the same experiment tried with a red squirrel with quite opposite results. The boy who had caught the squirrel in his wire trap had a very bright and nimble dog about the size of a fox, that seemed to be very sure he could catch a red squirrel under any circumstances if only the trees were out of the way. So the boy went to the middle of an open field with his caged squirrel, the dog, who seemed to know what was up, dancing and jumping about him. It was in midwinter; the snow had a

firm crust that held boy and dog alike. The
dog was drawn back a few yards and the squirrel liberated. Then began one of the most exciting races I have witnessed for a long time.
It was impossible for the lookers-on not to be
convulsed with laughter, though neither dog
nor squirrel seemed to regard the matter as much
of a joke. The squirrel had all his wits about
him, and kept them ready for instant use. He
did not show the slightest confusion. He was
no match for the dog in fair running, and he
discovered this fact in less than three seconds;
he must win, if at all, by strategy. Not a
straight course for the nearest tree, but a zigzag
course; yea, a double or treble zigzag course.
Every instant the dog was sure the squirrel was
his and every instant he was disappointed. It
was incredible and bewildering to him. The
squirrel dodged this way and that. The dog
looked astonished and vexed.

Then the squirrel issued from between his
hind legs and made three jumps toward the
woods before he was discovered. Our sides
ached with laughter, cruel as it may seem.

It was evident the squirrel would win. The
dog seemed to redouble his efforts. He would
overshoot the game, or shoot by it to the right
or left. The squirrel was the smaller craft and
could out-tack him easily. One more leap and
the squirrel was up a tree, and the dog was
overwhelmed with confusion and disgust.

He could not believe his senses. "Not catch
a squirrel in such a field as that? Go to, I

will have him yet!" and he bounds up the tree
as high as one's head, and then bites the bark
of it in his anger and chagrin.

The boy says his dog has never bragged since
about catching red squirrels "if only the trees
were out of reach!"

When any of the winged creatures are engaged in a life and death race in that way, or
in any other race, the tactics of the squirrel do
not work; the pursuer never overshoots nor
shoots by his mark. The flight of the two is
timed as if they were parts of one whole. A
hawk will pursue a sparrow or a robin through
a zigzag course and not lose a stroke or half a
stroke of the wing by reason of any darting to
the right or left. The clew is held with fatal
precision. No matter how quickly nor how
often the sparrow or the finch changes its
course, its enemy changes, simultaneously, as if
every move was known to it from the first.

The same thing may be noticed among the
birds in their love chasings; the pursuer seems
to know perfectly the mind of the pursued.
This concert of action among birds is very curious. When they are in the alert a flock of
sparrows, or pigeons, or cedar-birds, or snow-
buntings, or blackbirds, will all take flight as if
there was but one bird, instead of a hundred.
The same impulse seizes every individual bird
at the same instant, as if they were sprung by
electricity.

Or when a flock of birds is in flight, it is
still one body, one will; it will rise, or circle,

or swoop, with a unity that is truly astonishing.

A flock of snow-buntings will perform their aerial evolutions with a precision that the best-trained soldiery cannot equal. Have the birds an extra sense which we have not? A brood of young partridges in the woods will start up like an explosion, every brown particle and fragment hurled into the air at the same instant. Without word or signal, how is it done?

I

WE love nature with a different love at different periods of our lives. In youth our love is sensuous. It is not so much a conscious love as it is an irresistible attraction. The senses are keen and fresh, and they crave a field for their exercise. We delight in the color of flowers, the perfume of meadows and orchards, the moist, fresh smell of the woods. We eat the pungent roots and barks, we devour the wild fruits, we slay the small deer. Then nature also offers a field of adventure; it challenges and excites our animal spirits. The woods are full of game, the waters of fish; the river invites the oar, the breeze, the sail, the mountain-top promises a wide prospect. Hence the rod, the gun, the boat, the tent, the pedestrian club. In youth we are nearer the savage state, the primitive condition of mankind and wild nature is our proper home. The transient color of the young bird points its remote ancestry, and the taste of youth for rude nature in like manner is the survival of an earlier race instinct.

Later in life we go to nature as an escape from the tension and turmoil of business, or for

rest and recreation from study, or seeking solace
from grief and disappointment, or as a refuge
from the frivolity and hypocrisies of society.
We lie under trees, we stroll through lanes, or
in meadows and pastures, or muse on the shore.
Nature "salves" our worst wounds; she heals
and restores us.

Or we cultivate an intellectual pleasure in
nature, and follow up some branch of natural
science, as botany, or ornithology, or mineralogy.

Then there is the countryman's love of nature, the pleasure in cattle, horses, bees, growing crops, manual labor, sugar-making, gardening, harvesting, and the rural quietness and
repose.

Lastly we go to nature for solitude and for
communion with our own souls. Nature at-
tunes us to a higher and finer mood. This
love springs from our religious needs and instincts. This was the love of Thoreau, of
Wordsworth, and has been the inspiration of
much modern poetry and art.

Dr. Johnson said he had lived in London so
long that he had ceased to note the changes of
the seasons. But Dr. Johnson was not a lover
of nature. Of that feeling for the country of
which Wordsworth's poetry, for instance, is so
full, he probably had not a vestige. Think of
Wordsworth shut up year in and year out — in
the city! That lover of shepherds, of mountains, of lonely tarns, of sounding waterfalls, —

" Who looked upon the hills with tenderness,
  And made dear friendships with the streams and groves."

Dr. Johnson's delight was in men and in
verbal fisticuffs with them, but Wordsworth
seems to have loved nature more than men; at
least he was drawn most to those men who
lived closest to nature and were more a part
of her. Thus he says he loved shepherds,
"dwellers in the valleys,"

> " Not verily
> For their own sakes, but for the fields and hills
> Where was their occupation and abode."

Your real lover of nature does not love the
merely beautiful things which he culls here and
there; he loves the earth itself, the faces of the
hills and mountains, the rocks, the streams, the
naked trees no less than the leafy trees, — a
ploughed field no less than a green meadow.
He does not know what it is that draws him.
It is not beauty, any more than it is beauty in
his father and mother that makes him love
them. It is "something far more deeply in-
terfused," — something native and kindred that
calls to him. In certain moods how good the
earth, the soil, seems! One wants to feel it
with his hands and smell it — almost taste it.
Indeed, I never see a horse eat soil and sods
without a feeling that I would like to taste it
too. The rind of the earth, of this "round and
delicious globe" which has hung so long upon
the great Newtonian tree, ripening in the sun,
must be sweet.

I recall an Irish girl lately come to this country, who worked for us, and who, when I dug
and brought to the kitchen the first early pota-

toes, felt them, and stroked them with her
hand, and smelled them, and was loath to lay
them down, they were so full of suggestion of
the dear land and home she had so lately left.
I suppose it was a happy surprise to her to find
that the earth had the same fresh, moist smell
here that it had in Ireland, and yielded the
same crisp tubers. The canny creature had
always worked in the fields, and the love of the
soil and of homely country things was deep in
her heart. Another emigrant from over the
seas, a laboring man, confined to the town, said
to me in his last illness, that he believed he
would get well if he could again walk in the
fields. A Frenchman who fled the city and
came to the country said, with an impressive
gesture, that he wanted to be where he could
see the blue sky over his head.

These little incidents are but glints or faint
gleams of that love of nature to which I would
point, — an affection for the country itself, and
not a mere passing admiration for its beauties.
A great many people admire nature; they write
admiring things about her; they apostrophize
her beauties; they describe minutely pretty
scenes here and there; they climb mountains to
see the sun set, or the sun rise, or make long
journeys to find waterfalls, but nature's real
lover listens to their enthusiasm with coolness
and indifference. Nature is not to be praised
or patronized. You cannot go to her and describe her; she must speak through your heart.
The woods and fields must melt into your mind,

dissolved by your love for them. Did they not melt into Wordsworth's mind? They colored all his thoughts; the solitude of those green, rocky Westmoreland fells broods over every page. He does not tell us how beautiful he finds nature and how much he enjoys her, he makes us share his enjoyment.

Richard Jefferies was probably as genuine a lover of nature as was Wordsworth, but he had not the same power to make us share his enjoyment. His page is sometimes wearisome from mere description and enumeration. He is rarely interpretative; the mood, the frame of mind, which nature herself begets, he seldom imparts to us. What we finally love in nature is ourselves, some suggestion of the human spirit, and no labored description, or careful enumeration of details will bring us to this.

> "Nor do words
> Which practiced talent readily affords,
> Prove that her hand has touched responsive chords."

It has been aptly said that Jefferies was a reporter of genius but that he never (in his nature books) got beyond reporting. His "Wild Life" reads like a kind of field newspaper; he puts in everything, he is diligent and untiring, but for much of it one cares very little after he is through. For selecting and combining the things of permanent interest so as to excite curiosity and impart charm, he has but little power.

The passion for nature is by no means a mere curiosity about her, or an itching to portray certain of her features; it lies deeper and is probably a form of, or closely related to, our religious instincts. When you go to nature, bring us good science or else good literature, and not a mere inventory of what you have seen. One demonstrates, the other interprets.

Observation is selective and detective. A real observation begets warmth and joy in the mind. To see things in detail as they lie about you and enumerate them is not observation; but to see the significant things, to seize the quick movement and gesture, to disentangle the threads of relation, to know the nerves that thrill from the cords that bind, or the typical and vital from the commonplace and mechanical — that is to be an observer. In Thoreau's "Walden" there is observation; in the Journals published since his death there is close and patient scrutiny, but only now and then anything that we care to know. Considering that Thoreau spent half of each day for upward of twenty years in the open air, bent upon spying out nature's ways and doings, it is remarkable that he made so few real observations.

Yet how closely he looked! He even saw that mysterious waving line which one may sometimes note in little running brooks. "I see stretched from side to side of this smooth brook where it is three or four feet wide what seems to indicate an invisible waving line, like a cobweb against which the water is heaped up a very little. This line is constantly swayed to and fro, as if by the current or wind, belly-

ing forward here and there. I try repeatedly
to catch and break it with my hand and let the
water run free, but still to my surprise I clutch
nothing but fluid, and the imaginary line keeps
its place."

A little closer scrutiny would have shown him
that this waving water line was probably caused
in some way by the meeting of two volumes or
currents of water.

The most novel and interesting observation I
can now recall is his discovery of how the wild
apple-tree in the pastures triumphs over the
browsing cattle, namely, by hedging itself about
by a dense thorny growth, keeping the cows at
arm's length as it were, and then sending up a
central shoot beyond their reach.

One of the most acute observations Thoreau's
Journals contain is not upon nature at all, but
upon the difference between men and women
"in respect to the adornment of their heads:"
"Do you ever see an old or jammed bonnet on
the head of a woman at a public meeting? But
look at any assembly of men with their hats
on; how large a proportion of the hats will be
old, weather-beaten, and indented; but, I think,
so much more picturesque and interesting.
One farmer rides by my door in a hat which it
does me good to see, there is so much character
in it, so much independence, to begin with, and
then affection for his old friends, etc., etc. I
should not wonder if there were lichens on it.
. . . Men wear their hats for use, women
theirs for ornament. I have seen the greatest

philosopher in the town with what the traders would call a 'shocking bad hat' on, but the woman whose bonnet does not come up to the mark is at best a blue-stocking."

So clever an observation upon anything in nature as that is hard to find in the Journals.

To observe is to discriminate and take note of all the factors.

One day while walking in my vineyard, lamenting the damage the storm of yesterday had wrought in it, my ear caught, amid the medley of other sounds and songs, an unfamiliar bird-note from the air overhead. Gradually it dawned upon my consciousness that this was not the call of any of our native birds, but of a stranger. Looking steadily in the direction the sound came, after some moments I made out the form of a bird flying round and round in a large circle high in air, and momentarily uttering its loud sharp call. The size, the shape, the manner, and the voice of the bird were all strange. In a moment I knew it to be an English skylark, apparently adrift and undecided which way to go. Finally it seemed to make up its mind, and then bore away to the north. My ear had been true to its charge.

The man who told me that some of our birds took an earth bath, and some of them a water bath, and a few of them took both, had looked closer into this matter than I had. The sparrows usually earth their plumage, but the English sparrow does both. The farm boy who told a naturalist a piece of news about the tur-

tles, namely, that the reason why we never see
any small turtles about the fields is because for
two or three years the young turtles bury themselves in the ground and keep quite hidden from
sight, had used his eyes to some purpose.
This was a real observation.

Just as a skilled physician, in diagnosing a
case, picks out the significant symptoms and
separates them from the rest, so the real observer, with eye and ear, seizes what is novel
and characteristic in the scenes about him.
His attention goes through the play at the surface and reaches the rarer incidents beneath or
beyond.

Richard Jefferies was not strictly an observer; he was a loving and sympathetic spectator
of the nature about him, a poet if you please,
but he tells us little that is memorable or suggestive.   His best books are such as the
"Gamekeeper at Home," and the "Amateur
Poacher," where the human element is brought
in, and the descriptions of nature are relieved
by racy bits of character drawing.   By far the
best thing of all is a paper which he wrote
shortly before his death, called "My Old Village."   It is very beautiful and pathetic, and
reveals the heart and soul of the man as nothing else he has written does.   I must permit
myself to transcribe one paragraph of it.   It
shows how he, too, was under the spell of the
past, and such a recent past, too: —

"I think I have heard that the oaks are
down.   They may be standing or down, it mat-

ters nothing to me; the leaves I last saw upon
them are gone for evermore, nor shall I ever
see them come there again, ruddy in spring.
I would not see them again, even if I could;
they could never look again, as they used to do.
There are too many memories there.   The hap-
piest days become the saddest afterward; let
us never go back, lest we too die.   There are
no such oaks anywhere else, none so tall and
straight, and with such massive heads, on which
the sun used to shine as if on the globe of the
earth, one side in shadow, the other in bright
light.   How often I have looked at oaks since,
and yet have never been able to get the same
effect from them!   Like an old author printed
in another type, the words are the same, but
the sentiment is different.   The brooks have
ceased to run.   There is no music now at the
old hatch where we used to sit, in danger of
our lives, happy as kings, on the narrow bar
over the deep water.   The barred pike that
used to come up in such numbers are no more
among the flags.   The perch used to drift down
the stream and then bring up again.   The sun
shone there for a very long time, and the water
rippled and sang, and it always seemed to me
that I could feel the rippling and the singing
and the sparkling back through the centuries.
The brook is dead, for where man goes, nature
ends.   I dare say there is water there still, but
it is not the brook; the brook is gone like John
Brown's soul [not our John Brown].   There
used to be clouds over the fields, white clouds

in blue summer skies. I have lived a good deal on clouds; they have been meat to me often; they bring something to the spirit which even the trees do not. I see clouds now sometimes when the iron gripe of hell permits for a minute or two; they are very different clouds and speak differently. I long for some of the old clouds that had no memories. There were nights in those times over those fields, not darkness, but Night, full of glowing suns and glowing richness of life that sprang up to meet them. The nights are there still; they are everywhere, nothing local in the night; but it is not the Night to me seen through the window."

In the literature of nature I know of no page so pathetic and human.

Moralizing about nature or through nature is tedious enough, and yet unless the piece has some moral or emotional background it does not touch us. In other words, to describe a thing for the mere sake of describing it, to make a dead set at it like a reporter, whatever may be the case in painting, it will not do in literature. The object must be informed with meaning, and to do this the creative touch of the imagination is required. Take this passage from Whitman on the night, and see if there is not more than mere description there: —

" A large part of the sky seemed just laid in great splashes of phosphorus. You could look deeper in, farther through, than usual ; the orbs thick as heads of wheat in a field. Not that

there was any special brilliancy either — nothing near as sharp as I have seen of keen winter nights, but a curious general luminousness
throughout to sight, sense, and soul.   The latter
had much to do with it. . . . Now, indeed,
if never before, the heavens declared the glory
of God.   It was to the full the sky of the Bible,
oi Arabia, of the prophets, and of the oldest
poems."

Or this touch of a January night on the Delaware River: —

"Overhead, the splendor indescribable; yet
something haughty, almost supercilious, in the
night; never did I realize more latent sentiment, almost *passion*, in the silent intermin-
able stars up there.   One can understand on such
a night why, from the days of the Pharaohs or
Job, the dome of heaven, sprinkled with planets,
has supplied the subtlest, deepest criticism on
human pride, glory, ambition."

Matthew Arnold quotes this passage from
Obermann as showing a rare feeling for nature: —

"My path lay beside the green waters of the
Thiele.   Feeling inclined to muse, and finding
the night so warm that there was no hardship
in being all night out of doors, I took the road
to Saint Blaise.   I descended a steep bank,
and got upon the shore of the lake where its
ripple came up and expired.   The air was
calm; every one was at rest; I remained there
for hours.   Toward morning the moon shed
over the earth and waters the ineffable melan-

choly of her last gleams. Nature seems un-
speakably grand, when, plunged in a long rev-
erie, one hears the rippling of the waters upon
a solitary strand, in the calm of a night still
enkindled and luminous with the setting moon.

"Sensibility beyond utterance, charm and
torment of our vain years; vast consciousness
of a nature everywhere greater than we are, and
everywhere impenetrable; all-embracing passion, ripened wisdom, delicious self-abandon-
ment — everything that a mortal heart can contain of life-weariness and yearning, I felt it all.
I experienced it all, in this memorable night.
I have made a grave step toward the age of de-
cline.   I have swallowed up ten years of life at
once.   Happy the simple whose heart is always
young!"

The moral element is behind this also, and
is the source of its value and charm.   In literature never nature for her own sake, but for the
sake of the soul which is over and above all.

II

One of the most desirable things in life is a
fresh impression of an old fact or scene.   One's
love of nature may be a constant factor, yet it
is only now and then that he gets a fresh impression of the charm and meaning of nature;
only now and then that the objects without and
the mood within so fit together that we have a
vivid and original sense of the beauty and significance that surround us.   How often do we

really see the stars? Probably a great many people never see them at all — that is, never look upon them with any thrill of emotion. If I see them a few times a year, I think myself in luck. If I deliberately go out to see them, I am quite sure to miss them; but occasionally, as one glances up to them in his lonely night walk, the mind opens, or the heaven opens — which is it? — and he has a momentary glimpse of their ineffable splendor and significance. How overwhelming, how awe-inspiring! His thought goes like a lightning flash into that serene abyss, and then the veil is drawn again. One's science, one's understanding, tells him he is a voyager on the celestial deep, that the earth beneath his feet is a star among stars, that we can never be any more in the heavens than we are now, or any more within reach of the celestial laws and forces; but how rare the mood in which we can realize this astounding fact, in which we can get a fresh and vivid impression of it! To have it ever present with one in all its naked grandeur would perhaps be more than we could bear.

The common and the familiar — how soon they cease to impress us! The great service of genius, speaking through art and literature, is to pierce through our callousness and indifference and give us fresh impressions of things as they really are; to present things in new combinations, or from new points of view, so that they shall surprise and delight us like a new revelation. When poetry does this, or when art does

it, or when science does it, it recreates the
world for us, and for the moment we are again
Adam in paradise.

Herein lies one compensation to the lover of
nature who is an enforced dweller in the town:
the indifference which familiarity breeds is not
his. His weekly or monthly sallies into the
country yield him a rare delight. To his fresh,
eager senses the charm of novelty is over all.
Country people look with a kind of pitying
amusement upon the delight of their newly arrived city friends; but would we not, after all,
give something if we could exchange eyes with
them for a little while?

We who write about nature pick out, I suspect, only the rare moments when we have had
glimpses of her, and make much of them. Our
lives are dull, and our minds crusted over with
rubbish like those of other people. Then
writing about nature, as about most other sub-
jects, is an expansive process; we are under the
law of evolution; we grow the germ into the
tree; a little original observation goes a good
ways. Life is a compendium. The record in
our minds and hearts is in shorthand. When
we come to write it out, we are surprised at its
length and significance. What we feel in a
twinkling it takes a long time to tell to another.

When I pass along by a meadow in June,
where the bobolinks are singing and the daisies
dancing in the wind, and the scent of the clover
is in the air, and where the boys and girls are
looking for wild strawberries in the grass, I

take it all in in a glance, it enters swiftly
through all my senses; but if I set about writing an account of my experience for my reader,
how long and tedious the process, how I must
beat about the bush! And then, if I would
have him see and feel it, I must avoid a point-
blank description and bring it to him, or him
to it, by a kind of indirection, so as to surprise
him and give him more than I at first seemed
to promise.

To a countryman like myself the presence of
natural objects, the open face of the country,
sheds a cheering and soothing influence at all
times; but it is only at rare intervals that he
experiences the thrill of a fresh impression. I
find that a kind of preoccupation, as the farmer
with his work, the angler with his rod, the
sportsman with his gun, the walker with his
friend, the lounger with his book, affords conditions that are not to be neglected. So much
will steal in at the corners of your eyes; the
unpremeditated glance, when the mind is passive
and receptive, often stirs the soul. Upon
whom does the brook make such an impression
as upon the angler? How he comes to know
its character! how he studies its every phase!
how he feels it through that rod and line as if
they were a part of himself! I pity the person who does not get at least one or two fresh
impressions of the charm and sweetness of nature in the spring. Later in the season it gets
to be more of an old story; but in March when
the season is early, and in April when the sea-

son is late, there occasionally come days which awaken a new joy in the heart. Every recurring spring one experiences this fresh delight. There is nothing very tangible yet in awakening nature, but there is something in the air, some sentiment in the sunshine and in the look of things, a prophecy of life and renewal, that sends a thrill through the frame. The first sparrow's song, the first robin's call, the first bluebird's warble, the first phœbe's note — who can hear it without emotion? Or the first flock of migrating geese or ducks — how much they bring north with them! When the red-shouldered starlings begin to gurgle in the elms or golden willows along the marshes and watercourses, you will feel spring then; and if you look closely upon the ground beneath them, you will find that sturdy advanced guard of our floral army, the skunk cabbage, thrusting his spear-point up through the ooze, and spring will again quicken your pulse.

One seems to get nearer to nature in the early spring days: all screens are removed, the earth everywhere speaks directly to you; she is not hidden by verdure and foliage; there is a peculiar delight in walking over the brown turf of the fields that one cannot feel later on. How welcome the smell of it, warmed by the sun; the first breath of the reviving earth. How welcome the full, sparkling watercourses too, everywhere drawing the eye; by and by they will be veiled by the verdure and shrunken by the heat. When March is kind, for how much

her slightest favors count!   The other evening,
as I stood on the slope of a hill in the twilight,
I heard a whistling of approaching wings, and
presently a woodcock flying low passed near
me.   I could see his form and his long curved
wings dimly against the horizon; his whistling
slowly vanished in the gathering night, but his
passage made something stir and respond within
me.   March was on the wing, she was abroad
in the soft still twilight searching out the
moist, springy places where the worms first
come to the surface and where the grass first
starts; and her course was up the valley from
the south.   A day or two later I sat on a hill-
side in the woods late in the day, amid the
pines and hemlocks, and heard the soft, elusive
spring call of the little owl — a curious musical
undertone hardly separable from the silence; a
bell, muffled in feathers, tolling in the twilight
of the woods and discernible only to the most
alert ear.   But it was the voice of spring, the
voice of the same impulse that sent the woodcock winging his way through the dusk, that
was just beginning to make the pussy willows
swell and the grass to freshen in the spring
runs.

Occasionally, of a bright, warm, still day in
March, such as we have had the present season,
the little flying spider is abroad.   It is the
most delicate of all March tokens, but very
suggestive.   Its long, waving threads of gossamer, invisible except when the sunlight falls
upon them at a particular angle, stream out here

and there upon the air, a filament of life, reaching and reaching as if to catch and detain the most subtle of the skyey influences.

Nature is always new in the spring, and lucky are we if it finds us new also.

A TASTE OF KENTUCKY BLUE-GRASS

How beautiful is fertility! A landscape of fruitful and well-cultivated fields; an unbroken expanse of grass; a thick, uniform growth of grain — how each of these fills and satisfies the eye! And it is not because we are essentially utilitarian and see the rich loaf and the fat beef as the outcome of it all, but because we read in it an expression of the beneficence and good-will of the earth. We love to see harmony between man and nature; we love peace and not war; we love the adequate, the complete. A perfect issue of grass or grain is a satisfaction to look upon, because it is a success. These things have the beauty of an end exactly fulfilled, the beauty of perfect fitness and proportion. The barren in nature is ugly and repels us, unless it be on such a scale and convey such a suggestion of power as to awaken the emotion of the sublime. What can be less inviting than a neglected and exhausted Virginia farm, the thin red soil showing here and there through the ragged and scanty turf? and what, on the other hand, can please the eye of a countryman more than the unbroken verdancy and fertility of a Kentucky blue-grass farm? I find I am very apt to take a farmer's view of a

country. That long line of toiling and thrifty
yoemen back of me seems to have bequeathed
something to my blood that makes me respond
very quickly to a fertile and well-kept landscape, and that, on the other hand, makes me
equally discontented in a poor, shabby one.
All the way from Washington till I struck the
heart of Kentucky, the farmer in me was un-
happy; he saw hardly a rood of land that he
would like to call his own. But that remnant
of the wild man of the woods, which most of
us still carry, saw much that delighted him,
especially down the New River, where the
rocks and the waters, and the steep forest-clad
mountains were as wild and as savage as anything he had known in his early Darwinian
ages. But when we emerged upon the banks
of the Great Kanawha, the man of the woods
lost his interest and the man of the fields saw
little that was comforting.

When we cross the line into Kentucky, I
said, we shall see a change. But no, we did
not. The farmer still groaned in spirit; no
thrifty farms, no substantial homes, no neat
villages, no good roads anywhere, but squalor
and sterility on every hand. Nearly all the
afternoon we rode through a country like the
poorer parts of New England, unredeemed by
anything like New England thrift. It was a
country of coal, a very new country, geologi-
cally speaking, and the top-soil did not seem to
have had time to become deepened and enriched
by vegetable mould. Near sundown, as I

glanced out of the window, I thought I began to
see a change. Presently I was very sure I did.
It began to appear in the more grassy character
of the woods. Then I caught sight of peculiarly soft and uniform grassy patches here and
there in the open. Then in a few moments
more the train had shot us fairly into the edge
of the blue-grass region, and the farmer in me
began to be on the alert. We had passed in a
twinkling from a portion of the earth's surface
which is new, which is of yesterday, to a portion which is of the oldest, from the carboni-
ferous to the lower silurian. Here, upon this
lower silurian, the earth that saw and nourished
the great monsters and dragons was growing
the delicate blue-grass. It had taken all these
millions upon millions of years to prepare the
way for this little plant to grow to perfection.
I thought I had never seen fields and low hills
look so soft in the twilight; they seemed clad
in greenish-gray fur. As we neared Mount
Sterling, how fat and smooth the land looked;
what long, even, gently flowing lines against
the fading western sky, broken here and there
by herds of slowly grazing or else reposing and
ruminating cattle! What peace and plenty it
suggested! From a land raw and crude and
bitter like unripe fruit, we had suddenly been
transported into the midst of one ripe and mellow with the fullness of time. It was sweet
to look upon. I was seized with a strong desire to go forth and taste it by a stroll through
it in the twilight.

In the course of the ten days that followed, the last ten days of May, I had an opportunity to taste it pretty well, and my mind has had a grassy flavor ever since. I had an opportunity to see this restless and fitful American nature of ours in a more equable and beneficent mood than I had ever before seen it in; all its savageness and acridness gone, no thought now but submission to the hand and wants of man. I afterward saw the prairies of Illinois, and the vast level stretches of farming country of northern Ohio and Indiana, but these lands were nowhere quite so human, quite so beautiful, or quite so productive as the blue-grass region. One likes to see the earth's surface lifted up and undulating a little, as if it heaved and swelled with emotion; it suggests more life, and at the same time that the sense of repose is greater. There is no repose in a prairie; it is stagnation, it is a *dead* level. Those immense stretches of flat land pain the eye, as if all life and expression had gone from the face of the earth. There is just unevenness enough in the blue-grass region to give mobility and variety to the landscape. From almost any given point one commands broad and extensive views — immense fields of wheat or barley, or corn or hemp, or grass or clover, or of woodland pastures.

With Professor Proctor I drove a hundred miles or more about the country in a buggy. First from Frankfort to Versailles, the capital of Woodford County; then to Lexington, where we passed a couple of days with Major McDowell at Ashland, the old Henry Clay place; then to Georgetown in Scott County; thence back to Frankfort again. The following week I passed three days on the great stock farm of Colonel Alexander, where I saw more and finer blooded stock in the way of horses, cattle, and sheep than I had ever seen before. From thence we went south to Colonel Shelby's, where we passed a couple of days on the extreme edge of the blue-grass circle in Boyle County. Here we strike the rim of sharp low hills that run quite around this garden of the State, from the Ohio River on the west to the Ohio again on the north and east. Kentucky is a great country for licks; there are any number of streams and springs that bear the name of some lick. Probably the soil of no State in the Union has been so much licked and smacked over as that of Kentucky. Colonel Shelby's farm is near a stream called Knob Lick, and within a few miles of a place called Blue Lick. I expected to see some sort of salt spring where the buffalo and deer used to come to lick; but instead of that saw a raw, naked spot of earth, an acre or two in extent, which had apparently been licked into the shape of a clay model of some scene in Colorado or the Rocky Mountains. There were gullies and chasms and sharp knobs and peaks as blue and barren as could be, and no sign of a spring or of water visible. The buffalo had licked the clay for the saline matter it held, and had certainly made a deep and lasting impression.

From Shelby City we went west sixty or more miles, skirting the blue-grass region, to Lebanon Junction, where I took the train for Cave City. The blue-grass region is as large as the State of Massachusetts, and is, on the whole, the finest bit of the earth's surface, with the exception of parts of England, I have yet seen. In one way it is more pleasing than anything one sees in England, on account of the greater sense of freedom and roominess which it gives one. Everything is on a large, generous scale. The fields are not so cut up, nor the roadways so narrow, nor the fences so prohibitory. Indeed, the distinguishing feature of this country is its breadth: one sees fields of corn or wheat or clover of from fifty to one hundred acres each. At Colonel Alexander's I saw three fields of clover lying side by side which contained three hundred acres : as the clover was just in full bloom, the sight was a very pleasing one. The farms are larger, ranging from several hundred to several thousand acres. The farmhouses are larger, with wide doors, broad halls, high ceilings, ample grounds, and hospitality to match. There is nothing niggardly or small in the people or in their country. One sees none of the New York or New England primness and trimness, but the ample, flowing Southern way of life. It is common to see horses and cattle grazing in the grounds immediately about the house; there is nothing but grass, and the great forest trees, which they cannot hurt. The farmhouses rarely stand near the highway, but are set after the English fashion, from a third to half a mile distant, amid a grove of primitive forest trees, and flanked or backed up by the many lesser buildings that the times of slavery made necessary. Educated gentlemen farmers are probably the rule more than in the North. There are not so many small or so many leased farms. The proprietors are men of means, and come the nearest to forming a landed gentry of any class of men we have in this country. They are not city men running a brief and rapid career on a fancy farm, but genuine countrymen, who love the land and mean to keep it. I remember with pleasure one rosy-faced young farmer, whose place we casually invaded in Lincoln County. He was a graduate of Harvard University and of the law school, but here he was with his trousers tucked into his boot-legs, helping to cultivate his corn, or looking after his herds upon his broad acres. He was nearly the ideal of a simple, hearty, educated country farmer and gentleman.

But the feature of this part of Kentucky which struck me the most forcibly, and which is perhaps the most unique, are the immense sylvan or woodland pastures. The forests are simply vast grassy orchards of maple and oak, or other trees, where the herds graze and repose. They everywhere give a look to the land as of royal parks and commons. They are as clean as a meadow and as inviting as long, grassy vistas and circles of cool shade can make them.

All the saplings and bushy undergrowths common to forests have been removed, leaving only the large trees scattered here and there, which seem to protect rather than occupy the ground Such a look of leisure, of freedom, of amplitude, as these forest groves give to the landscape!

What vistas, what aisles, what retreats, what depths of sunshine and shadow! The grass is as uniform as a carpet, and grows quite up to the boles of the trees. One peculiarity of the blue-grass is that it takes complete possession of the soil; it suffers no rival; it is as uniform as a fall of snow. Only one weed seems to hold its own against it, and that is ironweed, a plant like a robust purple aster five or six feet high. This is Kentucky's one weed, so far as I saw. It was low and inconspicuous while I was there, but before fall it gets tall and rank, and its masses of purple flowers make a very striking spectacle. Through these forest glades roam the herds of cattle or horses. I know no prettier sight than a troop of blooded mares with their colts slowly grazing through these stately aisles, some of them in sunshine, and some in shadow. In riding along the highway there was hardly an hour when such a scene was not in view. Very often the great farmhouse stands amid one of these open forests and is approached by a graveled road that winds amid the trees. At Colonel Alexander's the cottage of his foreman, as well as many of the farm buildings and stables, stands in a grassy

forest, and the mares with their colts roam far
and wide. Sometimes when they were going
for water, or were being started in for the night,
they would come charging along like the wind,
and what a pleasing sight it was to see their
glossy coats glancing adown the long sun-flecked
vistas! Sometimes the more open of these
forest lands are tilled; I saw fine crops of hemp
growing on them, and in one or two cases corn.
But where the land has never been under cul·
tivation it is remarkably smooth — one can drive
with a buggy with perfect ease and freedom
anywhere through these woods. The ground is
as smooth as if it had been rolled. In Kentucky we are beyond the southern limit of the
glacial drift; there are no surface boulders and
no abrupt knolls or gravel banks. Another
feature which shows how gentle and uniform
the forces which have moulded this land have
been are the beautiful depressions which go by
the ugly name of "sink-holes." They are
broad turf-lined bowls sunk in the surface here
and there, and as smooth and symmetrical as if
they had been turned out by a lathe. Those
about the woodlands of Colonel Alexander were
from one to two hundred feet across and fifteen
or twenty feet deep. The green turf sweeps
down into them without a break, and the great
trees grow from their sides and bottoms the
same as elsewhere. They look as if they might
have been carved out by the action of whirling
water, but are probably the result of the surface
water seeking a hidden channel in the under·

lying rock, and thus slowly carrying away the
soil with it. They all still have underground
drainage through the bottom. By reason of
these depressions this part of the State has been
called "goose-nest land," their shape suggesting the nests of immense geese. On my way
southward to the Mammoth Cave, over the
formation known as the subcarboniferous, they
formed the most noticeable feature of the landscape. An immense flock of geese had nested
here, so that in places the rims of their nests
touched one another. As you near the great
cave you see a mammoth depression, nothing
less than a broad, oval valley which holds entire
farms, and which has no outlet save through
the bottom. In England these depressions
would be called punch-bowls; and though they
know well in Kentucky what punch is made
of, and can furnish the main ingredient of superb quality, and in quantity that would quite
fill some of these grassy basins, yet I do not
know that they apply this term to them. But
in the good old times before the war, when the
spirit of politics ran much higher than now,
these punch-bowls and the forests about them
were the frequent scenes of happy and convi-
vial gatherings. Under the great trees the
political orators held forth; a whole ox would
be roasted to feed the hungry crowd, and something stronger than punch flowed freely. One
farmer showed us in our walk where Crittenden
and Breckinridge had frequently held forth, but
the grass had long been growing over the ashes
where the ox had been roasted.

What a land for picnics and open-air meetings! The look of it suggested something more large and leisurely than the stress and hurry of our American life. What was there about it that made me think of Walter Scott and the age of romance and chivalry? and of Robin Hood and his adventurous band under the greenwood tree? Probably it was those stately, open forests, with their clear, grassy vistas where a tournament might be held, and those superb breeds of horses wandering through them upon which it was so easy to fancy knights and ladies riding. The land has not the mellow, time-enriched look of England; it could not have it under our harder, fiercer climate; but it has a sense of breadth and a roominess which one never sees in England except in the great royal parks.

The fences are mainly posts and rails, which fall a little short of giving the look of permanence which a hedge or a wall and dike afford.

The Kentuckians have an unhandsome way of treating their forests when they want to get rid of them; they girdle the trees and let them die, instead of cutting them down at once. A girdled tree dies hard; the struggle is painful to look upon; inch by inch, leaf by leaf, it yields, and the agony is protracted nearly through the whole season. The land looked accursed when its noble trees were all dying or had died, as if smitten by a plague. One hardly expected to see grass or grain growing upon it. The girdled trees stand for years,

their gaunt skeletons blistering in the sun or
blackening in the rain. Through southern Indiana and Illinois I noticed this same lazy,
ugly custom of getting rid of the trees.

The most noticeable want of the blue-grass
region is water. The streams bore underground through the limestone rock so readily
that they rarely come to the surface. With
plenty of sparkling streams and rivers like New
England, it would indeed be a land of infinite
attractions. The most unsightly feature the
country afforded was the numerous shallow
basins, scooped out of the soil and filled with
stagnant water, where the flocks and herds
drank. These, with the girdled trees, were
about the only things the landscape presented
to which the eye did not turn with pleasure. Yet when one does chance upon a spring,
it is apt to be a strikingly beautiful one.
The limestone rock, draped with dark, dripping
moss, opens a cavernous mouth from which in
most instances a considerable stream flows. I
saw three or four such springs, about which one
wanted to linger long. The largest was at
Georgetown, where a stream ten or twelve feet
broad and three or four feet deep came gliding
from a cavernous cliff without a ripple. It is
situated in the very edge of the town, and could
easily be made a feature singularly attractive.
As we approached its head, a little colored girl
rose up from its brink with a pail of water. I
asked her name. "Venus, sir; Venus." It
was the nearest I had ever come to seeing
Venus rising from the foam.

There are three hard things in Kentucky, only one of which is to my taste; namely, hard bread, hard beds, and hard roads. The roads are excellent, macadamized as in England, and nearly as well kept; but that "beat-biscuit," a sort of domestic hardtack, in the making of which the flour or dough is beaten long and hard with the rolling-pin, is, in my opinion, a poor substitute for Yankee bread; and those mercilessly hard beds — the macadamizing principle is out of place there too. It would not be exact to call Kentucky butter bad; but with all their fine grass and fancy stock, they do not succeed well in this article of domestic manufacture. But Kentucky whiskey is soft, seductively so, and I caution all travelers to beware how they suck any iced preparation of it through a straw of a hot day; it is not half so innocent as it tastes.

The blue-grass region has sent out, and continues to send out, the most famous trotting horses in the world. Within a small circle not half a dozen miles across were produced all the more celebrated horses of the past ten years; but it has as yet done nothing of equal excellence in the way of men. I could but ask myself why this ripe and mellow geology, this stately and bountiful landscape, these large and substantial homesteads, have not yet produced a crop of men to match. Cold and sterile Massachusetts is far in the lead in this respect. Granite seems a better nurse of genius than the lime-rock. The one great man born in Kentucky, Abraham Lincoln, was not a product of this fertile region. Henry Clay was a Virginian. The two most eminent native blue-grass men were John C. Breckinridge and John J. Crittenden. It seems that it takes something more than a fertile soil to produce great men; a deep and rich human soil is much more important. Kentucky has been too far to one side of the main current of our national life; she has felt the influence of New England but very little; neither has she been aroused by the stir and enterprise of the great West. Her schoolhouses are too far apart, even in this rich section, and she values a fast trotter or racer more than she does a fine scholar.

What gives the great fertility to the blue-grass region is the old limestone rock, laid down in the ancient silurian seas, which comes to the surface over all this part of the State and makes the soil by its disintegration. The earth surface seems once to have bulged up here like a great bubble, and then have been planed or ground off by the elements. This wearing away process removed all the more recent formations, the coal beds and the conglomerate or other rocks beneath them, and left this ancient limestone exposed. Its continued decay keeps up the fertility of the soil. Wheat and corn and clover are rotated for fifty years upon the same fields without manure, and without any falling off in their productiveness. Where the soil is removed, the rock presents that rough, honeycombed appearance which surfaces do that have been worm-eaten instead of worn. The tooth which has gnawed, and is still gnawing it, is the carbonic acid carried into the earth by rain-water. Hence, unlike the prairies of the West, the fertility of this soil perpetually renews itself. The blue-grass seems native to this region; any field left to itself will presently be covered with blue-grass. It is not cut for hay, but is for grazing alone. Fields which have been protected during the fall yield good pasturage even in winter. And a Kentucky winter is no light affair, the mercury often falling fifteen or twenty degrees below zero.

I saw but one new bird in Kentucky, namely, the lark-finch, and but one pair of those. This is a Western bird of the sparrow kind which is slowly making its way eastward, having been found as far east as Long Island. I was daily on the lookout for it, but saw none till I was about leaving this part of the State. Near old Governor Shelby's place in Boyle County, as we were driving along the road, my eye caught a grayish-brown bird like the skylark, but with a much more broad and beautifully marked tail. It suggested both a lark and a sparrow, and I knew at once it was the lark-finch I had been looking for. It alighted on some low object in a ploughed field, and with a glass I had a good view of it — a very elegant, distinguished-appearing bird for one clad in the sparrow suit, the tail large and dark, with white markings on the outer web of the quills. Much as I wanted to hear his voice, he would not sing, and it was

not till I reached Adams County, Illinois, that
I saw another one and heard the song. Driving
about the country here — which, by the way,
reminded me more of the blue-grass region than
anything I saw outside of Kentucky — with a
friend, I was again on the lookout for the new
bird, but had begun to think it was not a resident, when I espied one on the fence by the
roadside. It failed to sing, but farther on we
saw another one which alighted upon a fruit
tree near us. We paused to look and to listen,
when instantly it struck up and gave us a good
sample of its musical ability. It was both a
lark and a sparrow song; or, rather, the notes
of a sparrow uttered in the continuous and rapid
manner of the skylark — a pleasing performance, but not meriting the praise I had heard
bestowed upon it.

In Kentucky and Illinois, and probably
throughout the West and Southwest, certain
birds come to the front and are conspicuous
which we see much less of in the East. The
blue jay seems to be a garden and orchard bird,
and to build about dwellings as familiarly as
the robin does with us. There must be dozens
of these birds in this part of the country where
there is but one in New England. And the
brown thrashers — in Illinois they were as common along the highways as song sparrows or
chippies are with us, and nearly as familiar.
So also were the turtle-doves and meadow-larks.
That the Western birds should be more tame
and familiar than the same species in the East

is curious enough. From the semi-domestica-
tion of so many of the English birds, when
compared with our own, we infer that the older
the country, the more the birds are changed in
this respect; yet the birds of the Mississippi
Valley are less afraid of man than those of the
valley of the Hudson or the Connecticut. Is it
because the homestead, with its trees and buildings, affords the birds on the great treeless prairies their first and almost only covert? Where
could the perchers perch till trees and fences
and buildings offered? For this reason they
would at once seek the vicinity of man and become familiar with him.

In Kentucky the summer redbird everywhere
attracted my attention. Its song is much like
that of its relative the tanager, and its general
habits and manners are nearly the same.

The oriole is as common in Kentucky as in
New York or New England. One day we saw
one weave into her nest unusual material.
As we sat upon the lawn in front of the cottage, we had noticed the bird just beginning
her structure, suspending it from a long, low
branch of the Kentucky coffee-tree that grew
but a few feet away. I suggested to my host
that if he would take some brilliant yarn and
scatter it about upon the shrubbery, the fence,
and the walks, the bird would probably avail
herself of it, and weave a novel nest. I had
heard of it being done, but had never tried it
myself. The suggestion was at once acted upon
and in a few moments a handful of zephyr yarn,

crimson, orange, green, yellow, and blue, was
distributed about the grounds. As we sat at
dinner a few moments later I saw the eager bird
flying up toward her nest with one of these
brilliant yarns streaming behind her. They
had caught her eye at once, and she fell to
work upon them with a will; not a bit daunted
by their brilliant color, she soon had a crimson spot there amid the green leaves. She afforded us rare amusement all the afternoon
and the next morning. How she seemed to
congratulate herself over her rare find! How
vigorously she knotted those strings to her
branch and gathered the ends in and sewed
them through and through the structure, jerking them spitefully like a housewife burdened
with many cares! How savagely she would fly
at her neighbor, an oriole that had a nest just
over the fence a few yards away, when she invaded her territory! The male looked on approvingly, but did not offer to lend a hand.
There is something in the manner of the female
on such occasions, something so decisive and
emphatic, that one entirely approves of the
course of the male in not meddling or offering
any suggestions. It is the wife's enterprise, and
she evidently knows her own mind so well that
the husband keeps aloof, or plays the part of
an approving spectator.

The woolen yarn was ill-suited to the Kentucky climate. This fact the bird seemed to
appreciate, for she used it only in the upper
part of her nest, in attaching it to the branch

and in binding and compacting the rim, making the sides and bottom of hemp, leaving it thin and airy, much more so than are the same nests with us. No other bird would, perhaps, have used such brilliant material; their instincts of concealment would have revolted, but the oriole aims more to make its nest inaccessible than to hide it. Its position and depth insure its safety.

The red-headed woodpecker was about the only bird of this class I saw, and it was very common. Almost any moment, in riding along, their conspicuous white markings as they flew from tree to tree were to be seen festooning the woods. Yet I was told that they were far less numerous than formerly. Governor Knott said he believed there were ten times as many when he was a boy as now. But what beautiful thing is there in this world that was not ten times more abundant when one was a boy than he finds it on becoming a man? Youth is the principal factor in the problem. If one could only have the leisure, the alertness, and the freedom from care that he had when a boy, he would probably find that the world had not deteriorated so much as he is apt to suspect.

The field or meadow bird, everywhere heard in Kentucky and Illinois, is the black-throated bunting, a heavy-beaked bird the size and color of an English sparrow, with a harsh, rasping song, which it indulges in incessantly. Among bird-songs it is like a rather coarse weed among our wild-flowers.

I could not find the mocking-bird in song,

though it breeds in the blue-grass counties. I saw only two specimens of the bird in all my wanderings. The Virginia cardinal was common, and in places the yellow-breasted chat was heard. Once I heard from across a broad field a burst of bobolink melody from a score or more of throats — a flock of the birds probably pausing on their way north. In Chicago I was told that the Illinois bobolink had a different song from the New England species, but I could detect no essential difference. The song of certain birds, notably that of the bobolink, seems to vary slightly in different localities, and also to change during a series of years. I no longer hear the exact bobolink song which I heard in my boyhood, in the localities where I then heard it. Not a season passes but I hear marked departures in the songs of our birds from what appears to be the standard song of a given species.

SOME idea of the impression which Mammoth
Cave makes upon the senses, irrespective even
of sight, may be had from the fact that blind
people go there to see it, and are greatly struck
with it. I was assured that this is a fact.
The blind seem as much impressed by it as
those who have their sight. When the guide
pauses at the more interesting point, or lights
the scene up with a great torch or with Bengal
lights, and points out the more striking features, the blind exclaim, "How wonderful! how
beautiful!" They can feel it if they cannot
see it. They get some idea of the spacious-
ness when words are uttered. The voice goes
forth in these colossal chambers like a bird.
When no word is spoken, the silence is of a
kind never experienced on the surface of the
earth, it is so profound and abysmal. This,
and the absolute darkness, to a person with eyes
makes him feel as if he were face to face with
the primordial nothingness. The objective
universe is gone; only the subjective remains;
the sense of hearing is inverted, and reports
only the murmurs from within. The blind
miss much, but much remains to them. The
great cave is not merely a spectacle to the eye;

it is a wonder to the ear, a strangeness to the
smell and to the touch.   The body feels the
presence of unusual conditions through every
pore.

For my part, my thoughts took a decidedly
sepulchral turn; I thought of my dead and of
all the dead of the earth, and said to myself, the
darkness and the silence of their last resting-
place is like this; to this we must all come at
last.   No vicissitudes of earth, no changes of
seasons, no sound of storm or thunder penetrate
here; winter and summer, day and night, peace
or war, it is all one; a world beyond the reach
of change, because beyond the reach of life.
What peace, what repose, what desolation!
The marks and relics of the Indian, which disappear so quickly from the light of day above,
are here beyond the reach of natural change.
The imprint of his moccasin in the dust might
remain undisturbed for a thousand years.   At
one point the guide reaches his arm beneath the
rocks that strew the floor and pulls out the
burnt ends of canes used, when probably filled
with oil or grease, by the natives to light their
way into the cave doubtless centuries ago.

Here in the loose soil are ruts worn by cart-
wheels in 1812, when, during the war with
Great Britain, the earth was leached to make
saltpetre.   The guide kicks corn-cobs out of
the dust where the oxen were fed at noon, and
they look nearly as fresh as ever they did.   In
those frail corn-cobs and in those wheel tracks
as if the carts had but just gone along, one

seemed to come very near to the youth of the century, almost to overtake it.

At a point in one of the great avenues, if you stop and listen, you hear a slow, solemn ticking like a great clock in a deserted hall; you hear the slight echo as it fathoms and sets off the silence. It is called the clock, and is caused by a single large drop of water falling every second into a little pool. A ghostly kind of clock there in the darkness, that is never wound up and that never runs down. It seemed like a mockery where time is not, and change does not come — the clock of the dead. This sombre and mortuary cast of one's thoughts seems so natural in the great cave, that I could well understand the emotions of a lady who visited the cave with a party a few days before I was there. She went forward very reluctantly from the first; the silence and the darkness of the huge mausoleum evidently impressed her imagination, so that when she got to the spot where the guide points out the "Giant's Coffin," a huge, fallen rock, which, in the dim light takes exactly the form of an enormous coffin, her fear quite overcame her, and she begged piteously to be taken back. Timid, highly imaginative people, especially women, are quite sure to have a sense of fear in this strange underground world. The guide told me of a lady in one of the parties he was conducting through, who wanted to linger behind a little all alone; he suffered her to do so, but presently heard a piercing scream. Rushing back he found her lying prone upon

the ground in a dead faint. She had accidentally put out her lamp, and was so appalled by
the darkness that instantly closed around her
that she swooned at once.

Sometimes it seemed to me as if I was
threading the streets of some buried city of the
fore-world. With your little lantern in your
hand, you follow your guide through those end-
less and silent avenues, catching glimpses on
either hand of what appears to be some strange
antique architecture, the hoary and crumbling
walls rising high up into the darkness. Now
we turn a sharp corner, or turn down a street
which crosses our course at right angles; now
we come out into a great circle, or spacious
court, which the guide lights up with a quick-
paper torch, or a colored chemical light.
There are streets above you and streets below
you. As this was a city where day never entered, no provision for light needed to be made,
and it is built one layer above another to the
number of four or five, or on the plan of an
enormous ant hill, the lowest avenues being several hundred feet beneath the uppermost. The
main avenue leading in from the entrance is
called the Broadway, and if Broadway, New
York, was arched over and reduced to utter
darkness and silence, and its roadway blocked
with mounds of earth and fragments of rock, it
would perhaps, only lack that gray, cosmic,
elemental look, to make it resemble this. A
mile or so from the entrance we pass a couple
of rude stone houses, built forty or more years

ago by some consumptives, who hoped to prolong their lives by a residence in this pure, antiseptic air. Five months they lived here, poor creatures, a half dozen of them, without ever going forth into the world of light. But the long entombment did not arrest the disease; the mountain did not draw the virus out, but seemed to draw the strength and vitality out, so that when the victims did go forth into the light and air, bleached as white as chalk, they succumbed at once, and nearly all died before they could reach the hotel, a few hundred yards away

Probably the prettiest thing they have to show you in Mammoth Cave is the Star Chamber. This seems to have made an impression upon Emerson when he visited the cave, for he mentions it in one of his essays, "Illusions." The guide takes your lantern from you and leaves you seated upon a bench by the wayside, in the profound cosmic darkness. He retreats along a side alley that seems to go down to a lower level, and at a certain point shades his lamp with his hat, so that the light falls upon the ceiling over your head. You look up, and the first thought is that there is an opening just there that permits you to look forth upon the midnight skies. You see the darker horizon line where the sky ends and the mountains begin. The sky is blue-black and is thickly studded with stars, rather small stars, but apparently genuine. At one point a long, luminous streak simulates exactly the form and effect of a comet. As you gaze, the guide slowly moves his hat, and a black cloud gradually creeps over the sky, and all is blackness again. Then you hear footsteps retreating and dying away in the distance. Presently all is still, save the ringing in your own ears. Then after a few moments, during which you have sat in a silence like that of the interstellar spaces, you hear over your left shoulder a distant flapping of wings, followed by the crowing of a cock. You turn your head in that direction and behold a faint dawn breaking on the horizon. It slowly increases till you hear footsteps approaching, and your dusky companion, playing the part of Apollo, with lamp in hand ushers in the light of day. It is rather theatrical, but a very pleasant diversion nevertheless.

Another surprise was when we paused at a certain point, and the guide asked me to shout or call in a loud voice. I did so without any unusual effect following. Then he spoke in a very deep base, and instantly the rocks all about and beneath us became like the strings of an Æolian harp. They seemed transformed as if by enchantment. Then I tried, but did not strike the right key; the rocks were dumb; I tried again, but got no response; flat and dead the sounds came back as if in mockery; then I struck a deeper base, the chord was hit, and the solid walls seemed to become as thin and frail as a drum head or as the frame of a violin. They fairly seemed to dance about us, and to recede away from us. Such wild, sweet music

I had never before heard rocks discourse. Ah, the magic of the right key! "Why leap ye, ye high hills?" why, but that they had been spoken to in the right voice? Is not the whole secret of life to pitch our voices in the right key? Responses come from the very rocks when we do so. I thought of the lines of our poet of Democracy: —

"Surely, whoever speaks to me in the right voice, him or
    her I shall follow,
As the water follows the moon, silently, with fluid steps,
    anywhere around the globe."

Where we were standing was upon an arch over an avenue which crossed our course beneath us. The reverberations on Echo River, a point I did not reach, can hardly be more surprising, though they are described as wonderful.

There are four or five levels in the cave, and a series of avenues upon each. The lowest is some two hundred and fifty feet below the entrance. Here the stream which has done all this carving and tunneling has got to the end of its tether. It is here on a level with Green River in the valley below and flows directly into it. I say the end of its tether, though if Green River cuts its valley deeper, the stream will of course follow suit. The bed of the·river has probably, at successive periods, been on a level with each series of avenues of the cave. The stream is now doubtless but a mere fraction of its former self. Indeed, every feature of the cave attests the greater volume and activity of the forces which carved it, in the

earlier geologic ages. The waters have worn
the rock as if it were but ice. The domes and
pits are carved and fluted in precisely the way
dripping water flutes snow or ice. The rainfall
must have been enormous in those early days,
and it must have had a much stronger and
sharper tooth of carbonic acid gas than now.
It has carved out enormous pits with perpendicular sides, two or three hundred feet deep.
Goring Dome I remember particularly. You
put your head through an irregularly shaped
window in the wall at the side of one of the
avenues, and there is this huge shaft or well,
starting from some higher level and going down
two hundred feet below you. There must have
been such wells in the old glaciers, worn by a
rill of water slowly eating its way down. It
was probably ten feet across, still moist and
dripping. The guide threw down a lighted
torch, and it fell and fell, till I had to crane
my neck far out to see it finally reach the bottom. Some of these pits are simply appalling,
and where the way is narrow, have been covered
over to prevent accidents.

No part of Mammoth Cave was to me more
impressive than its entrance, probably because
here its gigantic proportions are first revealed to
you, and can be clearly seen. That strange
colossal underworld here looks out into the light
of day, and comes in contrast with familiar
scenes and objects. When you are fairly in the
cave, you cannot see it; that is, with your
above-ground eyes; you walk along by the dim

light of your lamp as in a huge wood at night;
when the guide lights up the more interesting
portions with his torches and colored lights, the
effect is weird and spectral; it seems like a
dream; it is an unfamiliar world; you hardly
know whether this is the emotion of grandeur
which you experience, or of mere strangeness.
If you could have the light of day in there,
you would come to your senses, and could test
the reality of your impressions.   At the entrance you have the light of day, and you look
fairly in the face of this underground monster,
yea, into his open mouth, which has a span of
fifty feet or more, and down into his contracting
throat, where a man can barely stand upright,
and where the light fades and darkness begins.
As you come down the hill through the woods
from the hotel, you see no sign of the cave till
you emerge into a small opening where the
grass grows and the sunshine falls, when you
turn slightly to the right, and there at your feet
yawns this terrible pit; and you feel indeed as
if the mountain had opened its mouth and was
lying in wait to swallow you down, as a whale
might swallow a shrimp.   I never grew tired
of sitting or standing here by this entrance and
gazing into it.   It had for me something of the
same fascination that the display of the huge
elemental forces of nature have, as seen in
thunder-storms, or in a roaring ocean surf.
Two phœbe-birds had their nests in little niches
of the rocks, and delicate ferns and wild-flowers
fringed the edges.

Another very interesting feature to me was
the behavior of the cool air which welled up
out of the mouth of the cave. It simulated
exactly a fountain of water. It rose up to a
certain level, or until it filled the depression
immediately about the mouth of the cave, and
then flowing over at the lowest point, ran down
the hill towards Green River, along a little
watercourse, exactly as if it had been a liquid.
I amused myself by wading down into it as into
a fountain. The air above was muggy and hot,
the thermometer standing at about eighty-six
degrees, and this cooler air of the cave, which
was at a temperature of about fifty-two degrees,
was separated in the little pool or lakelet which
is formed from the hotter air above it by a perfectly horizontal line. As I stepped down into
it I could feel it close over my feet, then it
was at my knees, then I was immersed to my
hips, then to my waist, then I stood neck deep
in it, my body almost chilled while my face
and head were bathed by a sultry, oppressive
air. Where the two bodies of air came into
contact, a slight film of vapor was formed by
condensation; I waded in till I could look under
this as under a ceiling. It was as level, and
as well defined as a sheet of ice on a pond.
A few moments' immersion into this aerial
fountain made one turn to the warmer air again.
At the depression in the rim of the basin one
had but to put his hand down to feel the cold
air flowing over like water. Fifty yards below,
you could still wade into it as into a creek, and

at a hundred yards it was still quickly perceptible, but broader and higher; it had begun to
lose some of its coldness, and to mingle with
the general air; all the plants growing on the
margin of the watercourse were in motion, as
well as the leaves on the low branches of the
trees near by. Gradually this cool current was
dissipated and lost in the warmth of the day.

HASTY OBSERVATION

WHEN Boswell told Dr. Johnson that while in Italy he had several times seen the experiment tried of placing a scorpion within a circle of burning coals, and that in every instance the scorpion, after trying to break through the fiery circle, retired to the centre and committed suicide by darting its sting into its head, the doctor showed the true scientific spirit by demanding further proof of the fact. The mere testimony of the eye under such circumstances was not enough; appearances are often deceptive. "If the great anatomist Morgagni," said the doctor, "after dissecting a scorpion on which the experiment had been tried, should certify that its sting had penetrated its head, that would be convincing." For almost the only time in his life, I say, the superstitious doctor showed himself a true scientist, a man refusing to accept the truth of appearances.

But this frame of mind was not habitual to him, for the next moment he said that swallows sleep all winter in the bed of a river or pond, "conglobulated" into a ball. The scientific spirit would have required him to insist upon the proof of the alleged fact in this case the same as in the other. Has any competent ob-

server verified this statement? Have swallows
been taken out of the mud, or been seen to
throw themselves into the water?

Albertus Magnus (1193–1280), in his book
on animals, says that the eel leaves the water in
the night time, and invades the fields and gardens to feed upon peas and lentils. A scientific man makes this statement, and probably
upon no stronger proof than that some eels
dropped by poachers in their hasty retreat, had
been found in a pea patch. If peas had been
found, and found in many cases, in the stom-
achs of eels, that would have been pretty con-
clusive proof that eels eat peas.

The great thing in observation is not to be
influenced by our preconceived notions, or by
what we want to be true, or by our fears, hopes,
or any personal element, and to see the thing
just as it is.

A person who believes in ghosts and appari-
tions cannot be depended upon to investigate
an alleged phenomenon of this sort, because he
will not press his inquiry far enough, and will
take for granted the very fact we want proof of.

The eye does not always see what is in front
of it. Indeed it might almost be said, it sees
only what is back of it, in the mind. Whenever I have any particular subject in mind,
every walk gives me new material. If I am
thinking about tree-toads, I find tree-toads. If
I am dwelling upon birds' nests, I find plenty
of nests which otherwise I should have passed
by. If bird-songs occupy me, I am bound to
hear some new or peculiar note.

Every one has observed how, after he has made the acquaintance of a new word, that word is perpetually turning up in his reading, as if it had suddenly become the fashion. When you have a thing in mind, it is not long till you have it in hand. Torrey and Drummond, the botanists, were one day walking in the woods near West Point. "I have never yet found so and so," said Drummond, naming a rare kind of moss. "Find it anywhere," said Torrey, and stooped and picked it up at their feet. Thoreau could pick up arrowheads with the same ease. Many people have the same quick eye for a four-leafed clover. I may say of myself without vanity, that I see birds with like ease. It is no effort, I cannot help it. Either my eye or my ear is on duty quite unbeknown to me. When I visit my friends, I leave a trail of birds behind me, as old Amphion left a plantation of trees wherever he sat down and played.

The scientific habit of mind leads a man to take into account all possible sources of error in such observations. The senses are all so easily deceived.

People of undoubted veracity tell you of the strange things they have known to rain down, or of some strange bird or beast they have seen. But if you question them closely, you are pretty sure to find some flaw in the observation, or some link of evidence wanting. We are so apt to jump to conclusions; we take one or two steps in following up the evidence, and then

leap to the result that seems to be indicated.
If you find a trout in the milk, you may be jus-
tified in jumping to a conclusion not flattering
to your milkman, but if you find angle-worms
in the barrel of rain-water after a shower, you
are not to conclude that therefore they rained
down, as many people think they do.

Or if after a shower in summer you find the
ground swarming with little toads, you are not
to infer that the shower brought them down.
I have frequently seen large numbers of little
toads hopping about after a shower, but only in
particular localities. Upon a small, gravelly
hill in the highway along which I was in the
habit of walking, I have seen them several seasons, but in no other place upon that road.
Just why they come out on such occasions is a
question; probably to get their jackets wet.
There was a pond and marshy ground not far
off where they doubtless hatched. Because the
frogs are heard in the marshes in spring as soon
as the ice and snow are gone, it is a popular belief that they hibernate in these places. But
the two earliest frogs, I am convinced, pass the
winter in the ground in the woods, and seek
the marshes as soon as the frost and ice are
gone. I have heard the *hyla* pipe in a feeble
tentative manner in localities where the ground
was free from frost, while the marshes near by
were yet covered with solid ice; and in spring
I have dug out another species from beneath the
leaf mould in the woods. Both these species
are properly land-frogs, and only take to the

water to breed, returning again to the woods later in the season. The same is true of the tree-frog, which passes the winter in the ground or in hollow trees, and takes to the marshes in May to deposit its eggs. The common bull-frog and the pickerel-frog doubtless pass the winter in the bed of ponds and streams. I think it is quite certain that hibernating animals in the ground do not freeze, though by no means beyond the reach of frost. The frogs, ants, and crickets are probably protected by some sort of acid which their bodies secrete, though this is only a guess of my own. The frog I dug out of the leaves one spring day, while the ground above and below him was frozen hard, was entirely free from frost, though his joints were apparently very stiff. A friend of mine in balling some trees in winter cut through a den of field crickets; the ground was frozen about their galleries, but the crickets themselves, though motionless, were free from frost. Cut the large, black tree ants out of a pine log in winter and though apparently lifeless they are not frozen.

There is something in most of us that welcomes a departure from the ordinary routine of natural causes; we like to believe that the impossible happens; we like to see the marvelous and mysterious crop out of ordinary occurrences. We like to believe, for instance, that snakes can charm their prey; can exert some mysterious influence over bird or beast at a distance of many feet, which deprives it of power to escape.

But there is probably little truth in this popular notion. Fear often paralyzes, and doubtless this is the whole secret of the power of snakes and cats to charm their prey.   It is what is called a subjective phenomenon; the victim is fascinated or spellbound by the sudden and near appearance of its enemy.   A sportsman in whose veracity I have full confidence, told me that his pointer dog had several times worked up to a woodcock or partridge and seized it in his mouth.   Of course the dog brought no mysterious power to bear upon the bird.   He could hardly have seen the bird till he came plump upon it; he was wholly intent upon unraveling its trail.   The bird, in watching the eager motions and the gradual approach of the dog, must have been thrown into such a state of fear or consternation as to quite paralyze its powers, and suffered the dog to pick it up.   In the case of snakes, they doubtless in most instances approach and seize their prey unawares.   I have seen a little snake in the woods pursue and overtake a lizard that was trying to escape from it.   There was no attempt at charming; superior speed alone gave the victory to the snake. I have known a red squirrel to be caught and swallowed by a black snake, but I have no belief that the squirrel was charmed; it was more probably seized from some ambush.

One can hardly understand how a mouse can be caught by a hawk except upon the theory that the mouse is suddenly paralyzed by fear. The meadow-mouse when exposed to view is

very wary and quick in its movements; it is
nibbling grass in the meadow bottom, or clearing its runway, or shaping its nest, when the
hawk poises on wing high in the air above it.
When the hawk discovers its victim, it descends
with extended talons to the earth and seizes it.
It does not drop like a bolt from heaven; its
descent, on the contrary, is quite deliberate,
and must be attended by a sound of rushing
wings that ought to reach the mouse's ear, if
the form escapes its eye.

There is doubtless just as much "charming"
in this case as in any other, or when a fish-
hawk falls through the air and seizes a fish near
the surface in perfectly clear water — what hin-
ders the fish from seeing and avoiding its enemy? Apparently nothing; apparently it allows
itself to be seized. Every fisherman knows
how alert most fish are, how quickly they discover him and dart away, even when he is immediately above them. All I contend for is
that the snake, the cat, the hawk, does not exert some mysterious power over its prey, but
that its prey in many cases loses its power to
escape through fear. It is said that a stuffed
snake's skin will charm a bird as well as the live
snake.

I came near reaching a hasty conclusion the
other day with regard to a chickadee's nest.
The nest is in a small cavity in the limb of a
pear-tree near my study, and the birds and I
are on very friendly terms. As the nest of
a pair of chickadees had been broken up here a

few seasons ago by a mouse or squirrel, I was apprehensive lest this nest share the same fate. Hence when, one morning, the birds were missing, and I found on inspection what appeared to be the hair of some small animal adhering to the edges of the hole that leads to the nest, I concluded that the birds had been cleaned out again.   Later in the day I examined the supposed hair with my pocket glass, and found it was not hair, but some vegetable fibre.   My next conclusion was that the birds had not been molested, but that they were furnishing their apartment, and some of the material had stuck to the door jambs.   This proved to be the correct inference.   The chickadee makes a little felt-like mat or carpet with which it covers the bottom of the nest-cavity.   A day or two later, in my vineyard near by, I found where a piece of heavy twine that held a young grapevine to a stake had been pulled down to the ground and picked and beaten, and parts of it reduced to its original tow.   Here, doubtless, the birds had got some of their carpeting material.

I recently read in a work on ornithology that the rings of small holes which we see in the trunks and limbs of perfectly sound apple-trees are made by woodpeckers in search of grubs and insects.   This is a hasty inference.   These holes are made by woodpeckers, but the food they obtain at the bottom of them is not the flesh of worm or insect, but the flesh of the apple-tree — the soft, milky inner bark.   The same writer says these holes are not hurtful to the tree, but conducive to its health. Yet I have seen the limbs of large apple-trees nearly killed by being encompassed by numerous rings of large, deep holes made by the yellow-bellied woodpecker. This bird drills holes in the sugar maple in the spring for the sap. I have known him to spend the greater part of a bright March day on the sunny side of a maple, indulging in a tipple of maple sap every four or five minutes. As fast as his well holes filled up he would sip them dry.

A lady told me that a woodpecker drilled holes in the boards that form the eaves of her house, for the grubs of the carpenter bumblebee. This also seemed to me a hasty conclusion, because the woodpeckers made holes so large that the next season the bluebirds nested there. The woodpeckers were probably drilling for a place to nest. A large ice-house stands on the river bank near me, and every season the man in charge has to shoot or drive away the highholes that cut numerous openings through the outer sheathing of hemlock boards into the spaces filled with sawdust, where they find the digging easy and a nesting-place safe and snug.

My neighbor caught a small hawk in his shad-net, and therefore concluded the hawk ate fish. He put him in a cage, and offered him fragments of shad. The little hawk was probably in pursuit of a bird which took refuge under the net as it hung upon the drying-poles; or he may have swooped down upon the net in the spirit of pure bluster and bravado, and thus come to grief in a hurry. The fine, strong threads of the net defied his murderous beak and talons. He was engulfed as completely as is a fly in a spider's web, and the more he struggled the more hopeless his case became. It was a pigeon-hawk, and these little marauders are very saucy.

My neighbor says that in the city of Brooklyn he has known kingbirds to nest in boxes like martins and bluebirds. I question this observation, though it may be true. The cousin of the kingbird, the great crested flycatcher, builds in cavities in trees, and its relative, the phœbe-bird, nests under bridges and hay-sheds. Hence there is this fact to start with in favor of my neighbor's observation.

But when a lady from Pennsylvania writes me that she has seen "swallows rolling and dabbling in the mud in early spring, their breasts so covered with it that it would take but little stretch of imagination to believe they had just emerged from the bottom of the pond beside which they were playing," I am more than skeptical. The lady has not seen straight. The swallows were not rolling in the mud; there was probably not a speck of mud upon their plumage, but a little upon their beaks and feet. The red of their breasts was their own proper color. They were building their nests, as my correspondent knew, but they did not carefully mix and knead the mud, as she thought they did; they had selected mortar already of the proper sort.

The careful observer is not long in learning that there is truth in the poet's remark, that "things are not what they seem." Everywhere on the surface of nature things seem one thing, and mean quite another. The hasty observer is misled by the seeming, and thus misses the real truth.

The little green snake that I saw among the "live-for-evers" the other day, how nearly it escaped detection by the close resemblance of its color to that of the plant! And when, a few days later, I saw one carelessly disposed across the top of the bending grass and daisies, but a few feet from where I sat, my eye again came near being baffled.

The little snake was probably lying in wait for some insect. Presently it slid gently down into the grass, moving so slowly as to escape any but the most watchful eye. After its head and a part of its body were upon the ground, its tail still pointed straight up and exactly resembled some fresh vegetable growth. The safeguard of this little snake is in his protective coloring; hence his movements are slower and more deliberate than those of the other snakes.

This simulation is very common in nature. Every creature has its enemy, and pretends to be that which it is not, in order to escape detection. The true frog pretends to be a piece of bark, or a lichen upon a tree; the wood-frog is the color of the dry leaves upon which it hops, though when spawning in the little black pools and tarns in spring, its color is very dark, like the element it inhabits.

One day, in my walk in the woods, I disturbed a whippoorwill where she sat upon her eggs on the ground. When I returned to the spot some hours afterward, and tried to make out the bird upon her nest, my eye was baffled for some moments, so successful was she in pretending to be only a mottled stick or piece of fallen bark.

Only the most practiced eye can detect the partridge (ruffled grouse) when she sits or stands in full view upon the ground in the woods. How well she plays her part, rarely moving, till she suddenly bursts up before you, and is gone in a twinkling! How well her young are disciplined always to take their cue from her! Not one will stir till she gives the signal.

One day in my walk, as I paused on the side of a steep hill in the edge of the woods, my eye chanced to fall upon a partridge, sitting upon the leaves beside a stump scarcely three paces from me. "Can she have a nest there?" was my first thought. Then I remembered it was late in the summer, and she certainly could not be incubating. Then why is she sitting there in that exposed manner?

Keeping my eye upon her, I took a step forward, when, quick as a flash, she sprang into the air and went humming away. At the same moment, all about me, almost from under my feet, her nearly grown young sprang up and went booming through the woods after her. Not one of them had moved or showed fear till their mother gave the word.

To observe nature and know her secrets, one needs not only a sharp eye, but a steady and patient eye. You must look again and again, and not be misled by appearances. All the misinformation about the objects and phenomena of nature afloat among country people is the result of hasty and incomplete observation.

In parts of the country where wheat is grown there is quite a prevalent belief among the farmers that if the land is poor or neglected, the wheat will turn into chess or cheat grass. Have they not seen it, have they not known the wheat to disappear entirely, and the chess to be there in its place?

But like so many strange notions that are current in the rural districts, this notion is the result of incomplete observation. The cheat grass was there all the while, feebler and inconspicuous, but biding its time; when the wheat failed and gave up possession of the soil the grass sprang forward and took its place.

Nature always has a card to play in that way. There is no miracle nor case of spontaneous generation about the curious succession of forest trees — oak succeeding pine, or poplar succeeding birch or maple — if we could get at the facts. Nature only lets loose germs which the winds or the birds and animals have long since stored there, and which have only been waiting their opportunity to grow.

A great many people are sure there is such a creature as a glass snake, a snake which breaks up into pieces to escape its enemies, and then when danger is past gets itself together again and goes its way.

Not long since a man published an account in a scientific journal of a glass snake which he had encountered in a hay-field, and which, when he attempted to break its head, had broken itself up into five or six pieces.

He carefully examined the pieces and found them of regular lengths of three or four inches, and that they dovetailed together by a nice and regular process. He left the fragments in the grass, and when he returned from dinner they were all gone. He therefore inferred the snake had reconstructed itself and traveled on.

If he had waited to see this process, his observation would have been complete.

On another occasion, he cut one in two with his scythe, when the snake again made small change of itself. Again he went to his dinner just at the critical time, and when he returned the fragments of the reptile had disappeared.

This will not do. We must see the play out, before we can report upon the last act.

There is, of course, a small basis of fact in the superstition of the glass snake. The creature is no snake at all, but a species of limbless lizard, quite common in the West. And it has the curious power of voluntarily breaking itself up into regular pieces when disturbed, but it is only the tail which is so broken up; the body part remains intact.

Break this up and the snake is dead. The tail is disproportionately long, and is severed at certain points, evidently to mislead its enemies. It is the old trick of throwing a tub to a whale. The creature sacrifices its tail to secure the safety of its body. These fragments have no power to unite themselves again, but a new tail is grown in place of the part lost. When a real observer encountered the glass or joint-snake, these facts were settled.

The superstition of the hair-snake is founded upon a like incomplete observation. Everywhere may be found intelligent people who will tell you they know that a horse-hair, if put into the spring, will turn into a snake, and that all hair-snakes have this origin. But a hair never turns into a snake any more than wheat is transformed into chess. The so-called hair-snake is a parasitical worm which lives in the bodies of various insects, and which at maturity takes to the water to lay its eggs.

What boy, while trout-fishing in July and August, and using grasshoppers for bait, has not been vexed to find the body of the insect, when snapped at by the trout, yielding a long, white, brittle thread, which clogged his hook, and spoiled the attractiveness of the bait? This thread is the hair-worm.

How the germ first gets into the body of the grasshopper I do not know. After the creature leaves the insect, it becomes darker in color, and harder and firmer in texture, and more closely resembles a large hair.

See what pains the trapper will take to outwit the fox; see what art the angler will practice

to deceive the wary trout.   One must pursue
the truth with the like patience and diligence.

The farmers all think, or used to think, that
the hen-hawk was their enemy, but last spring
the Agricultural Department procured three
hundred hen-hawks, and examined the craw of
each of them, and made the valuable discovery
that this hawk subsisted almost entirely upon
meadow mice, thus proving them to be one of
the farmer's best friends.

The crow, also, when our observations upon
his food habits are complete, is found to be a
friend, and not an enemy.   The smaller hawks
do prey upon birds and chickens, though the
pretty little sparrow-hawk lives largely upon
insects.

Gilbert White quotes the great Linnæus as
saying that "Hawks make a truce with other
birds as long as the cuckoo is heard."   This is
also a superstition.   Watch closely, and you
will see the small hawks in pursuit of birds at
all seasons; and when a hawk pursues a bird,
or when one bird pursues another, it has the
power to tack and turn, and to time its movements to that of the bird pursued, which is
quite marvelous.

The sparrow might as well dodge its own
shadow as to dodge the sharp-shinned hawk.
It escapes, if at all, by rushing into a bush or
tree, where the movements of its enemy are impeded by the leaves and branches.

Speaking of hawks, reminds me that I read
the other day in one of the magazines a very

pretty poem, in which a hawk was represented poised in mid-air, on motionless wing, during the calm of a midsummer day.

Now, of a still day, this is an impossible feat for a hawk or any other bird. The poet had not observed quite closely enough. She had noted (as who has not?) the hawk stationary in the air on motionless wing, but she failed to note, or she had forgotten, that the wind was blowing.

He cannot do it on a calm day; the blowing wind furnishes the power necessary to buoy him up. He so adjusts his wings to the moving currents that he hangs stationary upon them. When the hawk hovers in the air of a still day, he is compelled to beat his wings rapidly. He must expend upon the air the power which, in the former case, is expended upon him.

Thus does hasty and incomplete observation mislead one.

One day in early April as I was riding along the road I heard the song of the brown thrasher. The thrasher is not due yet, I said to myself, but there was its song, and no mistake, with all its quibs and quirks and interludes, being chanted from some tree-top a few yards in advance of me. Let us have a view of the bird, I said, as I approached the tree upon which I fancied he was perched. The song ceased and no thrasher was visible, but there sat a robin, which, as I paused, flew to a lower tree in a field at some distance from the road. Then I moved on, thinking the songster had eluded me. On looking back I chanced to see the robin fly back

to the top of the tree where I had first disturbed
it, and in a moment or two more, forth came
the thrasher's song again.   Then I went cautiously back and caught the robin in the very
act of reproducing perfectly the song of the
brown thrasher.   A bolder plagiarist I had
never seen; not only had he got the words, as
it were correctly, but he delivered them in the
same self-conscious manner.   His performance
would probably have deceived the brown
thrasher himself.   How did the robin come by
this song?   I can suggest no other explanation
than that he must have learned it from the
brown thrasher.   Probably the latter bird sang
near the nest of the robin, so that the young
heard this song and not that of their own kind.
If so it would be interesting to know if all the
young males learned the song.

Close attention is the secret of learning from
nature's book, as from every other.   Most
persons only look at the pictures, but the real
student studies the text; he alone knows what
the pictures really mean.   There is a great deal
of by-play going on in the life of nature about
us, a great deal of variation and out-cropping of
individual traits, that we entirely miss unless
we have our eyes and ears open.

It is not like the play at the theatre, where
everything is made conspicuous and aims to
catch the eye, and where the story clearly and
fully unfolds itself.   On nature's stage many
dramas are being played at once, and without
any reference to the lookers-on, unless it be to

escape their notice. The actors rush or strut across the stage, the curtain rises or falls, the significant thing happens, and we heed it not because our wits are dull or else our minds are preoccupied. We do not pay strict attention. Nature will not come to you; you must go to her; that is, you must put yourself in communication with her; you must open the correspondence; you must train your eye to pick out the significant things. A quick open sense, and a lively curiosity like that of a boy are necessary. Indeed, the sensitiveness and alertness of youth and the care and patience of later years are what make the successful observer.

The other morning my little boy and I set out to find the horse who had got out of the pasture and gone off. Had he gone up the road or down? We did not know, but we imagined we could distinguish his track going down the road, so we began our search in that direction. The road presently led through a piece of woods. Suddenly my little boy stopped me.

"Papa, see that spider's web stretched across the road; our horse has not gone this way."

My face had nearly touched the web or cable of the little spider, which stretched completely across the road, and which certainly would have been swept away had the horse or any other creature passed along there in the early morning. The boy's eye was sharper than my own. He had been paying stricter attention to the signs and objects about him. We turned back and soon found the horse in the opposite direction.

This same little boy, by looking closely, has discovered that there are certain stingless wasps. When he sees one which bears the marks he boldly catches him in his hand. The wasp goes through the motions of stinging so perfectly, so works and thrusts with its flexible body, that nearly every hand to which it is offered draws back. The mark by which the boy is guided is the light color of the wasp's face. Most country boys know that white-faced bumble-bees are stingless, but I have not before known a boy bold enough to follow the principle out and apply it to wasps as well. These white-faces are the males, and answer to the drones in the bee hive; though the drones have not a white face.

We cannot all find the same things in nature. She is all things to all men. She is like the manna that came down from heaven. "He made manna to descend for them, in which were all manner of tastes; and every Israelite found in it what his palate was chiefly pleased with. If he desired fat in it, he had it. In it the young men tasted bread; the old men, honey; and the children, oil." But all found in it substance and strength. So with nature. In her are "all manner of tastes," science, art, poetry, utility, and good in all. The botanist has one pleasure in her, the ornithologist another, the explorer another, the walker and sportsman another; what all may have is the refreshment and the exhilaration which come from a loving and intelligent scrutiny of her manifold works.

BIRD LIFE IN AN OLD APPLE-TREE

NEAR my study there used to stand several old apple-trees that bore fair crops of apples, but better crops of birds. Every year these old trees were the scenes of bird incidents and bird histories that were a source of much interest and amusement.

Young trees may be the best for apples, but old trees are sure to bear the most birds. If they are very decrepit, and full of dead and hollow branches, they will bear birds in winter as well as summer. The downy woodpecker wants no better place than the brittle, dozy trunk of an apple-tree in which to excavate his winter home.

My old apple-trees are all down but one, and this one is probably an octogenarian, and I am afraid cannot stand in another winter. Its body is a mere shell not much over one inch thick, the heart and main interior structure having turned to black mould long ago.

An old tree, unlike an old person, as long as it lives at all, always has a young streak, or rather ring, in it. It wears a girdle of perpetual youth.

My old tree has never yet failed to yield me

a bushel or more of gillyflowers, and it has turned out at least a dozen broods of the great crested flycatcher, and robins and bluebirds in proportion. It carries up one large decayed trunk which some one sawed off at the top before my time, and in this a downy woodpecker is now, January 12, making a home.

Several years ago a downy woodpecker excavated a retreat in this branch, which the following season was appropriated by the bluebirds, and has been occupied by them nearly every season since.

When the bluebirds first examined the cavity in the spring, I suppose they did not find the woodpecker at home, as he is a pretty early riser.

I happened to be passing near the tree when, on again surveying the premises one afternoon, they found him in.

The male bluebird was very angry, and I suppose looked upon the innocent downy as an intruder. He seized on him, and the two fell to the ground, the speckled woodpecker quite covered by the blue coat of his antagonist. Downy screamed vigorously, and got away as soon as he could, but not till the bluebird had tweaked out a feather or two.

He is evidently no fighter, though one would think that a bird that had an instrument with which it could drill a hole into a tree could defend itself against the soft-billed bluebird.

Two seasons the English sparrows ejected the bluebirds and established themselves in it, but were in turn ejected by myself, their furniture of hens' feathers and straws pitched out, and the bluebirds invited to return, which later in the season they did.

The new cavity which downy is now drilling is just above the old one and near the top of the stub. Its wells are usually sunk to a depth of six or eight inches, but in the present case it cannot be sunk more than four inches without breaking through into the old cavity.

Downy seems to have considered the situation, and is proceeding cautiously. As she passed last night in her new quarters I am inclined to think it is about finished, and there must be at least one inch of wood beneath her. She worked vigorously the greater part of the day, her yellow chips strewing the snow beneath.

I paused several times to observe her proceedings.

After her chips accumulate she stops her drilling and throws them out. This she does with her beak, shaking them out very rapidly with a flirt of her head.

She did not disappear from sight each time to load her beak, but withdrew her head and appeared to seize the fragments as if from her feet. If she had had a companion I should have thought he was handing them up to her from the bottom of the cavity. Maybe she had them piled up near the doorway.

The woodpeckers, both the hairy and the downy, usually excavate these winter retreats in the fall. They pass the nights and the stormy days in them. So far as I have observed they do not use them as nesting-places the following season.

Last night when I rapped on the trunk of the old apple-tree near sundown, downy put out her head with a surprised and inquiring look, and then withdrew it again as I passed on.

I have spoken of the broods of the great crested flycatchers that have been reared in the old apple-tree. This is by no means a common bird, and as it destroys many noxious insects I look upon it with a friendly eye, though it is the most uncouth and unmusical of the flycatchers.

Indeed, among the other birds of the garden and orchard it seems quite like a barbarian.

It has a harsh, froglike scream, form and manners to suit, and is clad in a suit of butternut brown. It seeks a cast-off snakeskin to weave into its nest, and not finding one, will take an onion skin, a piece of oiled paper, or large fish scales.

It builds in a cavity in a tree, rears one brood, and is off early in the season. I never see or hear it after August 1st.

A pair have built in a large, hollow limb in my old apple-tree for many years. Whether it is the same pair or not I do not know. Probably it is, or else some of their descendants.

I looked into the cavity one day while the mother bird was upon the nest, but before she had laid any eggs. A sudden explosive sound came up out of the dark depths of the limb, much like that made by an alarmed cat. It made me jerk my head back, when out came the bird and hurried off.

For several days I saw no more of the pair, and feared they had deserted the spot. But they had not; they were only more sly than usual. I soon discovered an egg in the nest, and then another and another.

One day, as I stood near by, a male bluebird came along with his mate, prospecting for a spot for a second nest. He alighted at the entrance of this hole and peeped in.

Instantly the flycatcher was upon him. The blue was enveloped by the butternut brown. The two fell to the ground, where the bluebird got away, and in a moment more came back and looked in the hole again, as much as to say, "I will look into that hole now at all hazards."

The barbarian made a dash for him again, but he was now on his guard and avoided her.

Not long after, the bluebirds decided to occupy the old cavity of the downy woodpecker from which I had earlier in the season expelled the English sparrows. After they had established themselves here a kind of border war broke out between the male bluebird and the flycatchers, and was kept up for weeks.

The bluebird is very jealous and very bold. He will not even tolerate a house-wren in the vicinity of his nest. Every bird that builds in a cavity he looks upon as his natural rival and enemy. The flycatchers did not seek any quarrel with him as long as he kept to his own domicile, but he could not tolerate them in the same tree.

It was a pretty sight to see this little blue-coat charging the butternut through the trees. The beak of the latter would click like a gun-lock, and its harsh, savage voice was full of anger, but the bluebird never flinched, and was always ready to renew the fight.

The English sparrow will sometimes worst the bluebird by getting possession of the box or cavity ahead of him. Once inside the sparrow can hold the fort, and the bluebird will soon give up the siege; but in a fair field and no favors, the native bird will quickly rout the foreigner.

Speaking of birds that build in cavities reminds me of a curious trait the high-hole has developed in my vicinity, one which I have never noticed or heard of elsewhere.

It drills into buildings and steeples and telegraph poles, and in some instances makes itself a serious nuisance.

One season the large imitation Greek columns of an unoccupied old-fashioned summer residence near me were badly marred by them. The bird bored into one column, and finding the cavity — a foot or more across — not just what it was looking for, cut into another one, and still into another. Then he bored into the ice-house on the premises, and in the sawdust filling between the outer and inner sheathing found a place to his liking.

One bird seemed like a monomaniac, and drilled holes up and down and right and left as if possessed of an evil spirit. It is quite probable that if a high-hole or other woodpecker should go crazy, it would take to just this sort of thing, drilling into seasoned timber till it used its strength up. The one I refer to would cut through a dry hemlock board in a very short time, making the slivers fly. The sound was like that of a carpenter's hammer. It may have been that he was an unmated bird, a bachelor whose suit had not prospered that season, and who was giving vent to his outraged instincts in drilling these mock nesting-places.

I HAVE often had occasion to notice how much more intelligence the bird carries in its eye than does the animal or quadruped.

The animal will see you, too, if you are moving, but if you stand quite still even the wary fox will pass within a few yards of you and not know you from a stump, unless the wind brings him your scent.

But a crow or a hawk will discern you when you think yourself quite hidden. His eye is as keen as the fox's sense of smell, and seems fairly to penetrate veils and screens. Most of the water-fowl are equally sharp-eyed.

The chief reliance of the animals for their safety, as well as for their food, is upon the keenness of their scent, while the fowls of the air depend mainly upon the eye.

A hunter out in Missouri relates how closely a deer approached him one day in the woods. The hunter was standing on the top of a log, about four feet from the ground, when the deer bounded playfully into a glade in the forest, a couple of hundred yards away. The animal began to feed and to move slowly toward the hunter. He was on the alert, but did not see or scent his enemy. He never took a bite of grass, says the sportsman, without first putting his nose to it, and then instantly raising his head and looking about.

In about ten minutes the deer had approached within fifty yards of the gunner; then the murderous instinct of the latter began to assert itself. His gun was loaded with fine shot, but he dared not make a move to change his shells lest the deer see him. He had one shell loaded with No. 4 shot in his pocket. Oh! if he could only get that shell into his gun.

The unsuspecting deer kept approaching; presently he passed behind a big tree, and his head was for a moment hidden. The hunter sprang to his work; he got one of the No. 8 shells out of his gun and got his hand into his pocket and a hold of the No. 4. Then the shining eyes of the deer were in view again. The hunter stood in this attitude five minutes. How we wish he had been compelled to stand for five hundred!

Then another tree shut off the buck's gaze for a moment; in went the No. 4 shell into the barrel and the gun was closed quickly, but there was no time to bring it to the shoulder. The animal was now only thirty yards away. His hair was smooth and glossy, and every movement was full of grace and beauty. Time after time he seemed to look straight at the hunter, and once or twice a look of suspicion seemed to cross his face.

The man began to realize how painful it was to stand perfectly still on the top of a log for fifteen minutes. Every muscle ached and seemed about to rebel against his will. If the buck held to his course he would pass not more than fifteen feet to one side of the gun, and the man that held it thought he might almost blow his heart out.

There was one more tree for him to pass behind, when the gun could be raised. He approached the tree, rubbed his nose against it, and for a moment was half hidden behind it. When his head appeared on the other side the gun was pointed straight at his eye — and with only No. 4 shot, which could only wound him, but could not kill him.

The deer stops; he does not expose his body back of the fore leg, as the hunter had wished. The latter begins to be ashamed of himself, and has about made up his mind to let the beautiful creature pass unharmed, when the buck suddenly gets his scent, his head goes up, his nostrils expand, and a look of terror comes over his face. This is too much for the good resolutions of the hunter. Bang! goes the gun, the deer leaps into the air, wheels around a couple of times, recovers himself and is off in a twinkling, no doubt carrying, the narrator says, a hundred No. 4 shot in his face and neck. The man says: "I've always regretted shooting at him."

I should think he would. But a man in the woods, with a gun in his hand, is no longer a man — he is a brute. The devil is in the gun to make brutes of us all.

If the game on this occasion had been, say a wild turkey or a grouse, its discriminating eye would have figured out the hunter there on that log very quickly.

This manly exploit of the Western hunter reminds me of an exploit of a Brooklyn man, who last winter killed a bull moose in Maine. It was a more sportsmanlike proceeding, but my sympathies were entirely with the moose. The hero tells his story in a New York paper. With his guides, all armed with Winchester rifles, he penetrated far into the wilderness till he found a moose yard. It was near the top of a mountain.

They started one of the animals and then took up its trail.

As soon as the moose found it was being followed, it led right off in hopes of outwalking its enemies. But they had snow-shoes and he did not; they had food and he did not. On they went, pursued and pursuers, through the snow-clogged wilderness, day after day. The moose led them the most difficult route he could find.

At night the men would make camp, build a fire, eat and smoke, and roll themselves in their blankets and sleep. In the morning they would soon come up to the camping place of the poor moose, where the imprint of his great body showed in the snow, and where he had passed a cold, supperless night.

On the fifth day the moose began to show signs of fatigue; he rested often, he also tried to get around and behind his pursuers and let them pass on. Think how inadequate his wit was to cope with the problem — he thought they would pass by him if he went to one side.

On the morning of the sixth day he had made up his mind to travel no farther, but to face his enemies and have it out with them.

As he heard them approach he rose up from his couch of snow, mane erect, his look fierce and determined. Poor creature, he did not know how unequal the contest was. How I wish he could at that moment have had a Winchester rifle too, and had known how to use it. There would have been fair play then.

With such weapons as God had given him he had determined to meet the foe, and if they had had only such weapons as God had given them, he would have been safe. But they had weapons which the devil had given them, and their deadly bullets soon cut him down, and now probably his noble antlers decorate the hall of his murderer.

To teach young people or old people how to observe nature is a good deal like trying to teach them how to eat their dinner. The first thing necessary in the latter case is a good appetite; this given, the rest follows very easily. And in observing nature, unless you have the appetite, the love, the spontaneous desire, you will get little satisfaction. It is the heart that sees more than the mind. To love nature is the first step in observing her. If a boy had to learn fishing as a task, what slow progress he would make; but as his heart is in it, how soon he becomes an adept.

The eye sees quickly and easily those things in which we are interested. A man interested in horses sees every fine horse in the country he passes through; the dairyman notes the cattle; the bee culturist counts the skips of bees; the sheep-grower notes the flocks, etc. Is it any effort for the ladies to note the new bonnets and the new cloaks upon the street? We all see and observe easily in the line of our business, our tasks, our desires.

If one is a lover of the birds, he sees birds everywhere, plenty of them. I think I seldom miss a bird in my walk if he is within eye or ear shot, even though my mind be not intent upon that subject. Walking along the road this very day, feeling a cold, driving snow-storm, I saw some large birds in the top of a maple as I passed by. I do not know how I came to see them, for I was not in an ornitho-logical frame of mind. But I did. There were three of them feeding upon the buds of the maple. They were nearly as large as rob-ins, of a dark ash color, very plump, with tails much forked. What were they? My neigh-bor did not know; had never seen such birds before. I instantly knew them to be pine grosbeaks from the far north. I had not seen them before for ten years. A few days pre-viously I had heard one call from the air as it passed over; I recognized the note, and hence knew that the birds were about. They come down from the north at irregular intervals, and are seen in flocks in various parts of the States. They seem just as likely to come mild winters as severe ones. Later in the day the birds came about my study. I sat reading with my back to the window when I was advised of their presence by catching a glimpse of one reflected in my eye-glasses as it flew up from the ground to the branch of an apple-tree only a few feet away. I only mention the circumstance to show how quick an observer is to take the hint. I was absorbed in my reading, but the moment that little shadow flitted athwart that luminous reflection of the window in the corner of my glasses, something said "that was a bird." Approaching the window, I saw several of them sitting not five feet away. I could inspect them perfectly. They were a slate color, with a tinge of bronze upon the head and rump. In full plumage the old males are a dusky red. Hence these were all either young males or females. Occasionally among these flocks an old male may be seen. It would seem as if only a very few of the older and wiser birds accompanied these younger birds in their excursions into more southern climes.

Presently the birds left the apple-bough that nearly brushed my window, and, with a dozen or more of their fellows that I had not seen, settled in a Norway spruce a few yards away, and began to feed upon the buds. They looked very pretty there amid the driving snow. I was flattered that these visitants from the far north should find entertainment on my premises. How plump, contented, and entirely at home they looked. But they made such havoc with the spruce buds that after a while I began to fear a bud would not be left upon the trees; the spruces would be checked in their growth the next year. So I presently went out to remonstrate with them and ask them to move on. I approached them very slowly, and when beside the tree within a few feet of several of them, they heeded me not. One bird kept its position and went on snipping off the buds till I raised my hand ready to seize it, before it moved a yard or two higher up. I think it was only my white, uncovered hand that disturbed it. Indeed,

> " They were so unacquainted with man,
> Their tameness was shocking to see."

The snow was covered with the yellow chaffy scales of the buds and still the birds sifted them down, till I was compelled to "shoo" them away, when they moved to a tree nearer the house beneath which they left more yellow chaff upon the snow.

The mind of an observer is like a gun with a hair trigger — it goes at a touch, while the minds of most persons require very vigorous nudging. You must take the hint and take it quickly if you would get up any profitable intimacy with nature. Above all, don't jump to conclusions; look again and again; verify your observations. Be sure the crow is pulling corn, and not probing for grubs, before you kill him. Be sure it is the oriole purloining your grapes, and not the sparrows, before you declare them your enemies. I one day saw humming-birds apparently probing the ripe yellow cheeks of my finest peaches, but I was not certain till I saw a bird hovering over a particular peach, and then mounting upon a ladder I examined it, when sure enough, the golden cheek was full of pin-holes. The orioles destroy many of my earliest pears, but it required much watching to catch them in the very act. I once saw a phœbe-bird swoop down upon a raspberry bush and carry a berry to a rail on a near fence, but

I did not therefore jump to the conclusion that the phœbe was a berry-eater. What it wanted was the worm in the berry. How do I know? Because I saw it extract something from the berry and fly away.

A French missionary, said to have been a good naturalist, writing in this country in 1634, makes this curious statement about our humming-bird: "This bird, as one might say, dies, or, to speak more correctly, puts itself to sleep in the month of October, living fastened to some little branchlet of a tree by the feet, and wakes up in the month of April when the flowers are in abundance, and sometimes later, and for that cause is called in the Mexican tongue the "Revived." How could the good missionary ever have been led to make such a statement? The actual finding of the bird wintering in that way would have been the proof science demands, and nothing short of that.

A boy in the interior of the State wrote to me the other day that while in the field looking after Indian arrow-heads he had seen a brown and gray bird with a black mark running through the eye, and that the bird walked instead of hopped. He said it had a high, shrill whistle and flew like a meadow-lark. This boy is a natural observer; he noted that the bird was a walker. Most of the birds hop or jump, keeping both feet together. This boy heard his bird afterward in the edge of the evening, and "followed it quite a ways, but could not get a glimpse of it." He had failed to note the crest on its head and the black spot on its breast, for doubtless his strange bird was the shore-lark, a northern bird, that comes to us in flocks in the late fall or early winter, and in recent years has become a permanent resident of certain parts of New York State. I have heard it in full song above the hills in Delaware County, after the manner of the English skylark, but its song was a crude, feeble, broken affair compared with that of the skylark. These birds thrive well in confinement. I had one seven months in a cage while living in Washington. It was disabled in the wing by a gunner, who brought it to me. Its wound soon healed; it took food readily; it soon became tame, and was an object of much interest and amusement. The cage in which I had hastily put it was formerly a case filled with stuffed birds. Its front was glass. As it was left out upon the porch over night, a strange cat discovered the bird through this glass, and through the glass she plunged and captured the bird. In the morning there was the large hole in this glass, and the pretty lark was gone. I have always indulged a faint hope that the glass was such a surprise to the cat, and made such a racket about her eyes and ears as she sprang against it, that she beat a hasty retreat, and that the bird escaped through the break.

II

In May two boys in town wrote to me to explain to them the meaning of the egg-shells, mostly those of robins, that were to be seen lying about on the ground here and there. I supposed every boy knew where most of these egg-shells came from. As soon as the young birds are out, the mother bird removes the fragments of shells from the nest, carrying them in her beak some distance, and dropping them here and there. All our song-birds, so far as I know, do this.

Sometimes, however, these shells are dropped by blue-jays after their contents have been swallowed. The jay will seize a robin's egg by thrusting his beak into it, and hurry off lest he be caught in the act by the owner. At a safe distance he will devour the contents at his leisure, and drop the shell.

The robins, however, have more than once caught the jay in the act. He has the reputation among them of being a sneak thief. Many and many a time during the nesting season you may see a lot of robins mob a jay. The jay comes slyly prowling through the trees, looking for his favorite morsel, when he is discovered by a vigilant robin, who instantly rushes at him crying, "Thief! thief!" at the top of his voice. All the robins that have nests within hearing gather to the spot and join in the pursuit of the jay, screaming and scolding.

The jay is hustled out of the tree in a hurry, and goes sneaking away with the robins at his heels. He is usually silent, like other thieves, but sometimes the birds make it so hot for him that he screams in anger and disgust.

Of the smaller birds, like the vireos and warblers, the jay will devour the young.

My little boy one day saw a jay sitting beside a nest in a tree, probably that of the red-eyed vireo, and coolly swallowing the just-hatched young, while the parent birds were powerless to prevent him.   They flew at him and snapped their beaks in his face, but he heeded them not.   A robin would have knocked him off his feet at her first dive.

One is sometimes puzzled by seeing a punctured egg lying upon the ground.   One day I came near stepping upon one that was lying in the path that leads to the spring — a fresh egg with a little hole in it carefully placed upon the gravel.   I suspected it to be the work of the cowbird, and a few days later I had convincing proof that the cowbird is up to this sort of thing.   I was sitting in my summer house with a book, when I had a glimpse of a bird darting quickly down from the branches of the maple just above me toward the vineyard, with something in its beak.   Following up my first glance with more deliberate scrutiny, I saw a female cowbird alight upon the ground and carefully deposit some small object there, and then, moving a few inches away, remain quite motionless.   Without taking my eyes from the spot, I walked straight down there. The bird flew away, and I found the object she had dropped to be a little speckled bird's egg still warm.   I saw that it was the egg of the red-eyed vireo.   It was punctured with two holes where the bird had seized it; otherwise it had been very carefully handled. For some days I had been convinced that a pair of vireos had a nest in my maple, but much scrutiny had failed to reveal it to me.

Only a few moments before the cowbird appeared I had seen the happy pair leave the tree together, flying to a clump of trees lower down the slope of the hill. The female had evidently just deposited her egg, the cowbird had probably been watching near by, and had seized it the moment the nest was vacated. Her plan was of course to deposit one of her own in its place.

I now made a more thorough search for the nest, and soon found it, but it was beyond my reach on an outer branch, and whether or not the cowbird dropped one of her own eggs in place of the one she had removed I do not know. Certain am I that the vireos soon abandoned the nest, though they do not always do this when hoodwinked in this way.

I once met a gentleman on the train who told me about a brood of quails that had hatched out under his observation. He was convinced that the mother quail had broken the shells for the young birds. He sent me one of the shells to convince me that it had been broken from the outside.

At first glance it did appear so. It had been cut around near the large end, with the exception of a small space, as if by regular thrusts or taps from a bird's beak, so that this end opened

like the lid of a box on a hinge, and let the im-
prisoned bird escape. What convinced the
gentleman that the force had been applied from
the outside was that the edges of the cut or
break were bent in.

If we wish rightly to interpret nature, to get
at the exact truth of her ways and doings, we
must cultivate what is called the critical habit
of mind; that is, the habit of mind that does
not rest with mere appearances. One must sift
the evidence, must cross-question the facts.
This gentleman was a lawyer, but he laid aside
the cunning of his craft in dealing with this
question of these egg-shells.

The bending in, or the indented appearance
of the edge of the shells was owing to the fact
that the thin paper-like skin that lines the interior of the shell had dried and shrunken, and
had thus drawn the edges of the shell inward.
The cut was made by the beak of the young
bird, probably by turning its head from right
to left; one little point it could not reach, and
this formed the hinge of the lid I have spoken
of.

Is it at all probable that if the mother bird
had done this work she would have left this
hinge, and left it upon every egg, since the
hinge was of no use? The complete removal
of the cap would have been just as well.

Neither is it true that the parent bird shoves
its young from the nest when they are ready to
fly, unless it be in the case of doves and pigeons. Our small birds certainly do not do this.

The young birds will launch out of their own motion as soon as their wings will sustain them, and sometimes before.

There is usually one of the brood a little more forward than its mates, and this one is the first to venture forth. In the case of the bluebird, chickadee, highhole, nuthatch, and others, the young are usually a day or two in leaving the nest.

The past season I was much interested in seeing a brood of chickadees, reared on my premises, venture upon their first flight. Their heads had been seen at the door of their dwelling — a cavity in the limb of a pear-tree — at intervals for two or three days.

Evidently they liked the looks of the great outside world; and one evening, just before sundown, one of them came forth. His first flight was of several yards to a locust, where he alighted upon an inner branch, and after some chirping and calling proceeded to arrange his plumage, and compose himself for the night.

I watched him till it was nearly dark. He did not appear at all afraid there alone in the tree, but put his head under his wing and settled down for the night as if it were just what he had always been doing. There was a heavy shower a few hours later, but in the morning he was there upon his perch in good spirits.

I happened to be passing in the morning when another one came out. He hopped out upon a limb, shook himself, and chirped and called loudly. After some moments an idea seemed to strike him. His attitude changed, his form straightened up, and a thrill of excitement seemed to run through him. I knew what it all meant; something had whispered to the bird, "Fly!" With a spring and a cry he was in the air, and made good headway to a near hemlock.

Others left in a similar manner during that day and the next, till all were out.

Some birds seem to scatter as soon as they are out of the nest. With others the family keeps together the greater part of the season. Among birds that have this trait may be named the chickadee, the bluebird, the blue-jay, the nuthatch, the kingbird, the phœbe-bird, and others of the true flycatchers.

One frequently sees the young of the phœbe sitting in a row upon a limb, while the parents feed them in regular order. Twice I have come upon a brood of young but fully fledged screech-owls in a dense hemlock wood, sitting close together upon a low branch. They stood there like a row of mummies, the yellow curtains of their eyes drawn together to a mere crack, till they saw themselves discovered.

Then they all changed their attitudes as if an electric current had passed through the branch upon which they sat. Leaning this way and that, they stared at me like frightened cats till the mother took flight, when the young followed.

The family of chickadees above referred to kept in the trees about my place for two or three weeks. They hunted the same feeding-ground over and over, and always seemed to find an abundance. The parent birds did the hunting, the young did the calling and the eating. At any hour in the day you could find the troop slowly making their way over some part of their territory.

Later in the season one of the parent birds seemed smitten with some fatal malady. If birds have leprosy, this must have been leprosy. The poor thing dropped down through a maple-tree close by the house, barely able to flit a few feet at a time. Its plumage appeared greasy and filthy, and its strength was about gone. I placed it in the branches of a spruce-tree, and never saw it afterward.

III

A boy brought me a dead bird the other morning which his father had picked up on the railroad. It had probably been killed by striking the telegraph wires. As it was a bird the like of which he had never seen before, he wanted to know its name. It was a wee bird, mottled gray and brown like nearly all our ground birds, as the sparrows, the meadow-larks, the quail: a color that makes the bird practically invisible to its enemies in the air above. Unlike the common sparrows, its little round wings were edged with yellow, with a tinge of yellow on its shoulders; hence its name, the yellow-winged sparrow. It has also a yellowish line over the eye. It is by no means a common bird, though there are probably few farms in the Middle and Eastern States upon which one could not be found. It is one of the birds to be looked for. Ordinary observers do not see it or hear it.

It is small, shy, in every way inconspicuous. Its song is more like that of an insect than that of any other of our birds. If you hear in the fields in May and June a fine, stridulous song like that of a big grasshopper, it probably proceeds from this bird. Move in the direction of it and you will see the little brown bird flit a few yards before you. For several mornings lately I have heard and seen one on a dry, gravelly hillock in a field. Each time he has been near the path where I walk. Unless your ear is on the alert you will miss his song. Amid the other bird songs of May heard afield it is like a tiny, obscure plant amid tall, rank growths. The bird affords a capital subject for the country boy, or town boy, either, when he goes to the country, to exercise his powers of observation upon. If he finds this bird he will find a good many other interesting things. He may find the savannah sparrow also, which closely resembles the bird he is looking for. It is a trifle larger, has more bay about the wings, and is more common toward the coast. Its yellow markings are nearly the same. There is also a variety of the yellow-winged sparrow called Henslow's yellow-winged sparrow, but it bears so close a resemblance to the first-named that it requires a professional ornithologist to distinguish them. I confess I have never identified it.

I never see the yellow-wing without being reminded of a miniature meadow-lark. Its short tail, its round wings, its long and strong legs and feet, its short beak, its mottled coat, the touch of yellow, as if he had just rubbed against a newly-opened dandelion, but in this case on the wings instead of on the breast, the quality of its voice, and its general shape and habits, all suggest a tiny edition of this large emphatic walker of our meadows.

The song of this little sparrow is like the words "chick, chick-a-su-su," uttered with a peculiar buzzing sound. Its nest is placed upon the ground in the open field, with four or five speckled eggs. The eggs are rounder and their ground color whiter than the eggs of other sparrows.

I do not know whether this kind walks or hops. This would be an interesting point for the young observer to determine. All the other sparrows known to me are hoppers, but from the unusually long and strong legs of this species, its short tail and erect manner, I more than half suspect it is a walker. If so, this adds another meadow-lark feature.

Let the young observer follow up and identify any one bird, and he will be surprised to find how his love and enthusiasm for birds will kindle. He will not stop with the one bird. Carlyle wrote in a letter to his brother, "Attempt to explain what you do know, and you already know something more." Bring what powers of observation you already have to bear upon animate nature, and already your powers are increased. You can double your capital and more in a single season.

The first among the less common birds which I identified when I began the study of ornithology was the red-eyed vireo, the little gray bird with a line over its eye that moves about with its incessant cheerful warble all day, rain or shine, among the trees, and it so fired my enthusiasm that before the end of the season I had added a dozen or more (to me) new birds to my list. After a while the eye and ear become so sensitive and alert that they seem to see and hear of themselves, and like sleepless sentinels report to you whatever comes within their range. Driving briskly along the road the other day, I saw a phœbe-bird building her nest under a cliff of rocks. I had but a glimpse, probably two seconds, through an opening in the trees, but it was long enough for my eye to take in the whole situation: the gray wall of rock, the flitting form of the bird and the half-finished nest into which the builder settled. Yesterday, May 7, I went out for an hour's walk looking for birds' nests. I made a tour of some orchards, pastures and meadows, but found nothing, and then came home and found a blue-jay's nest by my very door. How did I find it? In the first place my mind was intent upon nest finding: I was ripe for a bird's

nest.   In the second place I had for some time
suspected that a pair of jays were nesting or in-
tending to nest in some of the evergreens about
my house; a pair had been quite familiar about
the premises for some weeks, and I had seen
the male feed the female, always a sure sign
that the birds are mated, and are building or
ready to build.   Many birds do this.   I have
even seen the crow feed its mate in April.
Just at this writing, a pair of chickadees attracted my attention in a spruce-tree in front of
my window.   One of them, of course the male,
is industriously feeding the other.   The female
hops about, imitating the voice and manner of
a young bird, her wings quivering, her cry
plaintive, while the male is very busy collecting
some sort of fine food out of the just-bursting
buds of the tree.   Every half minute or so he
approaches her and delivers his morsel into her
beak.   I should know from this fact alone that
the birds have a nest near by.   The truth is, it
is just on the other side of the study in a small
cavity in a limb of a pear-tree.   The female is
laying her eggs, one each day probably, and the
male is making life as easy for her as possible,
by collecting all her food for her.

Hence, when as I came down the drive and
a blue-jay alighted in a maple near me, I
paused to observe him.   He wiped his beak on
a limb, changed his position a couple of times,
then uttered a low mellow note.   The voice as
of a young jay, tender and appealing, came out
of a Norway spruce near by.   The cry was con-

tinued, when the bird I was watching flew in amid the top branches, and the cry became still more urgent and plaintive. I stepped along a few paces and saw the birds, the female standing up in her nest and the male feeding her. The nest was placed in a sort of basket formed by the whorl of up-curving branches at the top of the tree, the central shaft being gone.

It contained four eggs of a dirty brownish-greenish color. As I was climbing up to it, a turtle dove threw herself out of the tree and fluttered to the ground as if mortally wounded. My little boy was looking on, and seeing the dove apparently so helpless and in such distress, ran to see "what in the world ailed it." It fluttered along before him for a few yards, and then its mate appearing upon the scene, the two flew away, much to the surprise of the boy. We soon found the doves' nest, a shelf of twigs on a branch about midway of the tree. It held two young birds nearly fledged. How they seemed to pant as they crouched there, a shapeless mass of down and feathers, regarding us! The doves had been so sly about their nesting that I had never suspected them for a moment. The next tree held a robin's nest, and the nest of a purple finch is probably near by. One usually makes a mistake in going away from home to look for birds' nests. Search the trees about your door.

The blue-jay is a cruel nest-robber, but this pair had spared the doves in the same tree, and I think they have made their peace with the robins, as I do not see the latter hustling them about any more. Probably they want to stand well with their neighbors, and so go away from home to commit their robberies.

IV

If a new bird appears in my neighborhood, my eye or ear reports it at once. One April several of those rare thrushes, — Bicknell's or Slide Mountain thrush — stopped for two days in my currant-patch. How did I know? I heard their song as I went about the place, a fine elusive strain unlike that of any other thrush. To locate it exactly I found very difficult. It always seemed to be much farther off than it actually was. There is a hush and privacy about its song that makes it unique. It has a mild, fluty quality, very sweet, but in a subdued key. It is a bird of remote northern mountain-tops, and its song seems adjusted to the low, thick growths of such localities.

The past season a solitary Great Carolina wren took up its abode in a bushy land near one corner of my vineyard. It came late in the season, near the end of August, the only one I had ever heard north of the District of Columbia. During my Washington days, many years ago, this bird was one of the most notable songsters observed in my walks. His loud, rolling whistle and warble, his jocund calls and salutations — how closely they were blended with all my associations with nature on the Potomac.

When, therefore, one morning my ear caught the same blithe, ringing voice on the Hudson, be assured I was quickly on the alert. How it brought up the past. How it reopened a chapter of my life that had long been closed. It stood out amid other bird songs and calls with a distinctness that attracted the dullest ears. Such a southern Virginia air as it gave to that nook by the river's side!

I left my work amid the grapes and went down to interview the bird. He peeped at me inquisitively and suspiciously for a few moments from a little clump of weeds and bushes, then came out in fuller view, and finally hopped to the top of a grape-post, drooped his wings and tail, lifted up his head, and sung and warbled his best. If he had known exactly what I came for and had been intent upon doing his best to please me, he could not have succeeded better.

The Great Carolina wren is a performer like the mocking-bird, and is sometimes called the mocking wren. He sings and acts as well. He seems bent on attracting the attention of somebody or something. A Southern poet has felicitously interpreted certain notes by the words, "Sweetheart, sweetheart, sweet."

Day after day and week after week, till the frosts of the late October came, the bird tarried in that spot, confining his wanderings to a very small area and calling and warbling at all hours. From my summer-house I could often hear his voice rise up from under the hill, seeming to

fill all the space down there with sound. What
brought this solitary bird there, so far from
the haunts of his kind, I know not. Maybe
he was simply spying out the land, and will
next season return with his mate. Mocking-
birds have wandered north as far as Connecticut,
and were found breeding there by a collector,
who robbed them of their eggs. The mocking
wren would be a great acquisition to our Northern river banks and bushy streams. It is the
largest of our wrens, and in the volume and
variety of its notes and the length of its song
season surpasses all others.

A lover of nature never takes a walk without
perceiving something new and interesting. All
life in the winter woods or fields as revealed
upon the snow, how interesting it is. I recently met a business man who regularly goes
camping to the Maine woods every winter from
the delight he has in various signs of wild life
written upon the snow. His morning paper,
he says, is the sheet of snow which he reads in
his walk. Every event is chronicled, every
new arrival registers his name, if you have eyes
to read it!

In December my little boy and I took our
skates and went a mile distant from home into
the woods to a series of long, still pools in a
wild, rocky stream for an hour's skating.
There was a light skim of snow upon the ice,
but not enough to seriously interfere with our
sport, while it was ample to reveal the course
of every wild creature that had passed the night

before. Here a fox had crossed, there a rabbit or a squirrel or muskrat.

Presently we saw a different track and a strange one. The creature that made it had come out of a hole in the ground about a yard from the edge of the long, narrow pool upon which we were skating, and had gone up the stream, leaving a track upon the snow as large as that of an ordinary sized dog, but of an entirely different character.

We had struck the track of an otter, a rare animal in the Hudson River Valley; in fact, rare in any part of the State. We followed it with deep interest; it threw over the familiar stream the air of some remote pool or current in the depths of the Adirondacks or the Maine woods. Every few rods the otter had apparently dropped upon his belly and drawn himself along a few feet by his fore paws, leaving a track as if a log or bag of meal had been drawn along there. He did this about every three rods.

At the head of the pool where the creek was open and the water came brawling down over rocks and stones, the track ended on the edge of the ice; the otter had taken to the water. A cold bath, one would say, in mid-December, but probably no colder to him than the air, as his coat is perfectly water-proof.

On another pool further up the track reappeared and was rubbed out here and there by the same heavy dragging in the snow, like a chain with a long solid bar at regular distances

in place of links. At one point the otter had
gone ashore and scratched a little upon the
ground. He had gone from pool to pool, taking the open rapids wherever they appeared.

The otter is a large mink or weasel, three
feet or more long and very savage. It feeds
upon fish, which it seems to capture with ease.
It is said that it will track them through the
water as a hound tracks a fox on land. It will
travel a large distance under the ice, on a single
breath of air. Every now and then it will ex-
hale this air, which will form a large bubble
next the ice, where in a few moments it becomes purified and ready to be taken into the
creature's lungs again. If by any accident the
bubble were to be broken up and scattered,
the otter might drown before he could collect
it together again. A man who lived near the
creek said the presence of the otter accounted
for the scarcity of the fish there.

V

The other day one of my farmer neighbors
asked me if I had seen the new bird that was
about. This man was an old hunter, and had
a sharp eye for all kinds of game, but he had
never before seen the bird, which was nearly as
large as a robin, of a dull blue or slate color
marked with white.

Another neighbor, who was standing by, said
the bird had appeared at his house the day before. A cage with two canaries was hanging

against the window, when suddenly a large bird swooped down as if to dash himself against it; but arresting himself when near the glass, he hovered a moment, eying the birds, and then flew to a near tree.

The poor canaries were so frightened that they fell from their perches and lay panting upon the floor of their cage.

No one had ever seen the bird before; what was it? It was the shrike, who thought he was sure of a dinner when he saw those canaries.

If you see, in late autumn or winter, a slim, ashen-gray bird, in size a little less than the robin, having white markings, flying heavily from point to point, and always alighting on the topmost branch of a tree, you may know it is the shrike.

He is very nearly the size and color of the mocking-bird, but with flight and manners entirely different. There is some music in his soul, though his murderous beak nearly spoils it in giving it forth.

One winter morning, just at sunrise, as I was walking along the streets of a city, I heard the shrike's harsh warble. Looking about me, I soon saw the bird perched upon the topmost twig of a near tree, saluting the sunrise. It was what the robin might have done, but the strain had none of the robin's melody.

Some have compared the shrike's song to the creaking of a rusty gate-hinge, but it is not quite so bad as that. Still it is unmistakably

the voice of a savage.   None of the birds of
prey have musical voices.

The shrike had probably come to town to try
his luck with English sparrows.   I do not know
that he caught any, but in a neighboring city I
heard of a shrike that made great havoc with
the sparrows.

VI

When nature made the flying squirrel she
seems to have whispered a hint or promise of
the same gift to the red squirrel.   At least
there is a distinct suggestion of the same power
in the latter.   When hard pressed the red
squirrel will trust himself to the air with the
same faith that the flying squirrel does, but, it
must be admitted, with only a fraction of the
success of the latter.   He makes himself into a
rude sort of parachute, which breaks the force
of his fall very much.   The other day my dog
ran one up the side of the house, through the
woodbine, upon the roof.   As I opened fire
upon him with handfuls of gravel, to give him
to understand he was not welcome there, he
boldly launched out into the air and came down
upon the gravel walk, thirty feet below, with
surprising lightness and apparently without the
least shock or injury, and was off in an instant
beyond the reach of the dog.   On another occasion I saw one leap from the top of a hickory
tree and fall through the air at least forty feet
and alight without injury.   During their descent upon such occasions their legs are widely

extended, their bodies are broadened and flat-
tened, the tail stiffened and slightly curved, and
a curious tremulous motion runs through all.
It is very obvious that a deliberate attempt is
made to present the broadest surface possible to
the air, and I think a red squirrel might leap
from almost any height to the ground without
serious injury.   Our flying squirrel is in no
proper sense a flyer.   On the ground he is more
helpless than a chipmunk because less agile.
He can only sail or slide down a steep incline
from the top of one tree to the foot of another.
The flying squirrel is active only at night;
hence its large, soft eyes, its soft fur and its
gentle, shrinking ways.   It is the gentlest and
most harmless of our rodents.   A pair of them
for two or three successive years had their nest
behind the blinds of an upper window of a
large, unoccupied country house near me.   You
could stand in the room inside and observe the
happy family through the window pane against
which their nest pressed.   There on the window sill lay a pile of large, shining chestnuts,
which they were evidently holding against a
time of scarcity, as the pile did not diminish
while I observed them.   The nest was composed of cotton and wool which they filched
from a bed in one of the chambers, and it was
always a mystery how they got into the room
to obtain it.   There seemed to be no other
avenue but the chimney flue.

   There are always gradations in nature, or in
natural life; no very abrupt departures.   If

you find any marked trait or gift in a species you will find hints and suggestions of it, or as it were, preliminary studies of it, in other allied species. I am not thinking of the law of evolution which binds together the animal life of the globe, but of a kind of overflow in nature which carries any marked endowment or characteristic of a species in lessened force or completion to other surrounding species. Or if looked at from the other way, a progressive series, the idea being more and more fully carried out in each succeeding type — a kind of lateral and secondary evolution. Thus there are progressive series among our song-birds. The brown thrasher is an advance upon the catbird and the mocking bird is an advance upon the brown thrasher in the same direction. Each one carries the special gift of song or mimicking some stages forward. The same among the larks, through the titlark, shore-lark, up to the crowning triumph of the skylark. The nightingale also finishes a series which starts with the hedge warbler, and includes the robin redbreast. Our ground-sparrow songs probably reach their highest perfection in the song of the fox-sparrow; our finches in that of the purple finch, etc.

The same thing may be observed in other fields. The idea of the flying fish, the fish that leaves the water and takes for a moment to the air, does not seem to have exhausted itself till we reach the walking fish of tropical America, or the tree-climbing fish of India. From the protective coloring of certain insects, animals, and birds the step is not far to actual mimicry of certain special forms and colors. The naturalists find in Java a spider that exactly copies upon a leaf the form and colors of bird droppings. How many studies of honey-gathering bees did nature make before she achieved her masterpiece in this line in the honey-bee of our hives? The skunk's peculiar weapon of defense is suggested by the mink and the weasel. Is not the beaver the head of the series of gnawers, the loon of divers, the condor of soarers? Always one species that goes beyond any other. Look over a collection of African animals and see how high shouldered they are, how many hints or prophecies of the giraffe there are before the giraffe is reached. After nature had made the common turtle, of course she would not stop till she had made the box tortoise. In him the idea is fully realized. On the body of the porcupine the quills are detached and stuck into the flesh of its enemy on being touched; but nature has not stopped here. With the tail the animal strikes its quills into its assailant. Now if some animal could be found that actually threw its quills, at a distance of several feet, the idea would be still further carried out.

The rattlesnake is not the only rattler. I have seen the black snake and the harmless little garter snake vibrate their tails when disturbed in precisely the same manner. The black snake's tail was in contact with a dry leaf, and it gave forth a loud humming sound which at once put me on the alert.

I met a little mouse in my travels the other day that interested me.   He was on his travels also, and we met in the middle of a mountain lake.   I was casting my fly there when I saw just sketched or etched upon the glassy surface a delicate V-shaped figure, the point of which reached about the middle of the lake, while the two sides as they diverged faded out toward the shore.   I saw the point of this V was being slowly pushed toward the opposite shore.   I drew near in my boat, and beheld a little mouse swimming vigorously for the opposite shore. His little legs appeared like swiftly revolving wheels beneath him.   As I came near he dived under the water to escape me, but came up again like a cork and just as quickly.   It was laughable to see him repeatedly duck beneath the surface and pop back again in a twinkling. He could not keep under water more than a second or two.   Presently I reached him my oar, when he ran up it and into the palm of my hand, where he sat for some time and arranged his fur and warmed himself.   He did not show the slightest fear.   It was probably the first time he had ever shaken hands with a human being.   He was what we call a meadow mouse, but he had doubtless lived all his life in the woods and was strangely unsophisticated.   How his little round eyes did shine, and how he sniffed me to find out if I was more dangerous than I appeared to his sight.

After a while I put him down in the bottom of the boat and resumed my fishing.   But it was not long before he became very restless and evidently wanted to go about his business. He would climb up to the edge of the boat and peer down into the water. Finally he could brook the delay no longer and plunged boldly overboard, but he had either changed his mind or lost his reckoning, for he started back in the direction he had come, and the last I saw of him he was a mere speck vanishing in the shadows near the other shore.

Later on I saw another mouse while we were at work in the fields that interested me also. This one was our native white-footed mouse. We disturbed the mother with her young in her nest and she rushed out with her little ones clinging to her teats. A curious spectacle she presented as she rushed along, as if slit and torn into rags. Her pace was so precipitate that two of the young could not keep their hold and were left in the weeds. We remained quiet and presently the mother came back looking for them. When she had found one she seized it as a cat seizes her kitten and made off with it. In a moment or two she came back and found the other one and carried it away. I was curious to see if the young would take hold of her teats again as at first and be dragged away in that manner, but they did not. It would be interesting to know if they seize hold of their mother by instinct when danger threatens, or if they simply retain the hold which they already have. I believe the flight of the family always takes place in this manner, with this species of mouse.

VII

The other day I was walking in the silent, naked April woods when I said to myself, "There is nothing in the woods."

I sat down upon a rock. Then I lifted up my eyes and beheld a newly constructed crow's nest in a hemlock tree near by. The nest was but little above the level of the top of a ledge of rocks only a few yards away that crowned the rim of the valley. But it was placed behind the stem of the tree from the rocks, so as to be secure from observation on that side. The crow evidently knew what she was about. Presently I heard what appeared to be the voice of a young crow in the treetops not far off. This I knew to be the voice of the female, and that she was being fed by the male. She was probably laying, or about beginning to lay, eggs in the nest. Crows, as well as most of our smaller birds, always go through the rehearsal of this act of the parent feeding the young many times while the young are yet a long way in the future. The mother bird seems timid and babyish, and both in voice and manner assumes the character of a young fledgling. The male brings the food and seems more than usually solicitous about her welfare. Is it to conserve her strength or to make an impression on the developing eggs? The same thing may be observed among the domestic pigeons, and is always a sign that a new brood is not far off.

When the young do come the female is usually more active in feeding them than the male. Among the birds of prey, like hawks and eagles, the female is the larger and more powerful, and therefore better able to defend and to care for her young. Among all animals, the affection of the mother for her offspring seems to be greater than that of her mate, though among the birds the male sometimes shows a superabundance of paternal regard that takes in the young of other species. Thus a correspondent sends me this curious incident of a male bluebird and some young vireos. A pair of bluebirds were rearing their second brood in a box on the porch of my correspondent, and a pair of vireos had a nest with young in some lilac bushes but a few feet away. The writer had observed the male bluebird perch in the lilacs near the young vireos, and, he feared, with murderous intent. On such occasions the mother vireo would move among the upper branches much agitated. If she grew demonstrative the bluebird would drive her away. One afternoon the observer pulled away the leaves so as to have a full view of the vireo's nest from the seat where he sat not ten feet away. Presently he saw the male bluebird come to the nest with a worm in its beak, and, as the young vireos stretched up their gaping mouths, he dropped the worm into one of them. Then he reached over and waited upon one of the young birds as its own mother would have done. A few moments after he came to his own brood, with a worm or insect, and then the next trip he visited the nest of the neighbor again, greatly to the displeasure of the vireo, who scolded him sharply as she watched his movements from a near branch. My correspondent says: "I watched them for several days; sometimes the bluebird would visit his own nest several times before lending a hand to the vireos. Sometimes he resented the vireos' plaintive fault-finding and drove them away. I never saw the female bluebird near the vireos' nest."

That the male bird should be broader in his sympathies and affections will not, to most men at least, seem strange.

Another correspondent relates an equally curious incident about a wren and some young robins. "One day last summer," he says, "while watching a robin feeding her young, I was surprised to see a wren alight on the edge of the nest in the absence of the robin, and deposit a little worm in the throat of one of the young robins. It then flew off about ten feet, and it seemed as if it would almost burst with excessive volubility. It then disappeared, and the robin came and went, just as the wren returned with another worm for the young robins. This was kept up for an hour. Once they arrived simultaneously, when the wren was apparently much agitated, but waited impatiently on its previous perch, some ten feet off, until the robin had left, when it visited the nest as before. I climbed the tree for a closer inspection and found only a well-regulated robin household, but nowhere a wren's nest. After

coming down I walked around the tree and dis‐
covered a hole, and upon looking in saw a nest
of sleeping featherless wrens. At no time
while I was in the vicinity had the wren vis‐
ited these little ones."

Of all our birds, the wren seems the most
overflowing with life and activity. Probably
in this instance it had stuffed its own young to
repletion, when its own activity bubbled over
into the nest of its neighbor. It is well known
that the male wren frequently builds what are
called "cock-nests." It is simply so full of life
and joy and of the propagating instinct, that
after the real nest is completed, and while the
eggs are being laid, it gives vent to itself in
constructing these sham, or cock-nests. I have
found the nest of the marsh-wren surrounded
by half a dozen or more of these make-believers.
The gushing ecstatic nature of the bird ex‐
presses itself in this way.

I have myself known but one instance of a
bird lending a hand in feeding young not its
own. This instance is to be set down to the
credit of a female English sparrow. A little
"chippie" had on her hands the task of supply‐
ing the wants of that horse-leech, young cow-
bunting. The sparrow looked on from its perch
a few yards away, and when the chippie was off
looking up food, it would now and then bring
something and place it in the beak of the clam‐
orous bunting. I think the "chippie" appre‐
ciated its good offices. Certainly its dusky
foster-child did. This bird, when young, seems

the most greedy of all fledgelings. It cries "More," "More," incessantly. When its foster parent is a small bird like "chippie" or one of the warblers, one would think it would swallow its parent when food is brought it. I suppose a similar spectacle is witnessed in England when the cuckoo is brought up by a smaller bird, as is always the case. Sings the fool in "Lear": —

> " The hedge-sparrow fed the cuckoo so long,
> That it had its head bit off by its young."

Last season I saw a cow-bunting fully grown following a "chippie" sparrow about, clamoring for food, and really looking large enough to bite off and swallow the head of its parent, and apparently hungry enough to do it. The "chippie" was evidently trying to shake it off and let it shift for itself, for it avoided it and flew from point to point to escape it. Its life was probably made wretched by the greedy monster it had unwittingly reared.

www.ingramcontent.com/pod-product-compliance
Lightning Source LLC
Chambersburg PA
CBHW060517030726
47498CB00004B/978